Jackie snorted. "Please keep it in your tutu, Mr. Spillane. I have absolutely no interest in molesting you. Sex is too much like snow — you never know how many inches you're going to get. Although," she said, glancing at the skimpy tutu, "I dare say I could make an accurate weather prediction from here."

"A lotta people like snow," said Spillane, trying to cover both his chest and his tutu at the same time.

"They don't live in California, do they?" said Jackie. "But you'll be buried here unless we can catch your elusive Alabama Sam. Judging by his handiwork, I'd say the cat has become tired of playing with the string and decided to put a bullet through it."

"Cats don't have guns," said Spillane.

"No," said Jackie, smiling and pulling a pistol out of her bustle. "But cougars do."

Skunks Dance

St John Karp

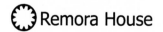 Remora House

Printed in the United States of America

First Edition
10 9 8 7 6 5 4 3 2 1

ISBN 978-0-9892630-6-1

Published by Remora House

St John Karp
www.fuzzjunket.com

Cover illustration copyright © 2016 by Kevin Alcantar
kevinalcantar.com
kevin.j.alcantar@gmail.com

Emoji art by EmojiOne
http://emojione.com

Chapter 1

Grandmammy Spillane always said there was only two good reasons to kill a man — for cheating on a woman and for serving drinks to a Yankee. That was why little Spivey grew up without a grandpappy, although on account of which one she never said. Spivey asked her if you couldn't also kill a man for cheating at cards, but she only shuffled the deck and said he had a lot to learn.

She'd been a sharp old crow, God rest her, but now Spivey Spillane reckoned he'd found another reason to kill — for money.

He'd spent such a long time telling himself it was for Christian reasons and he was doing the Lord's work. But really, when a man sets fire to your day's harvest, spooks your best milking cow, and makes off with the details of a buried fortune, is it God telling you to put a bullet in his belly? No sir, that's just good sense.

Spillane spat onto the dusty street to show the locals how much he thought of their town. No-one paid him much attention, but a few curious eyes glanced in his direction as he rode past the houses and storefronts. Spillane was young, but no younger than the dozens of other gold-diggers that came through Kansas on their way to the rush. He didn't seem to be tall, but he had the firm build of a man familiar with early mornings, hard labor, and vigorous milkings. He'd grown himself a fine mustache and sideburns, though they were now interspersed with rough and seldom-cut stubble. Spillane eyed the stores and dirty windows from under the brim of his hat. This town had a rat problem. He could smell it.

Spillane stabled his horse and tried to ignore the yawning in his stomach. A man had his priorities: kill, drink, and then get something to eat — if circumstances allowed. When he made sure his horse was watered and his revolver cocked, Spillane pushed open the doors of the Gravesend Saloon.

His eyes hadn't yet adjusted to the gloom, but Spillane's infallible sense of direction led him straight to the bar. He slammed down a few coins and glared from under his hat to where he imagined the bartender would be.

"Whiskey," he said. "And open up a fresh 'un, if y'don't mind obligin'. Never know what kinda vermin's been drinkin' from the bottle."

As the bartender turned to open a bottle, Spillane leaned over the bar and grabbed the guest book. He ran his finger down the list of names, sounding out each one under his breath. His finger stopped — room three, George Washington Dickey. Now he'd seen it all! The cur was Clancy Wellwater in Amity and Jebediah Balthrop in Bible Hill, but Spillane could smell that mangy thief a mile away. It was Alabama Sam.

Spillane replaced the guest book just before the barman turned back and placed a shot of whiskey on the counter. He affected an air of disinterest as he let his eyes wander across the saloon full of unhappy men with unhappier mustaches. Everything here seemed to droop and wither in the fog of cigar smoke and the constant squelch of chewing tobacco. Mangy deer heads were mounted above the bar, gazing eyelessly at the drinkers and soaking in the fetid atmosphere of that place. A woman in enormous petticoats and a shockingly prominent bustier attempted to cock an eyebrow in Spillane's direction, but he passed her over scornfully. At last he saw past the drinkers and gamblers and spittoons to where a staircase led to the second floor. Smoke curled around the landing, and through the haze Spillane caught sight of room number three. His jaw clenched and his eyes fixed themselves on that door with unstoppable malice.

"Keep that whiskey warm," he said without looking at the barman. "I ain't gonna be long."

Spillane walked across the saloon with slow, heavy footfalls. The drink-sodden gamblers and women of the night averted their eyes abruptly, sensing that something was about to go down.

Spillane could feel the ache in his thighs from the long ride. He savored the feeling. He had been at this filthy business for a very long time. The handle of his revolver stuck out of the holster at his side, ready, eager to feel the touch of his hand as if it had been waiting all these months just for this moment. Spillane scaled the stairs, old and damp, and heard them creak under his shoes. As he stepped onto the landing he shifted his weight very carefully so as not to make any noise on the treacherous floorboards. The revolver was in his hand now. The air was warm. The musty atmosphere had a different flavor now — it tingled, spicy and electric. His breath was still.

Then he kicked in the door. It flew off its hinges and Spillane charged into the room, gun blazing.

The reverberation of the shots faded, and the room fell to an unnatural silence. Spillane's chest was heaving and his heart felt ready to burst against his ribs. A gigantic tropical bird lay dead on the floor.

"Excuse me, can I help you with anything?"

Spillane jumped out of his skin. He spun around to find the voice and blast it, but he caught himself just in time. It wasn't Alabama Sam. It was a thin, white-haired old gentleman.

Spillane exhaled. "Lord help me, old-timer, if you sneak up on me like that again you're liable to wind up with a ribcage full o' lead."

The old man peered into his room and caught sight of the bird. "What on earth? You shot my macaw!"

"That's a spurious fabrication and you know it. You wasn't even in the room."

"The bird, you chucklehead. What convinced you to go do a damn fool thing like that?"

Spillane mumbled, "I thought it was someone else," but the old man only glared in response. "Anyhow," said Spillane, "what are you doin' with a critter like that in somebody else's room?"

"This is *my* room. I'm a naturalist."

"A nat-ur-alist?" asked Spillane, being careful to take the challenge one syllable at a time.

"Well naturally. How else do you think a macaw got all the way to Kansas? By flying?"

"Well why not?"

"Because it's dead! It's been dead for years. You don't think you killed it, do you? It's dead and stuffed and you just put three bullets into it."

The old man waved the bird in Spillane's face so he could see the stitching and sawdust.

"I do apologize," mumbled Spillane.

Spillane made to leave, but before he went more than two steps something seemed to strike the naturalist. "Young man, you're not, by any chance, looking for the gentleman who took this room before me? Only he left you a message."

"Yeah?"

"Indeed, now let me see…" The old man muttered to himself as he fished a notebook out of his pocket and began to read. "He told me to say your features are wormy and pustulent and he hopes your rectal cavity gets used as a burrow by a family of diseasy ferrets. Then he made an obscene noise that I wasn't sure how to spell."

Spillane grabbed the notebook in a rage and tore it clean in two.

As he stormed away he heard the old man mumbling, "Damn gunslingers, think they own the whole damn West. Vandals and Visigoths…"

Spillane made his way back down the stairs and collected his whiskey at the bar. The barman eyed him.

"Hope I didn't hear shootin' just now, kiddo."

"I'm 20," said Spillane, tipping his hat back in contempt. "Do I look like a kiddo to you?"

"We don't want no trouble, is all I'm sayin'."

"No, no trouble." Spillane thrust some coins at the barman. "Your obligin', a room for the night, an' another drink, on the house."

"Drinks is money too, mister."

"This one's on the house, on account o' me bein' such a valued customer an' all. Now what do you know about 'George Washington Dickey'?" he asked, saying the name like he was peeling a slug off his skin.

The barman scowled. "Only that he come through here, oh, three, four days ago. All he said, once he got himself good and liquored up, was he was makin' for a Skunks Dance. Only I never heard of any place called Skunks Dance in these parts."

Damnation! Sam was getting away. If Spillane knew an egg from an omelet, that two-timing pick-pocket was making for California. Sam was liable to get there weeks ahead of Spillane, even accounting for a detour around Great Bend where rumor held a staunch sheriff had staked out his turf. But that didn't worry Spillane. Let him get there first. Let him find it and dig it up. That's when Spivey Spillane would saunter into town and take it off him.

Spillane downed his whiskey all in one. It was a good sipping whiskey, which meant it was even better by the bottle. He waved for a refill and eyed a game of cards forming in the back corner. Spillane limbered up his fingers and checked his sleeves. If he remembered anything Grandmammy Spillane taught him about cards, this night in Gravesend was about to pay for itself.

Chapter 2

If it weren't summer Jet would never have found his mother until mid-afternoon, when she would surface from underneath the sofa or inside the utility closet. As it was she had been up early to take advantage of what she insisted were the prime trampolining hours between 5 and 7 a.m. Jet should have been used to the noises after all these years, but he was always startled awake by his mom's breathing exercises, the rusty springs on the trampoline, and her boisterous rendition of "I'm Going to Wash That Man Right Out of My Hair."

It was not easy being the son of the Amazing Allan and Ashwood. Stories about them would circulate at school, each one more extravagant and embarrassing than the last. Jet only wished they weren't true, but they almost always were. Even the mailmen of Skunks Dance had an uncharitable opinion of that house. They took turns doing the route and reporting back on the songs and dances they'd seen being rehearsed. The most popular nickname for the the duo was the Amazing Ass-Hats, but other names had their own charm too: the Flying Fruits, the Bouncy Melons, or simply Murder on the High Cs.

Jet slumped into a pair of baggy pants that flapped around his legs and put on a t-shirt with a picture of a cross-eyed Josephine Baker on it. He had always been a slightly pudgy kid, but in the last few years it had melted away. He gazed blearily into the mirror and ran his hands through his clipped blond hair until it was messy enough to look properly disrespectable. He always kept his hair short to avoid the dreaded blond afro that made him look like Harpo Marx or, worse, his mother.

He had his dad's nose, though — a pointy, Puckish thing that invited mischief. Although she never told anyone, Jet's mom quite liked that nose. Without it she might never have married her husband.

By the time Jet got to the kitchen his mom was walking around on her hands, still dressed in a spandex leotard. He knew her well enough to recognize her worried face, even when it was upside-down.

"Up early, I see," she said.

"Yeah, I guess."

"You know when *I* was 17 I used to take the morning off school sometimes, sit in the park with a pack of smokes, and practice my French kissing with the linebacker."

"Mom, gross."

"Well it wasn't in the French curriculum, I had to get the hang of it somehow. But you know, if you wanted you could take a little time off school once in a while. I'd even write you a note, I can forge the dentist's signature easy. Play hookey! You could go to the penny arcade. You never know, you might meet a pretty punk girl with purple hair," she said. "Or a boy…"

"Mom, for the millionth time, I'm not gay."

"I'm not saying you have to put up a big poster of Justin Bieber, but a little experimentation never hurt anyone. It's good for the soul. I remember when I was in high school there was this blond cheerleader who had *the* most amazing rack."

"Mom! Stop being gross."

She poured herself a cup of coffee and took a sip. Years of practice meant she could do this upside-down without spilling a drop. The trick, she delighted in telling the teachers at Jet's parent/teacher nights, was to draw the scalding hot coffee into your nasal cavity until it could be forced back up against gravity and into the stomach. These days the teachers tried to send the parent/teacher invitations to Jet's dad instead, but they were rarely successful.

"Jet, you know I love you more than life itself. You and Gina are the most precious things to me in the whole world. But sometimes I look at you and wonder how you came out of my vagina. It's a very real possibility you're actually the son of that Republican senator I had a fling with when your father and I were still poly."

Jet groaned. "Not the Republican story again."

She smiled and put her hand on Jet's knee. "Then cut class, what do you say? For me?"

"I can't do that," he said, snatching his leg away.

She stumbled to get her balance back, then threw her feet up in the air with dismay. "I don't know why you do this to me. Where did I go wrong? Am I a bad mother? Is that why you hate me?"

"You know it's summer break, right?"

The blood rushed to his mother's cheeks. "What do you mean, summer break? I gave Gina lunch money! See, she stole from me. Why can't you be more like your sister? It shows a free spirit."

"I dunno, Mom, how about I club you over the head with a crowbar next time you come in the door."

"Jet! I will not be spoken to in that tone."

But she smiled when Jet wasn't looking. She knew he didn't mean it, and if Jet needed an authority figure to rebel against, she was willing to be the patsy. She was about to forbid him to see his no-good friends when something exploded to her right. She fell off her hands and landed on the table amid a storm of shattered glass. Jet was already on his feet, staring blankly at the debris. For once he didn't know any more than his mom.

Jet's mom carefully stood back up on her feet and picked up the rock that had come clean through the kitchen window. To her surprise it was wrapped in a frilly lace doily. She shook off the shards of glass and unwrapped it.

A note on the doily read: "Dear Fat-flap. Die in a fire. Yours, A. S."

A smile crept across her face. "I think a certain someone has a secret admirer! A. S. wouldn't happen to be that Amanda Spillane, would it?"

"Mom, we hate each other! She just threw a rock through our window."

"Ah well, 'The course of true love never did run smooth,' as they say on TV. You two have been play-fighting since you were 12."

"She collects porcelain dolls! She puts doilies under everything. Oh, yeah, and I nearly forgot, she's a total bitch."

"Don't you use the b-word in this house. Who do you think you are?" Mrs. Ashwood glanced back over the wreckage. "Though I do think she got a bit carried away with the window. Just ask her for a check the next time you two have a play date."

"I'm not gonna ask her for money!"

Jet's mom contemplated the empty window and started framing it through her hands. "I suppose we could put some kind of curtain here. Maybe a tapestry. What do you think?"

Jet grabbed the note off the table and saw there was more. As he read, his face changed color.

"This is illegal — she stole my mail. I got a comic in the mail and she took it right off the doorstep. That *bitch*."

Jet's mom sighed. All Jet's comic books were a little too... *boring* for her. She'd hoped he might develop an interest in the performing arts, but now she really was starting to wonder if that Republican story was true. Still, he seemed to like collecting his picture books.

While his mom despaired, Jet quietly fumed. The comic he bought happened to be a first edition of *Fantastic Firecat* (1943), worth at least $400. He made a fair amount trading comics on the side, but they were small fry compared to a collector's item like this. He swore to himself that if anything happened to that comic book he was going to put Amanda Spillane's pigtails in the insinkerator and turn it on.

The benches in the town plaza were a kind of desiccated wood covered in flaky green paint. Every time Jet sat down he tried to do it as hard as possible to see if he could snap one of the beams. So far they had bent and creaked, but to his disappointment nothing ever broke.

Josue texted to say he was right down the street, but knowing Josue that could mean down the street, up the street, or at a strip club on the moon. You kind of just had to wait and see.

Jet picked up a pebble or two and hurled one of them at the big, ugly statue in the middle of the plaza. It bounced off with a really satisfying clang, then rebounded and hit a middle-aged man on the back of the head.

"Mother of God!" he screamed. "What in the name of —" The man turned around and spotted Jet. "Oh hello! It's young Jettison, isn't it?"

Crap, Jet thought. It was the mayor, Mr. Franklin. Normally Jet wouldn't know who the hell was mayor, only he'd gone to school with Franklin's son since the third grade. Franklin was in the plaza almost every day campaigning for something or another that threatened to destroy the fabric of their entire community but which a year later no-one could really remember. When one cause was won or lost, there was always another waiting to take its place.

Mr. Franklin had a kind of turkey neck that bulged voluptuously into his shirt collar. One of Jet's earliest memories of Franklin was during one of his election campaigns when he was handing out leaflets outside the polling station. Jet followed after his father and ran past Franklin with eyes glued to the man's grotesquely wobbling neck. When Franklin smiled — and he always did — it compressed his neck fat and made him look strangely like a pelican trying to smuggle a fish in its beak. It was almost endearing, and evidently Jet wasn't the only one who thought so — Franklin had been elected mayor for three straight terms.

"You're up bright and early, aren't you Mr. Ashwood?"

"Allan-Ashwood," said Jet, trying to hide the pebbles behind his back.

The mayor's eyes tracked the sudden movement. It was too late to stop him seeing.

"Oh, was that you?" said the mayor. "Think nothing of it, I was young once too. Throw as many rocks as you like. I used to hurl the odd igneous missile in my day, you know."

Franklin looked up at the statue Jet had thrown the rock at.

"Good old Spivey Spillane. Truth is we're about to tear the damn thing down. About time too, though the place just won't look the same without him. Here," he said, reaching for a pebble, "I can't tell you how long I've been wanting to do this."

He threw the pebble, then put his hand up to his eyes and squinted into the distance.

"Did I hit it?" he asked.

Jet shrugged. "Yeah, why not."

"Hot dog, I don't remember the last time I had this much fun. You know what I miss? It's been years since I saw your parents perform. Your father's quite a legend of the ol' legerdemain, if I may say, a prodigy of prestidigitation! Where are they performing these days?

"Circus Maximo's."

"Oh fancy," said Franklin, searching for his hairline nervously. "I didn't know Maximo was out again."

"Good behavior, apparently."

"Well I'll have to book a ticket to go see their show, anonymously," he said with a cautious glance around the plaza. "You know I remember seeing the Amazing Allan and Ashwood way back in, oh, must have been '96. Your mother was quite the little acrobat. There were things she could do on the back of a pony that still send shivers down my spine."

"Yeah, I know. I have to watch them practice over my breakfast cereal."

Jet's eyes wandered awkwardly, trying to avoid catching Franklin's. This was getting embarrassing. When was the old man going to leave?

In the awkward pause Jet spotted Nina at the far end of the plaza. Jet looked away and tried to hide half-heartedly behind his hand. The last thing he needed was her bugging him to get back together. He caught enough drama off his mother without adding Nina into the mix.

Franklin's eye had also been caught by someone in the crowd of shoppers. He started inching towards them, turning his head back only to mutter a distracted farewell at Jet.

"Nice talking to you, but I think I see a registered voter. Give my regards to your mother," he said, running his fingers through some imaginary hair.

A moment later Steve and Josue arrived on the scene. Josue had a big, goofy grin on his face. "Was that Drama-Llama-Ding-Dong I just saw?" he asked, looking back in Nina's direction.

"Shhh!" said Jet. "She'll hear you. Anyway, you can talk. Are you late enough?"

"What? You can't blame me for that. My alarm clock's broken."

"Isn't that the same excuse you used on Mr. Ricard?"

"Of course it is, it's the same alarm clock isn't it?" Josue asked, eyes twinkling with delight. "I don't know if I like this intrusion into everybody else's business. This exactly is how Hitler got started, *Herr Jet von Fritzenheimenberg.* Maybe someone should tell you this is America, where every citizen has the right to a broken alarm clock."

"All right!" said Jet. To be friends with Josue was to enjoy being conned, and Josue lived up to his end of the bargain with infallible flair. He'd probably been planning this little speech all morning.

Steve finally spoke. Jet didn't know why, but Steve never had to speak over anyone else — it seemed like everyone automatically listened. Jet hated him for it but had to admit that when Steve did speak, it tended to be good.

"School's empty," said Steve. "What say we find out what's in the teachers' lounge?"

"I'm betting it's an altar to Aleister Crowley with black candles and upside-down crosses," said Josue. "And the corpses of sacrificed cats scattered all over the ground like Dippin' Dots."

Jet laughed. "It's probably really boring. Like all the fireworks for the Fourth of July barbe—"

Slowly the laughter stopped. Jet, Josue, and Steve looked at each other as they realized Jet was right. The school must be packed with fireworks for next month's display.

"Could we?" breathed Josue. "Should we?"

"Yes," said Jet. "And no. Let's do it."

Jet didn't know why, but he loved breaking into his own school. It was weird — he spent enough of the rest of the time trying to break out of it. It was a pointless place anyway. He was already making better money than his parents, and that was just trading comics online. He kept wondering how much cooler it would be to have his own store, with a microbrewery in an annex out back and horror movies playing on the walls. He'd have to move out of Skunks Dance (Population: You and that old woman who wears too much makeup and smells like feet). Never mind the school — he'd outgrown this town years ago, let alone the school. But now he had the chance to turn it back on them, to do something that proved he dreamed bigger and better than the rest of them.

"I hear talking," Josue said as if he were picking up a psychic signal.

"That's you, you tard."

"When I talk it's like getting a hand-job from Natalie Portman wearing satin gloves. This is more like… rusty chains."

The noise got closer and they realized Josue was right. A group of chattering people were approaching, but a certain irritating voice seemed to carry over the others. Jet, Josue, and Steve all ducked into the stairwell and kept in the shadows as the voices walked past. Jet let himself peek out and sure enough, there she was — Spillane.

"God damn it!" hissed Jet. "Doesn't she have a life? She's at school during summer break."

"So are we," said Steve.

Jet glared back at him.

Amanda Spillane was tall but solidly built, the kind of figure that might have been child-bearing if she'd ever had a boyfriend. As it was she barely even had friends. She always wore her hair strictly plaited into pigtails, which gave her an air of Pippi Longstocking that made Jet want to chew his own face off.

Amanda was leading a tour group through the school, and Jet realized it must be for the prospective students. He saw a number of parents dragging their captive children through all the levels of the school and all the different cookie-cutter classrooms. She must be the only person in their grade who'd volunteer for this colossal waste of time.

"Look," said Steve after they passed by, "we've got a clear run at the teachers' lounge."

They crept out from under the stairs and nicked off down an empty hallway. The teachers' lounge was right in front of them. Steve stepped to the front and pushed his way inside.

The place had been furnished with chairs and chaise-longues that looked like they'd been found on the side of the street. The crushed velvet and embroidery, the soft leather and claw feet must have been very expensive when they were new, but now they were covered in tears and scratches and matted with dirt. Their stuffing had been deflated by generations of merciless academic bottoms.

The tables and shelves were littered with used martini glasses. To one side of the room Jet spotted an impromptu bar stocked with cheap gin and Spanish olives.

"I knew it," Josue breathed. "They're all drunks. I always thought Miss Bannister was flying high."

"She's taught you for three years in a row, hasn't she?" asked Steve.

"Yeah. What's your point?"

"Shut up and look!" said Jet.

At the far end of the teachers' lounge was a broom cupboard marked "Geography Supplies and Emergency Protractors — Highly Flammable."

"They hid them in here where no-one would ever want to look."

"But what happens if you want a protractor in a hurry?" asked Josue.

"You suck it up and *grow a pair.*"

He pulled open the door and walked into Fort Knox. The small, dusty, highly flammable room was loaded with fireworks of every kind — Roman candles, squawkers, squeakers, fizzlers and twizzlers, multi-stage exploding rockets, ones that went off with a bang and ones that peppered the children in the front row with white-hot phosphorus.

They gazed lovingly at the trove, eyes full of dollar signs.

"What are we going to do with them?" Josue asked.

A light bulb went on over Jet's head. "I know the perfect thing."

The school car park was underneath the main block. Not much sunlight got this far, so the parking lot was dusty, dim, and deliciously enclosed. The perfect place to set off explosive projectiles.

They had lined up the fireworks with unusual care. All were primed and loaded. All were facing the same target: a beat-up Volkswagen belonging to a certain student tour-guide, doily-fancier, and rock-thrower by the name of Amanda Spillane. Revenge was sweet.

"What the hell is that?" Jet asked, peering into the back seat. It was hard to make out in the gloom but it looked like Amanda's car was full of picks and shovels.

"Who cares? Get out of the way so we can torch this lemon."

They ran, ducked behind a concrete wall, and breathlessly looked at each other as if waiting for the first explosion.

"So," said Jet, "how do we light these things?"

"Do I look like Gandalf to you?" asked Steve.

Josue produced a lighter out of his pocket. "What's this I've found?" he said in awe. "It seems to be some kind of fire-maker. How did this miracle of rare device get into my pocket? What sorcery is this?"

Jet snatched it out of his hand and went to light the fuses. It was all he could do to jump back behind the wall and murmur, "Burn, baby, burn…"

There was a gentle hiss as the fuses burned down, then a heart-stopping silence for a fraction of a second. Jet cautiously peered over the wall.

The fireworks erupted, shrieking off into the darkness and sending Jet ducking for cover. Some of them showered the car in sparks and some ricocheted off and exploded onto the ground. Fire spewed in every direction. The noise stung Jet's ears, even with his hands clamped over them. So much fire was flying through the air that Jet barely had the courage to glance back and see what was going on.

A rocket bounced off the hood and shot off into the distance. Then one heavy, loaded bomb sailed straight towards the windshield. It struck the glass and embedded jagged shards into the front seats. The bomb itself lay wedged against the gear stick. A second later it exploded in a dazzling blossom of light and fire. It was so intense the whole car lit up like a Christmas tree. The upholstery and paintwork began to singe. Suddenly the whole car was ablaze.

"WHAT THE HELL WAS THAT?" screamed Josue.

The fireworks had fizzled their last now and only the quiet flames in the car remained to illuminate the parking lot.

Jet peered at it and, as his eyes adjusted, he saw the flames consuming Amanda's car.

"Ho-lee shit."

A shiver ran up Jet's spine, and he realized he was shaking. He made himself keep breathing. He never actually thought they'd nuke the thing.

But it was okay. No-one knew it was them.

Then he caught sight of Amanda Spillane on the other side of the parking lot staring slack-jawed at the wreck.

"Run!" he yelled.

The three boys all dashed off into the real world, leaving Amanda alone with her car. She realized the fire hadn't yet hit the fuel tank and leaped out of the way. The last thing Jet heard as he sprinted off the school grounds was the blast as the fire finally ignited the gas and tore the car to pieces.

The blood throbbed in his temples. He had the sinking feeling he'd regret this.

The problem with having acrobatic parents was they were always cooking healthy food. Gina made a face and pushed her asparagus away.

"No!" she muttered. "It's my birthday, I don't have to eat that if I don't want to."

Jet rolled his eyes. It wasn't Gina's birthday for days, but she treated the whole week like one long birthday and refused to let anyone forget it.

"Come on," said their dad, "you can eat what you like at your party but you don't want to die of malnutrition before then. Look at Jet, he's eating his asparagus."

Jet picked up the stalks of green slime and dropped them head-first into a glass of milk. He cocked an eyebrow at his dad, who just sighed.

"Really?" said Mr. Allan. "You couldn't back me up on this one?"

Mrs. Ashwood reached out and lazily plucked a stalk from Jet's glass. She munched curiously.

"You know this isn't as bad as you'd think."

"Jet, have you got a check for the window? Your mother and I aren't made of money."

Jet cast his eyes down at his food. There was no chance he'd get any money out of Amanda now he'd exploded her car.

"Can I break a window too?" Gina asked.

"Not till your father and I explain the birds and the bees," said Mrs. Ashwood.

"What do birds and bees do? Is it sex?"

"Yes, Gina, it's sex."

"Gross. I'm-a write a complaint to the Nature Channel."

Jet was about to say something, but closed his mouth quickly and lifted his head. He thought he'd heard a police siren. Probably nothing.

Jet's dad grinned at him. "I heard it was the ever-lovely Miss Spillane that threw the rock. You should ask her out, you two have been play-fighting for long enough. If you keep putting this off she'll think something's wrong with your equipment. There are many things a lady will put up with, Jet, but an overcooked noodle isn't one of them."

He leaned in close so Gina and Mrs. Ashwood couldn't hear. "*Is* there is something wrong with your equipment? Just let me know, I can hook you up with a little chemical 'inspiration.' Erectile dysfunction is nothing to be ashamed of."

"Dad! I don't even like her, she's a frickin' weirdo. You should see the crap she's got in the back of her car — shovels and ropes and stuff. She thinks she's digging to China."

"How d'you know what's in her car?" asked Gina. Jet stuck his tongue out at her in reply.

"That family have been digging for lost treasure since the Gold Rush," said Mr. Allan. "They're all descended from that Spivey Spillane."

"...who made a million dollars in Skunks Dance..." said Jet, rolling his eyes.

"Or might have, if someone didn't cut off his head before he could tell anyone where it was. All they ever found was the body stuck full of arrows and floating down the river."

Chapter 3

Nothing in Skunks Dance was more than a year old. The whole town grew up on the spur of the moment, and everything was geared towards the gold rush. Diggers from all around the country flocked to California, and those diggers needed food, drink, and whores — and not necessarily in that order. There were two saloons on every block, interspersed with hardware stores stocked to the brim with picks, shovels, and panning equipment. A digger wanted for nothing — when he struck gold there were bars and restaurants to take it off him, and when he was feeling blue he was never short of company. The only thing that wasn't here was Alabama Sam.

Spillane didn't understand it. He'd been in Skunks Dance for a month and there was still no sign of Sam, not under any of his fake names. He had to be here. He *had* to be.

Spillane trudged up to the house where he'd taken a room. It was a rather hasty-looking confabulation on the edge of town owned by a misguided Portuguese man looking for something he'd never find.

As he opened the door Spillane caught a strong whiff of cigar smoke. He couldn't help passing the living room where Mr. Nunes sat with a balloon of brandy and a leather-bound book. That was the problem with foreigners. They never seemed to realize they were in America. He was, as ever, wearing an immaculate suit the color of a baby's first teeth.

"Back already?" asked Nunes.

Spillane grunted.

"I do not allow grunting in my house, Mr. Spillane. It shows a weakness of character that I find unbecoming."

"You mind your business, Nunes. I'll mind mine."

"Cheery-bye," said Nunes, waving his fingers goodbye as Spillane trudged off to his room.

Spillane only scowled harder. Although Nunes was a bizarrely optimistic kind of gent, Spillane could smell the same hollow despair on him that seemed to drip off everyone in Skunks Dance. He couldn't wait to leave this place. It had been so long since he'd been in the company of familiar things and familiar people. His youngest brother would be 12 now. And what about Ma Spillane? The winters had been harder and harder on her these past few years. But he knew she must be okay. He had chased the curse away from their house now, and besides, he would know if his mother were dead. He would feel it.

Spillane shut himself in his room and, when the door clicked shut, he tried to relax. Some of the day's tension seemed to leave his tired arms, but it never left completely. He hadn't had one moment's real peace since he left Tennessee.

He sat down on the edge of his bed and focused himself on some proper scheming. He unrolled the map of Skunks Dance and tried to match it with what he could remember of the stolen map. It didn't work. No matter which way he turned the thing, none of the features looked familiar. Inexplicably the California surveyors hadn't marked anything with a big X and an arrow saying, "Buried treasure here."

Somebody knocked at the front door. The noise startled Spillane's caged goat, which gave the bars a half-hearted kick. Spillane eyed it menacingly and the animal began to settle down.

Somebody knocked again and the goat bucked hard.

"You're about this far from becoming shoes," Spillane growled at it.

He ignored whoever was at the door. There was no-one he wanted to talk to. Let Nunes get it. But the insistent knock came again and again until Spillane finally heaved himself up off the bed and went to see who was making all that racket. As he passed the living room he saw that Nunes had made himself scarce.

When he answered the door he found a doddering, elderly woman.

"Mr. Spillane?"

"Yes."

"I'm Maureen Delaney, First Skunks Dance Baptist Church. It's such a pleasure to finally meet you!" She pushed past him into the house. "Oh my, what a lovely place you have."

Mrs. Delaney ran her hands along the wall and let her wrinkled fingertips brush past the nails sticking out. "Still waiting for that big jackpot, I see. Well never you mind, I'm sure it's just around the corner."

"Ma'am, I have to confess I ain't got the first knowance what in the hell you're talkin' about."

"Your one-man play for the orphans, you silly-billy! We're all just busting to see your show. There's not much of a theater scene here in little ol' Skunks Dance, so you'll be quite a breath of fresh air."

Spillane just looked at her in disbelief.

"You're Mr. Spivey Spillane, aren't you? Well I have your letter right here: 'Dear Christian Soldiers' — that's my favorite bit — 'I am a traveling theatrical type who will be visiting Skunks Dance as part of my Grand Introduction to the West. I hope you'll allow me to perform for you and your orphans a new composition of my own entitled *Heliogabalus' Pursuit of the Sugar Plum Faeries (A Study in Lavender)*.'

"Why, the whole congregation has been waiting for weeks. I do hope you won't disappoint us."

Spillane was so speechless that saliva started to pool at the corner of his mouth. "I never wrote a letter like that in my whole life!" he shouted. "That two-timing son of a..." Spillane lost his words once again until the one he was looking for sprang to the tip of his tongue: "Whore!" he shouted at the old Baptist lady. "Whore! whore! whore! whore!... Ass!"

Mrs. Delaney gathered her skirts in umbrage. "Well! I certainly hope you're not going to use *that* kind of language in front of the orphans. I really ought to review a draft of this 'composition' if you have a copy around here somewhere."

"There ain't no composition, lady! You got tricked by the trickiest snake oil salesman in these United States. That Alabama Sam is somewhere in Skunks Dance pretending to be *me*, if y'please."

Mrs. Delaney scrutinized him carefully. "So, what you're trying to tell me is, you don't have a one-man play called *Heliogabalus' Pursuit of the Sugar Plum Faeries*."

"No!"

"And you're not going to come down to the church and perform for the orphans."

"No!"

Mrs. Delaney cast her eyes around and spied the open door to Spillane's room. "Then why is there a dog in your room?"

"When I lay hands on that no-good two-faced tapeworm I'm gonna tie him up in a sack with that there dog and throw him into the river."

Mrs. Delaney paused for a moment to take this in. "And why do you also have a cockerel?"

Spillane snarled, "That's going in the sack too."

"And a snake…?" she asked.

"Sack," said Spillane.

"And… a billy-goat?"

"That, ma'am, is because I couldn't find a monkey."

Spillane's reply made a few laps of the inside of Mrs. Delaney's head before she broke into a big grin. "Of course you've never heard of *Heliogabalus* — I didn't realize you were already in character. I know how you theatrical types have to warm up for a part. If your acting is this good for the orphans, I think this will be our best season yet."

"Get out! Get outta my house, woman!"

"See you on the 19th?" she asked.

"Out!"

Spillane propelled her out the door and onto the street. The commotion attracted the attention of a few people walking past. Spillane should have known better than to eject an old woman onto the street in broad daylight.

"Hey mister, you can't treat an old lady like that."

Mrs. Delaney walked up to the passer-by and said, "It's perfectly all right, young man. This is Mr. Spivey Spillane."

"Ohh, *you're* Mr. Spillane! I heard you was at the hospital demonstratin' your dangly bits — or what's left of 'em."

"That's not what I heard," added a newcomer. "I heard he was showin' off *all* his dangly bits — more'n the usual number if y'catch my meaning."

A crowd was starting to form outside Spillane's front door.

"Hey mister, just how many dangly bits d'you got? We all wanna know. Heck, I got five dollars ridin' on your weenies."

"That there's mah baby-daddy!" cried a woman.

"Then you seen them dangly bits! Did he use 'em both at the same time?"

Spillane was finding all new depths of hatred and indignation.

"Shut your yaps!" he spat at the crowd. "All of you! Now you listen up and listen good. I never met any o' you cowpokes in all my time in God's green creation. Someone came to town a coupla weeks ago and that man was a no-good scoundrelly con-artist who misfooled every single one o' you. I never wrote no letters, I don't know no Helliagabbles, an' there ain't nothin' the matter with my dangly bits — so's my ma always insisted.

"Now I'd be most obliged if every one o' you could step off o' my front lawn and go about your business."

Mrs. Delaney leaned over to one of the strangers and said, "He's *such* a good actor — never breaks character for a second."

"I had just about enough o' you time-wastin' Yankees! Get offa my property and get off now, an' if I hear any more yappin' about one-man plays or dangly bits I'm a-gonna come after you with the kinda firearm the good Lord intended for use on buffaloes."

The crowd seemed unmoved, and simply observed him like a fish in an aquarium. At the back someone asked, "Does anyone have a program guide? What did I miss?"

"That's it!" shouted Spillane. He drew his revolver and started firing into the air. "That's the last warning you're gonna get."

The crowd started to break up, or so it seemed until Spillane spotted two men in broad hats pushing their way to the front.

"You Spivey Spillane?"

Spillane wasn't stupid — he knew a sheriff's badge when he saw one.

"What if I am?" he demanded. "I ain't got no quarrel with the law."

"I'll be the judge of that, mister. Deputy, search this man's house. Mr. Spillane, I'm arresting you on suspicion of robbing the Skunks Dance Bank."

"It's a lie! I never robbed no bank. I never done a damn thing against the law."

The sheriff frowned at him. "Then would you like to explain how you come to be dischargin' a weapon in public?"

"I ain't in public, this is my house."

"Mighty fine house for a newcomer in town with no money to his name."

"I mean it's not *my* house…"

The sheriff began jotting notes — "Squatting," he said, "and theft of property."

A man in the crowd said, "Come on now, sheriff, he was just about to show us how many willies he got."

"Indecent exposure," mumbled the sheriff, jotting furiously.

The deputy reappeared from inside the house and reported, "Sheriff, there's a strange menagerie o' wildlife locked up in that there house."

"Operatin' a zoo without a license…" noted the sheriff.

"Includin' a goat," the deputy added.

"Devil worship! Idolatry of the cloven hoof. Boyo, you got quite a bit o' 'splainin' to do."

Then, without another word, the sheriff and the deputy dragged Spillane away.

Chapter 4

Amanda hoped the police station would be full of muggers, drug addicts, and serial rapists. It was the least Jet deserved after what he'd done to her car, but Skunks Dance was a far cry from New York or San Francisco. The worst that ever happened was someone calling after 9:30, watering the roses during water restrictions, or repairing the local monuments without a license. Amanda would be lucky just to find someone in the drunk tank.

The only disturbance that seemed likely to inconvenience anyone was caused by Jet himself — or at least his family. Outside the police station Amanda saw Jet's mom, Mrs. Ashwood, camped out with a big picket sign that said "OCCUPY SKUNKS DANCE" on one side and "KISS THE 99% OF MY ASS" on the other. Jet's dad, Mr. Allan, was sitting next to his wife and quietly putting some brie on crackers.

When she caught sight of Amanda, Mrs. Ashwood shouted, "Yes! The word has got around! The masses are rising up. Come join us in our protest against the police state. We are the many. We are Anonymous. Fear us." She turned to her husband and hissed, "Get the mask. The mask!"

Mr. Allan reached for something in his picnic basket and unenthusiastically put on a Guy Fawkes mask. "How's this?" he asked.

"Shhh! Your silence will intimidate them more than your words ever could." Mrs. Ashwood turned back to Amanda. "Do you realize what's going on in that jail at this very minute? The fascist pigs in this town are waterboarding my firstborn, putting a bag over his head and

25

attaching electrodes to his nipples. The charges are completely trumped up. I never heard anything so crazy in my entire life. Exploding a car indeed. Who do they think he is? They're the real terrorists."

Sergeant Murdock stuck his head out of the station door and shouted, "Ma'am, if you don't keep that racket down I'm going to take you in for creating a public disturbance."

"You do and I'll make a citizen's arrest! This is a peaceful protest. I know my rights. I didn't fight in Vietnam so people like you could ruin this country."

"You *didn't* fight in Vietnam," said Murdock.

"That's what I said, isn't it?" demanded Mrs. Ashwood. "You great dummy."

Mr. Allan tried and failed to insert a piece of cheese through the mouthpiece of his mask. Although the mask showed no emotion, Amanda thought it looked disappointed.

Amanda turned to Murdock and said, "Excuse me. I'm here to see you about Jet Allan-Ashwood?"

Murdock eyed her wearily. "All right, miss. Come in."

"That's the stuff," cried Mrs. Ashwood after her. "You give 'em what-for."

Amanda tried not to catch Mrs. Ashwood's eye as she passed by, and ducked quietly into the police station.

The police station was one of the older buildings in town. It was originally a haphazard wooden construction thrown together as a hasty sheriff's office back when Skunks Dance had been a Gold Rush town. There wasn't much of the original structure left any more except the wooden floorboards that creaked with the dust of 150 years and were polished smooth by generations of law-abiding footfalls. If it hadn't been for the faint odor of feces and vomit that persisted from the dysentery outbreak of 1898, Amanda would actually have liked the place.

"They hanged people outside here when it was still a sheriff's office," she said. "Back on the old survey maps from 1850 they marked the place with a little gallows. It must have been really convenient — they could get their policin' and their hangin' done all in the same place."

Amanda smiled as if she'd said something funny. Sergeant Murdock, bored already, faked the best smile he could. The girl before him was tall and sturdy. Her hair was tied back in two tightly braided pigtails that carried irritating overtones. The effect was not helped by black stockings and a conservative tartan skirt. On the whole she gave the impression that she thought it was impossible not to like her. She was wrong.

"The more you learn," mumbled Murdock. "Now about this statement —"

"Of course the California judicial laws were all pretty different back then. They'd only just become a state. But then I'm sure you know all about that."

"You're quite the little... *expert*, aren't you?"

Murdock would have loved to use a different word, but his job tended to get in the way of good, old-fashioned personal abuse. All this public service could be a real pain.

"Oh that's nothing," said Amanda. "My dad's the real expert. He can tell you everything there is to know about Skunks Dance in the early days."

Murdock couldn't help cracking a smile. "Still looking for that missing treasure?" he asked.

"Yeah," said Amanda wistfully. "And you'd be surprised how much evidence there is. Everything we know suggests —"

"There's gold in them thar hills!" he said in a hillbilly voice.

Amanda just pursed her lips. It was nothing she hadn't heard before.

"How about we get on with this car business."

"Right you are, ma'am. If you can fill out a formal complaint we'll be able to press charges against Mr. Allan-Ashwood. A prosecution should also help you get a pay-out from the insurance company. Sometimes they need a little encouragement."

Amanda hesitated for a second. "I don't suppose I could talk to Jet before I fill out the forms?"

Murdock groaned inwardly. "I won't stop you," he said, "but we advise against it. You understand, ma'am, it helps prevent people being intimidated and whatnot."

"He *is* behind bars, isn't he?"

"Well that's true and we can guarantee you'll be perfectly safe, but bars can't stop him threatening you. Remember he already committed arson all over your car. We don't know what else he's capable of."

Amanda was beginning to regret throwing that rock through Jet's window. She must have stood outside his house for ten minutes, clutching the rock in her hand and feeling the frills of the doily through her fingers. But try as she might, steel herself as hard as she could, she just didn't have it in her. She'd sighed and turned back to Bentley.

Bentley, as ever, looked like he was 12. It was as if Puberty had taken one look at him, despaired, and went off for a friendly round of chess with Death. Bentley was blond, but inside that irritatingly whiskerless head sat the brain of a ruthless genius.

"Well?" he'd said.

"Let's go. I've already got his package."

"Are you telling me I came all this way to watch you not throw a rock through that dick's window? He's made your life hell since seventh grade."

"I'll figure something out later," she'd said.

That was when Bentley had grabbed the rock out of her hand and hurled it through the window himself, shouting "Vive la Révolution!"

"Ben! What did you do that for?"

"My God," he'd said, looking at his hands. "I'm a criminal. And I feel *fantastic*."

"Run!" she'd screamed, and the two of them had legged it before anyone was the wiser.

Now she was wondering why she'd ever agreed to let Ben come see the great window-smashing, but as soon as he'd got wind of her plans he wouldn't take no for an answer. If he hadn't smashed that window, she'd still have a car.

Officer Murdock led Amanda round the back of the station to a small room made of damp, gritty masonry. The place was divided into two cells by bars and in between them was a narrow walkway. As she stepped into the room Amanda realized there wasn't even enough room to keep her out of arm's reach. Her footsteps echoed on the stone.

Someone threw himself at the metal bars. Amanda shrieked and leaped backwards, pressing herself against the bars of the other cell. Grizzly features leered at her, a prematurely wasted face whose gums were receding faster than its hairline. His black, wet teeth glistened in the low light.

A chuckle came from behind Amanda and she turned nervously. It was impossible to watch both cells at once.

"They brought him in at like 1 a.m. He didn't stop screaming for an hour. Then he just sort of cried quietly."

"Who is he?" asked Amanda.

Jet stood up and walked over to the bars. "Sad Stan," he said. "I'm pretty sure I've seen him in the plaza covered in newspaper. Kids throw peanuts at him. He's here nearly every night."

Amanda tried to ignore Sad Stan and concentrate on Jet. "How long have you...?"

"Since yesterday afternoon, waiting for you to file that damn complaint. If you don't do it soon they're gonna have to let me out of here. They can't lock up an innocent man forever."

"Innocent!" Amanda exclaimed.

"Yeah, give or take. How was I supposed to know the car would explode?"

"You shot fireworks at it," she said through gritted teeth.

"Ah. Is that what those were."

"Give me one good reason not to send you down," said Amanda.

For the first time Jet looked unsure of himself. "Don't you want to?"

"Listen," said Amanda. "You don't like me and I don't like you. I'll refuse to give a statement. You'll get out of here — no charges, no arson, theft, and reckless endangerment on your record. But only if you do something for me."

"What do you want?"

"Protection. You let up on me and stop your friends making fun of me. Any time your flunkeys decide to pick on me, you stop them. I don't care what you tell them, just as long as they leave me alone. What do you say?"

Jet twisted his mouth into a wry smile. His teeth seemed unnaturally white in the gloom.

"Well, throw in my comic book and you've got yourself a deal."

Amanda flicked her head upwards in what she hoped was a disingenuous look. "What comic book?"

"The one you stole off my doorstep," Jet said humorlessly.

"Oh, you mean that expensive-looking package? With all the tracking numbers and insurance labels on it?"

"Yes," he muttered.

Amanda shrugged. "Justice is a poet, isn't she? That comic was in my car when some vandalizing creep set fire to it. It suffered the same fate as my Volkswagen."

Jet gripped the bars of his cell so hard his knuckles turned white. "*What?* That comic was worth $400."

"So was my car," Amanda huffed.

"What? You paid $400 for that lemon? You got ripped off."

"Mind your own beeswax!" she snapped. "Look, the only thing you need to worry about now is whether you're a deranged pyro or whether you were just first on the scene trying to put it out. I'll say I got confused in the dark."

"Fat chance. That place was lit up like Joan of Arc."

"Do you want to get out of here or not?" she demanded.

In the end, Jet had to concede he did.

Amanda rode her cruiser over the curb and heard the basket jolt against the handlebars. She let herself coast regally up the driveway and executed a perfect dismount at the garage door. The Spillanes' two cars were always parked in the driveway or on the street because Mr. Spillane had long ago converted the garage into a study. These days it was more like a shrine to the family obsession. Amanda could see her father was in there now, hunched over a wooden work bench surrounded by haphazard stacks of reference books. The walls were papered with historical maps of Skunks Dance and the surrounding hills, particularly the regions exhausted by the gold miners and excavated by treasure-hunters hell-bent on finding Spillane's lost gold. All these years later and people were still looking.

Every now and then some wag or day-dreamy millionaire wanted to squeeze out a sixteenth minute of fame. They'd claim they'd found something hidden away in the mountains or on a dusty plain, and suddenly all the country's bored media descended on Skunks Dance to talk about the treasure again. Then it blew over. There was no treasure. The reporters left town and the locals went back to sleep until the next fortune-hunter came along and reignited old embers. Everyone in Skunks Dance was thoroughly sick of it — except for the Spillanes.

Mr. Spillane and his father before him — the family had been devoted to the mystery for generations. Evenings and weekends Mr. Spillane could often be found in his garage poring over old maps, diaries, letters, and county records. If the solution was to be found, Mr. Spillane was determined to be the one who found it.

"Hey, sweetie," said Mr. Spillane without taking his eyes off the computer screen.

From what Amanda could see he was combing the 1850 census.

"I didn't know you had work today," he mused.

"I didn't," she sighed. "I just… thought I might check out the police reports on Leverett. I made an appointment with Mr. Snodgrass on Monday."

"Still stuck on Leverett? I wouldn't bother too much with cases like that. They're a dime a dozen, you'll go mad trying to trace them all."

"I guess you're right."

"You're not going to listen to me, are you?" he asked.

"Not really."

"Atta girl," said Mr. Spillane with a distant smile. "When you burn yourself out on Leverett you can come back and help me with Alabama Sam. He's not in *any* of these censuses. I'm beginning to wonder if he wasn't some kind of agent for the Masons or an underground Royalist movement. 'Alabama Sam' is a pretty bad pseudonym."

He idly clicked through a few pages of census data, so Amanda left him to work. There was always another avenue to explore. It was maddening, but it was the perfect problem — seductive and yet impossible.

Amanda went through the door at the back of the garage, and emerged out into the kitchen. She breathed in heavily and put on the coffee machine. An iced coffee was just what she needed. As the pot bubbled away Amanda sat on the counter swinging her legs. Maybe things were looking up. Maybe her last year of school would be easier than the others — and then she would be out in the world, spreading her wings, and basking in freedom she could only dream about here at home.

"You look like the cat that caught the canary," said Mrs. Spillane. "Do you have a good lead?"

Amanda jumped down and her mom absent-mindedly started buffing the counter where Amanda's butt had been.

"Yeah, I think I do."

"Well don't tell your father, he'll only want a cut of the money. You can keep it all to yourself and buy me a nice big sofa to retire on."

Amanda smiled softly at her mom. "You shouldn't be working *now*."

"There's always more to do," she said with a distant look. In this light Amanda could see the heavy layer of powder collecting in the wrinkles and worry lines on her mother's face. Her hair dye was just a shade too dark to look natural for her age. That distant look seemed to be in her eyes more and more these days. "But there's an end in sight," she breathed. "Don't you worry about that."

Amanda hugged her. "I love you, Mom."

Her mother shushed her and cocked her ear into the air. "Do you hear that?"

Amanda shook her head.

"That neighbor's dog is in the yard again. I'm going to have it spayed."

Mrs. Spillane grabbed her dog whistle from her shirt pocket and started blowing furiously, ambling into the yard at full charge. Amanda heard a sudden rustling as the dog bolted away through one of the bushes.

With her coffee in one hand, Amanda went up to her room and checked the references she needed for Monday. She couldn't help her eyes lingering on her desk drawer for a second, nor could she stop a little smile playing around the corners of her mouth. Nobody knew about her secret. It was a happy little memory she could call upon any time she needed cheering up. She opened the bottom drawer to make sure it was still there. Tucked away between two vertical files was the comic she'd stolen from Jet.

Amanda briefly pondered selling the thing to pay for her car, but it was almost worth keeping it just to know Jet couldn't have it. She wondered where he was now — probably just getting home. Amanda was sorry she wouldn't be there to see his parents' wrath, and she hoped this would finally level him out. But in case it didn't, Amanda still had the comic.

She smiled to herself. She could handle herself pretty well in a scrap.

Chapter 5

"Stranger, you're fulla all kinds o' crazy today."

"I ain't crazy," said Spillane as he paced up and down his cell.

Cell was a big word for what was really just a barred-off section of the same room. On the other side of those bars was the sheriff's office. There was also the sheriff, who had his legs propped up on his desk and looked mightily unimpressed with what little he'd heard of the story so far.

"You reckon there's gold in Skunks Dance in the middle of a gold rush? Son, everyone from Peking to Paris thinks there's gold in Skunks Dance."

Spillane remained tight-lipped.

"Have it your own way," said the sheriff, getting to his feet and pacing in front of Spillane's cell. "But in this county, we take the law pretty serious-like. You are lookin'," he barked, turning viciously on Spillane, "at a town on the edge of the world, Mr. Spillane. We exist only by the breath o' the Lord himself. When them purdy trees catch fire they burn down whole states. We're fightin' off the likes o' cattle rustlers an' gunslingers. We been through two sheriffs in the past year, an' now even the mayor's taken his leave an' ain't come back. Right now I'm the highest authority there is in this here town, so you can believe me when I say that if'n we catch ourselves a bank robber he's gonna hang for it."

The deputy entered with a young man trailing nervously behind him. The young man wore an immaculate black suit and a collar so high it was a wonder he could even bend his neck. For that matter, in all the time Spillane watched him, he never did.

"Mr. Spillane," said the sheriff, "this here is Mr. Jeffrey Mulvehill of the Skunks Dance Bank. D'you old friends got anything to say to each other?"

Mulvehill spoke up before Spillane could. "That's not Spivey Spillane," he said. "You've arrested the wrong man."

"Yes I *am* Spivey Spillane!" he shouted.

"I don't think so," said Mulvehill. "The fellow who robbed the bank was taller, intelligent eyes, kind of a silver tongue on him. This is a completely different man. You seem to have arrested some kind of a hillbilly."

"Yes! I mean no — I mean, damn it!"

"Please, Mr. Spillane, we're a Godly folk round these parts."

"There's your proof," said Spillane, pointing to Mulvehill. "I didn't rob that bank. That Alabama Sam set me up."

"That would seem to make the most sense," said Mulvehill. "The gentleman did seem pretty keen for us to know his name. In my experience that's not all that common amongst bank robbers."

Spillane grabbed at the bars of his cell. "You seen him. You know where he's at. Lemme at him, I'll clean his plow good an' proper, you see if I don't."

"My good Mr. Spillane, if I knew where he was you'd hardly be behind bars right now, sweating and shouting and hankering for a hoedown with twelve of your comeliest cousins."

"Lemme at him!" shouted Spillane. "Lemme at him!" It was no longer clear whether he was talking about Alabama Sam or Jeffrey Mulvehill.

The sheriff waved dismissively. "Get the suit outta here. I wanna word with Mr. Spillane — if that *is* his real name."

The deputy led Mulvehill out of the office, leaving the sheriff alone with Spillane.

"Well," said the sheriff, "I think you better tell me everything."

Spillane hesitated. "Sheriff, are you under any kinda… oath of secrecy?"

"No, but you're under some kinda oath o' start talkin' or I'm gonna feed your kidneys to the coyotes."

Spillane mumbled awkwardly, but in the end had little choice. He began to tell the sheriff what had happened.

It began with the Spaniard. No-one knew who he was or how he came to Tennessee, only that he turned up one day half-dead from starvation and exposure. His limbs were brown and wiry, but so spindly from malnutrition it was a wonder he'd made it any distance at all. The man's beard was enormous, gray and tangled. The hairs were cemented together by spittle and mud, except for where twigs had managed to lodge themselves and could not be removed without ripping the hair from his face. He was so weathered that no-one could tell if he was very old or just very ill.

He arrived one evening as little Andrew was fetching the firewood. The Spaniard's footfalls made no sound in the snow, almost as if he made no impression on the ground at all. The first Andrew knew was that someone had grabbed his shoulder. He spun around to find the grisly face of the Spaniard leering at him, reeking of a thousand untaken baths, skin dry and warped, teeth black and glistening with light reflected off the snow.

Then Andrew was screaming, tearing back to the house, firewood forgotten and scattered across the ground.

Spivey took the shotgun and went to investigate. When he got there he found the Spaniard face-down in the snow surrounded by discarded wood.

The man was so light Spivey didn't need any help to carry him inside. He laid him down awkwardly before the fire. The Spillanes were unused to offering any hospitality. It wasn't that they were ill-disposed to strangers. It was just that nobody ever came all the way out to the farm. The Spillanes rode into Breakneck often enough, or else received house calls from the doctor whenever a tooth needed pulling or a baby delivering, but a stranger? On the farm? It was unheard of.

Now the family gathered around the fire to wonder at what had washed up on their shore. While Spivey and his brothers worked to force some whiskey between the man's purple gums, old Ma Spillane held back and watched with a wary eye.

The man surfaced from his shock for long enough to speak a language the Spillanes didn't recognize. Then he died.

They buried the man in the cemetery at the back of the property. It had traditionally only been a family cemetery, but then family were the only people who'd died here. The headstones were scattered and badly ordered — just a few roughly-hewn chunks of rock with misspelled names etched into them with a nail. Great-uncle George's grave had been missing since the earth subsided into the river one spring, but they had managed to recover the headstone and put it back with the others.

Now they had a problem. They had to make a headstone for a man when they didn't even know his name. All they found on the body were a bottle of gin and a Bible that no-one could read. This was partly because it was written in a foreign language and partly because the familiar pages were scrawled over with cabbalistic images of idols and ceremonies of human sacrifice. Huge stone gods stared with gaping mouths while men wore demonic headdresses, leaping about in pagan dances before a fire.

The defaced Bible sent shivers through Spivey's old mother and she demanded the unholy object be burned. He promised he would. But Spivey kept it. On some pages, where the chapter endings left enough space, the dead man had scribbled thousands of words of his own device. Sometimes these had diagrams of strange machines, fabulous treasures, or maps of hills and coastlines that Spivey didn't recognize. There was something about it he couldn't put his finger on. He pored over the maps by candlelight for hours on end, tracing his fingers over the spidery outlines and trying to make sense of the alien topography. These maps led to something important. He knew it. Spivey couldn't let them be destroyed.

Ma Spillane, however, couldn't sleep with the book in the house. She seemed to know the book had survived even though Spivey had done his best to keep it from her. The more suspicious she got, the more determined he was to hide it. Her accusing eyes followed him day and night until, in desperation, he took his own Bible to the fireplace when no-one was looking. He knew he had to burn it to show his mother the ashes — maybe that would finally satisfy her — but when it came to doing it he froze, hands gripping the Bible a little too firmly. He tried to tell himself it was only a book, but he knew better. It was his link to his God — the only real possession he had to his name. But he had to burn something, and it was either going to be his Bible or the stranger's. He stood, suddenly gripped by indecision, heart palpitating as if he might die here and now. Then before he knew what he was doing, he had thrown the Bible onto the flames. The pages of the book curled angrily, finally. He could hardly believe what he had done.

The ashes seemed to put an end to Ma Spillane's questions for the time being, and yet every night the book was under that roof she slept fitfully, or else wandered through the night haunted by visions that would not let her sleep.

She began to grow ill.

She was becoming too weak to walk now, and Spivey had to bring her meals in bed. Just when it seemed like she might be slipping away for good, she reached out a bony hand and snatched at Spivey's elbow.

"Burn it."

He shook his head, terrified of what he was doing. Eventually he convinced her to let him bury the book with the stranger's body. Spivey trudged out into the snow and down to where the frozen river ran still and ice hung from the trees. When he cleared away the snow the stranger's headstone stared up at him, blank, like a featureless face. Spivey spent all morning digging up the frozen ground and placing the Bible between the stranger's hands.

For the first time in weeks, his mother slept. The color began to return to her cheeks and now, when she looked at Spivey, she was able to smile.

But one night Spivey Spillane went back for the book. It was so cold the chill stabbed at his very bones, but there was no way he could have retrieved the book during the day. With only a lantern for light he began to dig away at the frozen ground. Each impact of the shovel juddered through his arms, but he found that the exertion was at least warming him up. That and a frequent nip of whiskey from a flask he'd secured inside his boot. His breath billowed out in front of him as he leaned over the coffin and pried open the lid.

And that is just how Alabama Sam found him.

"Ornery Dago," said the newcomer.

Spillane looked up and stood rooted to the spot. A man was standing over the grave. From what Spillane could see he was wearing travel-stained clothes, but it was hard to tell by the light of the lamp that threw the shadows upwards across his figure and cast a ghoulish half-light onto his face. He gazed stonily at the corpse of the old man.

"Never could leave nothin' alone. Never knew when to give up." He grinned sideways at Spillane, acknowledging him for the first time. "Sorta like me."

The man leaped down into the grave with the languid, confident strength of a snake. He reached for the Bible, but Spillane's hand was on it first.

The stranger tensed and Spillane felt his hackles rise.

"Now that was a very interestin' thing to do," the stranger said. "I might almost say uncharitable, seein' as that book belongs to me."

Spillane finally broke his silence. "Now, sir, it seems to me that this old feller was runnin' away from somethin' when he died. Or someone. But you wouldn't know nothin' about that, would you."

"Smart man. How smart, I wonder?" The man said nothing more for a moment. The only part of him that moved were the eyes, which searched every part of Spillane's face. Then he broke into a sly smile. "You don't know what it is..." he breathed.

"I know what it is just fine," said Spillane. "It's mine. If you got some claim on the man who took it, well that man's dead. Now get on your horse and ride on outta town. We wrestle bears in these parts, an' that's just for fun. I could bury you in this grave an' no-one would know you was ever here."

The man never stopped grinning, just clambered out of the grave as carefree as you please and bade Spillane goodbye.

Spillane filled the grave back in and hid the book in his room. Ma Spillane slept badly again that night, and Spivey was wracked with guilt. He had to hide it somewhere where everyone would be safe.

But before Spivey could figure out a good hiding place, the stranger turned up on their doorstep calling himself Alabama Sam and looking for work as a farmhand. Old mother Spillane hired him immediately, despite Spivey's protests. Spivey tied himself into knots. He could never reveal what he knew about Sam without also confessing he'd dug up the Bible. There was nothing he could do.

That was the beginning of their uneasy truce. They worked together for weeks without drawing attention to themselves, but each keeping a close watch on the other. Spillane spent every waking moment ensuring Sam was not left alone in the house. At night Spillane slept with the Bible under his pillow to ensure Sam couldn't get his hands on it. There was something about those hands, Spillane now realized — something that unsettled him. It wasn't so much the way they looked as the way they moved, with strange monkey-like grabbing motions or like the slimy feelers on a snail. Spillane didn't know if it was possible to hate hands — just that he hated those ones, and that he would do anything to prevent them taking his Bible.

Ma Spillane began to get sick again, but Spivey couldn't hide the book anywhere else without leaving it open to Sam's disgusting fingers.

But in the end that wasn't enough. Spillane was fast asleep and felt the gentlest tugging from under the pillow. He very nearly went back to sleep, but the strange emptiness triggered something in his brain. Before he even knew what he was doing, he was running.

The footsteps were getting away. Spillane was in time to see Sam's silhouette vanishing into the night. Spillane scrambled into some clothes and sprinted after him. He could no longer see the thief, but he heard a triumphant shout in the dark.

Spillane gasped and paused for breath. The ground was uneven beneath his feet. All he could see around him were the dim shadows thrown by the moonlight. He glanced behind him and saw the house — dark, sleepy. It would have been so easy just to go back to bed and forget the whole strange business with the Spaniard and his Bible. But Spivey Spillane, the Baptist farmer who had never even left Breakneck, Tennessee in all his 20 years, did a very strange thing.

He ran.

Chapter 6

The cake arrived while Mrs. Ashwood was trying to inflate the jumping castle using only her lips. This was supposed to be done by the contractors with their air pump, but she'd bossed them around so much that they told her where to stick the jumping castle and promised to come back to extract it at 5. The backyard was teeming with children running, screaming, shoving food in their faces, and skinning their knees, not to mention all the Allan-Ashwoods' friends and circus folk who were there to entertain the kids. The funambulist was taking a sip of something from a flask and was already looking a little unsteady on his feet, the sword-swallower looked like he'd eaten something that disagreed with him, and the tattooed lady was showing off the illustrations on her grotesquely huge bosom to the mortified children. Mrs. Ashwood was for once the one trying to rein in all this chaos — now the doorbell was ringing, and on the other side of that door was a seven-story cake with eleven candles and a candy Wolverine on top.

"Jet," called Mrs. Ashwood from the jumping castle, "go see who that is, will you?"

"Are you still angry about the car?" Jet asked apprehensively.

"You're damn right —" Mrs. Ashwood said a little too loudly before she caught herself. Then she hissed, so the children couldn't hear, "You're damn right I'm angry. Someone could have been killed."

"You and Dad play with fireworks all the time."

"Look, right now I just need you to help out with your sister's party. If you can do that without setting anything else on fire, then we'll talk."

Jet sighed and went to get the door. Mrs. Ashwood just put one hand to her forehead and moaned, "God help me, I'm beginning to sound just like my mother. Stay cool, Cerise. Whatever happens, you still have Lennon."

His mom was making such a big deal out of nothing that Jet almost regretted setting fired to that car in the first place. But it was too late for regrets now. You do the crime, you do the time, he supposed — he just had to get through this party and hopefully then his parents would stop busting his ass over this.

He pulled open the front door to find the teetering birthday cake and three increasingly unstable pastry chefs attempting to hold it upright. "Aren't you gonna come in?" he asked.

"It won't fit in the door," growled the head chef. "Idiot boy."

Jet waved them round the side of the house and let them sort themselves out. The pastry chefs were just about able to keep the cake stable as they led it round the side. The top of the cake brushed past low-hanging tree branches, and the intrusion seemed to disturb a roosting magpie. It circled out of the tree and started to dive at the chefs' heads. They only just ducked in time, but the magpie caught sight of the candy Wolverine, a smug little figure with pecs stashed in yellow spandex and a self-satisfied smirk on its mouth. The magpie narrowed its eyes at the hateful little figure. Wolverine seemed to narrow his eyes back.

It was *on*.

The magpie dived at Wolverine and pecked viciously at his face. The chefs stumbled, trying to protect their faces but determined not to let this cake die a violent death. The layers slid against each other lopsidedly, but the head chef managed to bat the magpie out of the way in time to bring the cake to rest in the back yard. The cake had survived, if a bit battle-scarred — but Wolverine was done for.

"I hope you're planning to eat this thing soon," said the chef. "It won't last much longer than midday in this sun."

"Oh dear," said Mrs. Ashwood as she secured the brass attachments onto her bra. "Do you have any more Wolverines?"

The chef coughed wetly into his hands and pulled a candy Batman out of his pants.

"No more Wolverine, but we got too many of these Batmans. Can't get rid of them for love or money."

Mrs. Ashwood grabbed the Batman and waved it in the air.

"You don't have children, do you? This is a DC superhero. Wolverine is a Marvel superhero. No 11-year-old on the planet will stand for this sort of malarkey."

Gina ran up and gasped when she saw the Batman.

"Is that for my cake? I get a Batman too? This is the awesomest cake in the universe."

Mrs. Ashwood put on a tight smile and turned back to the chef.

"Let me introduce myself," she said. "Cerise Ashwood, and my husband Max Allan."

She pulled a business card out of her costume and handed it to the chef. It read:

The Amazing Allan & Ashwood

Death-Defying Stunts and Derring-Do
Domes of Doom, Monster Truck Rallies,
& Old Folks' Homes a Specialty

"Call me," she said, "and we can review your business model."

She cast her arm around him and, as he inched away, he caught a glint of starlight in her eye. Mad, demented starlight.

"You and I are in the same business," she said.

"Cakes?" he asked, squinting uncertainly at the lumpy assortment of carnies around him.

"*Show business*," she insisted. "You have to know what your audience wants. You'll be twice as popular with a bit of spit and polish in your act, I guarantee it."

Mr. Allan was dragging an Olympic-size trampoline into the back yard. He stood back and took a moment to position it right.

Mrs. Ashwood dropped the relieved chef when she saw her husband adjusting the trampoline. She rushed over and said, "Oh honey, not there. I'll be right under the power lines. We don't want another Montreal."

Her husband grinned. "You won that suit for medical expenses."

"You could just as easily have been collecting my life insurance," she scolded.

"No chance. A million volts across the cranium and you walked away with a tan. You're the invincible lady. Hell," he said with a wink, "you're *my* invincible lady."

Mrs. Ashwood smiled, but not enough to encourage him.

Jet, on the other hand, just groaned. Nothing made him want to become celibate more than the sight of his parents flirting. Mrs. Ashwood, however, caught that groan before he could stifle it. She clamped an arm around Jet and guided him to the kitchen.

"You make yourself useful and frost your sister's cupcakes."

Jet made a face. "Is that legal?"

"What is the *matter* with you? You know I'm this close to setting Big Brenda on you. You wouldn't be the first teenager she scared straight."

Jet glanced over to the enormous bearded lady, who growled at him menacingly.

Mrs. Ashwood spotted her and said, "Thumbelina, have you seen Brenda? I think it's time for one of her talks."

Thumbelina shrugged, cleared her throat, and spat. "If I was you, I'd frost them cupcakes, kid. Brenda scares the bejeezus outta me."

"All right, all right," he said, avoiding his mother's gaze until she went back to the bouncy castle.

Jet boggled at the sight of 50 cupcakes on the kitchen counter waiting to be iced. He began stuffing as many of them into his mouth as he could fit at one time. He got about four before he gagged and vomited into the sink. There. Now he only had 46 cupcakes to frost.

Jet's dad stuck his head in the house.

"I smelled vomit and came as fast as I could. The pyrotechnics didn't get damp, did they?"

Jet shoved the frosting gun in his mouth to cover the smell.

"It's fine," he said with a mouthful of frosting. "To tell you the truth I think L'Estrange might be hitting the bottle again."

"Mmmm," said Mr. Allan, "we really ought to have an intervention. We'll wean him off the Hi-C one of these days. But about your mother, she didn't mean what she said earlier. She's just a bit stressed. It'd mean a lot to her if you could help out today."

"You know I'm sorry, right?"

"I know, but you know how parents work. We can't let you blow up a car and get away with it. Not till you're 18, anyway."

Jet smiled at his dad. Mr. Allan knew the feeling a bit too well. He and Cerise still weren't used to being on the responsible side of the law, and he half wished that he'd set fire to that car himself. It wouldn't have been the first time he'd been arrested. Hell, if it hadn't been for over-zealous law enforcement he would never have met Cerise at all. The smell of police-station doughnuts and burned coffee still filled him with happy memories.

His wife interrupted his train of thought when she walked by with an armful of tiki torches and thrust them at Jet.

"Set fire to these," she said. "That seems to be what you're good at. I'm going to get my wig."

"Little scarab, please not Brunhilda," Max begged. "They're 11-year-olds, not the Skunks Dance Opera Society."

"It worked for Bugs Bunny didn't it? And anyway, Brunhilda *killed* in San Diego."

"I know, and we were lucky to be acquitted."

Gina was in the backyard with a big stack of presents and torn wrapping paper. Jet peered out the window and saw her swinging a new baseball bat and daring her friends to pitch cupcakes at her.

The doorbell rang. Jet's mom was fussing with her bra plates so Jet was on door duty again. This time he found the members of the Happy Faces Carnival Club, who all wore giant plastic heads that smiled frighteningly like demented cast members at the Devil's Disneyland.

"Good to see you, young Jet! Here, smell my flower."

The man angled the flower in his lapel towards Jet and sprayed him in the face. Jet yanked his headphones off and wiped away the water, resisting the urge to hit the giant carnival mask in its plastic mouth.

Jet's dad came by and said, "Hey, come in guys! Jet, go grab my video camera from upstairs. Your mom wants to record her act."

Jet groaned internally and wondered if this birthday party would ever end. *Record Brunhilda, frost the balloons, set fire to the cupcakes…*

He returned in time to see his mom climb up onto the trampoline. She was wearing a huge blond wig with pigtails and a metal hat with horns. Her bra was so pointy she had to be careful when turning around in case she accidentally eviscerated someone. Mr. Allan made sure Jet had started recording and announced, "Ladies and gentlemen, I give you the Amazing Cerise Ashwood!"

Mrs. Ashwood took a very deep breath and started to sing — a horrifying, ear-curdling, spoon-bending war-cry that could peel paint off a house or summon the infernal machines that would bring about the end of the world. Then Mrs. Ashwood did the unthinkable — she began jumping up and down on the trampoline, pigtails flying as she somersaulted and shrieked her terrible song.

Jet was just glad Josue and Steve had never seen this. It was so embarrassing. All of Gina's friends were laughing, but the attention only encouraged Mrs. Ashwood.

Gina was still swinging her bat. That's when someone found a firework on the ground and pitched it to her. Gina thwacked it straight into one of the tiki torches. The firework ignited and shot into the air, trailing red and blue sparks like a patriotic comet, and hit Mrs. Ashwood square in the bottom. She shrieked and lost her footing. Her next bounce propelled her dangerously far, but she was lucky enough to have a soft landing — on the jumping castle. Mrs. Ashwood landed face-first on the North-West turret where her pointy metal bra ripped straight through the plastic. The castle began to deflate with Mrs. Ashwood still wailing from the North-West turret.

"Happy birthday, kid," said Jet, tousling Gina's hair. "You sure done good."

"Thank you, thank you," she said with a bow. "I do what I can."

Mr. Allan was trying to help his wife, but she was too high up to reach.

"Jet, call 911!"

But Jet was just watching the camera screen and videoing the chaos. Sometimes he wished it were only the first time his mother's bottom had caught fire, but by now he'd begun to savor these occasions like a fine wine. The only problem was he could never show this to anyone.

48

He'd never live it down.

One of Gina's friends came creeping up on Thumbelina and grabbed hold of her beard, screaming, "You're not the real Santa Claus!"

The boy pulled Thumbelina face-first into the cake. She shuddered, feeling the frosting ooze between her armpits. Then the candy Batman tumbled off the top and hit her head with an unhealthy thud.

"What happened to Batman?" whined Gina. "He and Wolverine were gonna get gay-married on top of the cake."

Mr. Allan snatched the Batman off Thumbelina's body and said, "There! Batman's perfectly okay."

A FedEx woman appeared in the kitchen and said, "Hello? I rang the doorbell, I have a package for Jet —"

"That's me," shouted Jet over the hullabaloo.

"Are you sure this is for you?" she asked. "Where are your parents?"

"In a castle and on fire," said Jet.

"*I'm* Jet's father," said Mr. Allan. He walked over to the kitchen door but tripped on one of Thumbelina's legs and went sprawling. He tumbled into the FedEx lady and dropped the candy Batman directly into her bosom. She screamed and went toppling over with Mr. Allan, scrambling to escape this madman with a Batman.

Jet didn't even care any more. His package had finally arrived.

A raven sat perched on a bust of Pallas above the door. Spackle's workshop was full of heads and carvings and busts. Above the door sat the familiar image of Athena and the raven, but tucked away underneath the sofa was the death mask of Vladimir Lenin, while the disembodied head of Robespierre hung from the ceiling, twisting slowly to and fro like a sociopathic piñata. But it was the painting of Medusa's head that took pride of place above the mantelpiece. She stared out across the room with a mixture of anger, surprise, and accusation. Spackle would never have said as much, but he loved her for that.

But Spackle wasn't looking at Medusa today. He was looking at another painting, this one locked away inside a vacuum-sealed, temperature-controlled cabinet made of lead glass.

Someone rang the doorbell.

Spackle began swearing hard. He cursed, in turn, God, orphans, and the disabled.

"Get in here!" he finally yelled as he unlatched the door. "And shut that thing behind you. You're ruining my light."

Jet pushed open the door and felt Spackle's supercooled air conditioning wash over him. He was still trying not to giggle at Spackle's tirade, but it was an uphill battle. The last thing he wanted to do was irritate Spackle with the sound of youthful laughter.

After they stopped watering, Jet's eyes took a moment to adjust to the gloom. Walking into Spackle's house was like delving into a five and a half minute hallway. The only light came from status LEDs and small luminescent displays scattered around the room. He didn't need to see Spackle clearly to know he would have thin, straggly white hair which did not believe in the benefits of shampoo or haircuts. Spackle always wore khaki chinos in a baggy cut, and sweat-stained polo shirts with the neck-buttons open even though he kept his house at a cadaverous 50 °F.

Jet could almost see again when a searing flash went off. For a second all he saw was a painting suspended in the air, a screaming dragon. Then Jet was blind again. Something mechanical cranked and he heard the camera go off, though this time without a flash. X-rays, Jet supposed.

"What is it?" he asked.

"Saint George. Legion of Honor is having me photograph their collections. Shows uncommonly good sense for anyone crass enough to live in a place called 'Frisco,'" he spat.

The sound of surf guitar came crashing through the silence and Jet cringed as he tried to muffle the noise. He'd forgotten to switch off his phone.

"What's that?" Spackle screamed.

The old man tackled Jet to the floor before he could answer. Spackle's age was hard to tell — he looked like he'd been 70 for the past 30 years, like Patrick Stewart but without the good looks. Jet knew better than to underestimate his strength, though. He tackled like a quarterback.

Jet couldn't even move until Spackle had ripped the phone from his pocket and smashed it on the ground. He polished it off by bringing his foot down on it again and again until there was nothing left but debris.

If Jet thought that was the end of the matter, he was wrong.

"What do you mean, bringing abominations into my house? I could have been recording Edison cylinders, sound waves on tinfoil, the music of the Goddamned spheres. Instruments delicate enough to hear every conversation in Skunks Dance from the way the wind is blowing. Then you blunder in here with your squawking and your squeaking. You know why I moved to this town, this great big zero on the map, the town that bored Time? To get away from all the cars and trains and lights and" — he glared at Jet — "*teenagers* who want to 'lay down some phat beats' and 'rock out with their sock out.'"

Jet didn't bother to correct him. He didn't even mind being shouted at, as long as it was by a genius. He was furious the first time Spackle went off at him, but after Jet complained to other collectors he realized Spackle shouted at everyone. It was just his way of acknowledging you were there. The only time Spackle ever *really* lost his temper was once in the '90s when the IRS attempted to audit him, but they preferred not to talk about that. Nowadays they liked to pretend that Spackle didn't exist.

The old man dusted himself off and returned to the painting of Saint George.

"What do you want here anyway. Disturbing my peace. Better be good."

"I got a little something."

"Comic books," Spackle scoffed.

"Bit stranger than that. It's this really old Bible that came from the estate of Spivey Spillane."

For the first time Jet had ever known him, a wry grin crept across Spackle's face.

"Show me."

Jet had never seen Spackle so talkative, so he fished the Bible out of his bag. It was old, bound up in ancient, battered boards. The text was so well-worn it was beginning to rub right off, which wouldn't have mattered much anyway as it had been scribbled over long before. Someone had scored so deeply into some of the pages with a pen that he had run right through to the pages underneath. In some places there was strange writing, and in others dark, chaotic illustrations of sacrifice.

"I can't read it," said Jet. "But I figured you might. Or at least know what the language is."

"Vulgate," murmured Spackle.

"Can you read Vulgate?"

"Latin, stupid boy! Sakes, don't they teach you anything?"

"Not if I can help it."

Spackle grunted, and looked at Jet with something approaching approval.

"Been a long time since I saw one of these. Why do you have this?"

"Well, there's this completely retarded girl —"

"— Amanda Spillane."

"How did you know that?" demanded Jet.

"What, you think I don't have a brain? Think I spend all day playing with my willy?"

"No, it's just… Well, she's obsessed with this Spivey Spillane and I figured I could beat her to it. You don't track down a first issue *Fantastic Firecat* without some mad skillz."

"Just what we need," scoffed Spackle. "Another treasure-hunter."

"Think again, old man. I'm not talking treasure — I'm talking Amanda Spillane. She is going to go *mental* when she finds out I have this Bible."

"You'll spend your whole summer antagonizing Amanda Spillane?"

Jet nodded solemnly. "Everyone should have a hobby."

Spackle only grunted.

"That's him, isn't it?" Jet asked, pointing to a small statue in the corner. "That's the same one in the plaza."

Spackle nodded. "The statue of Spivey Spillane, or a model of it. Council wants to replace the real one. I told them to jump in a lake."

Jet gazed at the statue. It was complete in every detail, down to the pick slung over one shoulder and the arrow sticking out of its leg. It seemed to be missing only one feature — the head. It was strange to see a body without a head when the rest of Spackle's place was full of heads without bodies.

"Where's the head?"

"Not supposed to have one," Spackle grunted. "They put that statue up in 1974, without the head, just like Spillane when they found him in the river. Not much to do in Skunks Dance in '74, a statue was a good reason for a party. Barbecues, beer, music. It was awful. Put streamers all over the place like a Fourth of July parade. Then the mayor got up, made a speech and unveiled the statue. Headless, of course. Everyone was happy, everyone went to bed. Next day the statue had a head on it."

"Who put a head on the statue?" Jet asked.

"Do you think I know? Just because I've been around forever, I know everything? How should I know who put a head on the statue."

"So what's the big deal?"

"They couldn't take it off again!" said Spackle. "Everyone said it was vandalism, wanted it back the way it was, but the council found out it was illegal to remove the head. Law against vandalism says it's illegal to deface public works. Can't remove the head without removing the face. So there you go. We're stuck with a Spivey Spillane with a head. People think we're the biggest bunch of hayseeds on the West coast.

"Council never listens to me anyway. Stopped funding the historical society, didn't they? Buffoons. They'll scrap that historical statue and never lose a night's sleep. All I hope is I get the old one when they put some new atrocity in its place. I could polish it up, take off that infernal head, make it nice the way it's supposed to be. Got some sketches of the original and all. Mayor doesn't know what he has. No-one does."

Jet got home and cranked up the stereo. He tossed the fraying Bible from one hand to the other, smiling to himself.

"Turn off that noise," said Jet's mom. "Can't you see I'm in pain?"

She really did look aggrieved. Mrs. Ashwood was sitting on the sofa on an inflatable doughnut the exact same shape as her heinie.

Jet smiled and turned down the volume. Sure, his mom was a pain, and God knew she was never at her best when anything had attacked her hindquarters, but Jet didn't know what he'd do if he were stuck with some empty suits for parents. His mom and dad embarrassed the hell out of him, but at least they guaranteed life would never be boring.

"Sorry your Brunhilda didn't work out," he said. "It was actually pretty cool. And in the end it wasn't your fault. It was the firework that did it. I got the whole thing on camera."

"I know, I've already seen myself on YouTube. I don't suppose you know who's responsible for that?"

Jet shook his head. "Nuh-uh. I don't want anyone from school seeing that."

"Thanks…" said Mrs. Ashwood uncertainly.

"Say Mom, Harvey said something about that statue in the plaza today."

"Oh that creepy Mr. Spackle. He's got a house full of heads, but he's never once asked me to model for him." She held out her head so Jet could admire it. She looked like a starved owl. "Why do you think that is?"

"He said your expressions are too subtle. He can't capture the depth of your emotions. He has a room full of failed attempts to sculpt you."

His mom looked at him suspiciously. "You're making fun of me."

"Well maybe about the rejects. But the rest was true."

"Yes," she said with a sigh, "my emotions *are* too deep. I've always thought that was my only flaw."

"Mmmm."

Chapter 7

The sheriff eyed Spillane for a few moments. Spillane just stood and sweated. He couldn't believe how stupid he sounded now he'd said it all out loud. What had felt like a bottomless well of curiosity and frustration now felt like a puddle burning away in the California sun. Right now, home was starting to sound pretty nice.

"Now lemme get this straight. You left your hard-workin' momma to come all the way to California to get a demon-Bible you stole from a coffin? You're chasin' a man you only ever met once because he took that same demon-Bible which, God knows, probably belonged to him in the first place? And now you're tryin' to track down that man here in Skunks Dance even though he's a hundred times smarter'n you? I'm-a keep my eye on you, stranger. You're one crazy-ass son of a —"

The door opened and the sheriff got interrupted by his own deputy.

"Deputy, come on in. I was just readin' Mr. Spillane here the crazy talk."

"Hell's bells! Where were you up to?"

" 'Crazy-ass,' " said the sheriff.

"Heck, that's my favorite bit." The deputy turned to Spillane and started pointing at him angrily. "You crazy-ass gold-digger, you come all the way to Skunks Dance to go diggin' and pannin' for gold? Are you a lemming? If I told you to jump off a cliff would you do that too?"

"Oh this ain't no ordinary digger," said the sheriff. "This one got him a demon-Bible."

"Demon-Bible! Tarnation, we got ourselves a real original. This

55

'demon-Bible,'" said the deputy, "what does it do?"

Spillane looked back and forth between the sheriff and his deputy in confusion.

"I don't understand…"

The sheriff just chuckled. "Heck, we get people from all over the *world* come here chasin' a dream that never happens. We can't keep an eye on 'em all. We just read 'em the crazy talk and tell 'em to keep outta trouble."

"Then I'm not under arrest?"

"Naw, 'less you really did rob that bank," said the sheriff, pulling open the rusty door to Spillane's cell. "Just keep your nose clean, try not to do anythin' illegal. Good luck with your demon-Bible there, but I tell you now, son, if I see any walkin' dead in Skunks Dance, I'm a-comin' for you."

Spillane took his hat in his hand and bolted out of the sheriff's station as innocently as he could. Something about this town was screwy. It was like the whole state of California was on Mars.

Spillane tried to ignore the awful heat. It might be green up in the hills, but Skunks Dance was baking and choked with dust. He'd never known anything like it. The heat even robbed the air from his lungs.

Everything seemed simpler with perspective. Now that he'd made up his mind to leave, he could see everything as it really was. He must have been mad to leave home and run across the whole country. Maybe it had been a touch of the strong fives or some other such spiritual malady. Whatever the case, it was gone now. Ever since he left Tennessee the world had just gone mad. Maybe that's what the world was like all the time and it was Tennessee that was crazy? Who knew. All he knew now was he was miles away from home. California was the Devil's armpit. And Alabama Sam? A con-artist, a trickster, nothing more. Spillane doubted this "Alabama Sam" wanted anything more than to hoodwink some unlicked rube who didn't know a ham from a hamster. Well it wasn't going to be *him*. He was going home.

No sooner had he put Alabama Sam out of his mind than Mrs. Delaney ambushed him in the middle of the road. Spillane was so wrapped in his thoughts that he had no idea where she came from — just that she was suddenly in front of him and demanding something about orphans and one-man plays.

"How did you find me?" Spillane demanded.

"Oh I didn't think the sheriff would keep you long," she said, grasping at Spillane's arm with her spindly fingers. "Probably just giving you the crazy talk, I expect. Him and the deputy are such gentlemen. They're always making up new stuff to keep the crazy talk fresh. That's what I call real professionalism, you know? It really shows they care."

"Get your talons off me, ma'am. I'm gettin' outta here. With no disrespect, you and everyone you know are *nuts*."

"Oh, well isn't that a shame. Don't you worry, I'm sure the real Spivey Spillane will turn up in no time and we'll have this whole mess sorted out."

"Ma'am, for the hundredth time, *I'm* the real Spivey Spillane. The man you knew was nothin' but a snake-oil salesman."

"Ohhhhh," she said, nodding her head uncertainly. Spillane was just turning his back on the old coot when she added, "Then you'd be the rightful owner of that funny-looking Bible."

Spillane froze. His jaw clenched uncontrollably. He forced himself to speak slowly.

"And what funny Bible would that be?"

"The one that *other* Mr. Spillane left at the church. I've never seen such a funny-looking Bible in all my born days. It's just covered in pictures and writing, like some kind of a demon-Bible. I just figured it was Mexican. But if this other Mr. Spillane was a bad man, I guess that Bible rightly belongs to you."

In the space of a second the crazy was back in him like a tapeworm.

The old woman took Spillane to the church. She nattered all the way, but Spillane had no trouble tuning it out. He was of only one mind now — he *had* to have that Bible.

And at last, there it was. The same battered leather, the same yellowed pages — it was unmistakable. He picked it up greedily and flicked through the pages. It was all there, from the scribbled and blackened pictures to the indecipherable notes at the end of the chapters. It was incredible. Spillane could hardly believe his luck. Sam had really screwed up this time. It was almost too good to be true.

"I'll just leave you alone with your nice book," said Mrs. Delaney.

Spillane waved her away without really listening. He was too engrossed in the book. Everything was just as he remembered it. Only... did that drawing seem different? It had been so many months since he saw the book, but surely the map hadn't looked like that before. Spillane knitted his brow.

He flicked through the pages, desperately trying to confirm his memories. That's when he spotted a note written on the inside cover, the only writing in the whole book in English. It said: "Look in the closet."

Spillane was utterly lost. He looked around to see who might be watching, but he was alone with the Bible. Then a door caught his eye. The door to a closet. It couldn't be.

Spillane's heart beat faster and he laid a hand on the grip of his revolver. If Alabama Sam thought he was going to leap out and get the better of Spivey Spillane, he had another thing coming. He brushed his fingertips along the doorknob as if he could sense what was on the other side. It felt firm beneath his fingertips, heavy and full of promise. Spillane had him now.

He yanked open the closet door.

The contents of the closet came crashing down on Spillane's head, and something heavy struck him right in the face. He fell to the ground too stunned to react.

If Sam really had been in there, he would surely have killed Spillane by now. But Spillane wasn't dead, just stunned, with a bloody nose, in the middle of an avalanche of identical demon-Bibles.

He pawed through the heap in disbelief. They were the same, every single one of them. The drawings, the mad writing... Alabama Sam had somehow managed to knock up a mountain of fakes. No wonder all the maps looked different — they weren't even real. What's worse, they were never even meant to pass for real. This whole thing was just a joke at his expense.

Spillane felt his hackles rise. That swindler! He picked up the Bibles and began hurling them around the room in a fury, stamping his feet and swearing uncontrollably.

Until the priest came in and demanded an explanation.

Spillane suddenly remembered he was in church. The blood drained from his face and left him with a clammy chill.

"What in Heaven do you think you're doing?" demanded the priest. "Are those Vulgate Bibles?"

Spillane was dumbstruck. "You know what these say?"

"Of course I do! You people think I spend all day in the rectory quaffing communion wine. I do read Latin, you know. I do have an education."

Spillane held up one of the books. "And these notes, can you read what they say?"

The priest took the Bible from him and examined the page. Next thing Spillane knew, the priest was blushing.

"Oh my Lord," tittered the priest, "this is quite obscene. Can I keep one of these?"

"What does it say?" Spillane demanded.

"Well, this one says: 'You have the brain of a pornographic pea-hen and your nipples look like cucumbers.'" Then the priest blew a long raspberry. "To be honest, I'm amazed he even managed to spell that. And in Latin, too."

Spivey Spillane was too appalled even to speak.

Chapter 8

No, thought Amanda. *This can't be happening.*

She stared at the envelope that had been couriered to her house first thing in the morning before she had even had time to rub the sleep from her eyes or apply hair tonic to what she called her "problem scalp." She hoped she had just misread the damn thing. It was from her boss, asking her to serve papers — on Max Allan.

Amanda called him right away and protested everything she could think of — she wasn't rostered on today, she was too close to the Allan-Ashwoods to —

"You're perfect," her boss said, cutting her off. "They'll never suspect you're about to serve them. You can get all the way into the house before you whip out that envelope. Life's been owing me big time since my daughter pierced her unmentionables. I'd have preferred a stripper in a chocolate cake, but I'll take what I can get. Now on your way, you want to catch him before he leaves for work."

Before she could say anything else, her boss had hung up. Amanda huffed and put the phone away. She supposed this was why he was such a good lawyer. He always got the last word.

She sighed and shoved the papers in her backpack. It was a decent summer job most of the time. She got to collect the legal documents from her boss, then take them down to the City Hall to have them properly filed and notarized. If all that standing in line and filling out legal paperwork seemed too good to be true, then Amanda supposed that having to serve papers to Jet's dad was only karma. She reckoned she could just about hit the Allan-Ashwood house before she went over to browse the town archives. She swung her leg over her bicycle and pedaled away down the street.

Jet's house loomed up a few blocks away. Amanda prayed Jet wouldn't be awake yet. It was almost too much to hope for. Either way, she knew this wasn't going to end well.

She leaned her bicycle against the wall and walked up the steps. She could see the living room through the windows. It almost looked like no-one was home. She couldn't even hear the Allan-Ashwoods stirring.

Amanda rang the doorbell, clutched the papers between sweaty fingers, and hoped.

A loud crash from upstairs dashed her dreams of escape. Slowly a clunking noise made its way down the stairs and struggled to open the front door.

"Yes?" Mr. Allan asked.

Amanda was too shocked to reply immediately. Her eyes were glued to Mr. Allan's indecent costume — a pair of undersized red Speedos (with gold trim and tassels) wrapped inadequately around his nether regions. He appeared to have yellow smiley faces pasted onto his nipples. Now that Amanda had taken in the whole spectacle, she realized he had also been limping.

"You interrupted a very complicated trick," he said. "You people should know better than to come knocking on people's doors when — oh! Sorry, Amanda. I was miles away."

"Yes," she mumbled, wishing she were too.

"I have to train every day to keep me in my prime, you know. My old lady says I have the body of a 19-year-old."

Amanda glanced unkindly at his Speedos again and shivered.

"And thanks," said Mr. Allan, "for not pressing charges against Jet. The whole thing was probably just a rotten mix-up. And while we're at it, I think we can forget about that broken window. All forgiven and forgotten, eh?"

"Sorry, Mr. Allan, but I've been asked to give you this." She handed him the papers. "You've been served."

"You're suing us? After you told Jet you'd drop the charges? I take it all back. You're a devious insect! Jet was right to set that car on fire, and don't think I've forgotten about that window either."

"I'm not suing you," said Amanda. "It's someone called Emily Beagle, I don't know anything about it. I'm just the delivery girl."

"Your summer job is serving papers on people?"

"It's mostly clerical work —"

"I don't care!" shouted Mr. Allan. "Some idiot's suing me! Is it the Skunks Dance Opera Company? The noise pollution people again? Surely not the Dallas Bureau of Orphanages — all those children were found to have crossed over the safety lines and we could not be held responsible for every single loss of vision or hearing…"

Mr. Allan trailed off as his eyes scanned down the page.

"Candy cake-topper?" he mumbled.

Mrs. Ashwood's voice came down the stairs: "What is it, Max? My mastiff's getting cold."

"It's that FedEx woman!" he shouted back. "She's suing me for sexual assault with a candy cake-topper."

"What? That's absurd. Anyone could have dropped a Batman into that woman's boobs. It was an accident waiting to happen."

Mr. Allan turned back to Amanda, who was looking increasingly pained.

"Well," he said, "thank you for delivering these. I don't… I'm not supposed to tip you or anything, am I?"

Amanda shook her head. Mr. Allan nodded faintly, said goodbye, and shut the door. But as Amanda turned to walk away, she caught sight of Jet through the living room window, staring at her with burning eyes.

The wind whistled through Amanda's hair as she pedaled through downtown Skunks Dance. After the unpleasantness at the Allan-Ashwood house, she couldn't repress a happy sigh as she contemplated a day of research in the Skunks Dance archives.

Although she couldn't say why, Amanda liked Mayor Franklin. He was always happy to see her, always keen to share in her academic successes, though he had very little to do with it. Sure, this didn't make her too popular with Franklin's own kids, who would probably have liked a slice of that attention themselves, but that never seemed to bother

Franklin. Amanda just stayed away from them, if she could. In her opinion that was the easiest way to deal with anyone she didn't like — she just hoped they wouldn't see her. But every now and then they would deliberately bump into her in the hall or go out of their way to say something nasty over her shoulder in the cafeteria. She bore it with bad grace and scratched ever deeper grooves into the underside of her tray with her fingernails.

It was hard, though, to hold this against Mayor Franklin himself. He was always friendly and, Amanda thought, very genuine. No-one else could have got her into the town archives. She'd tried asking the archivist, of course, but he was one of the old guard who seemed to think the point of having records was so no-one could ever look at them. It sounded absurd, but Amanda knew enough librarians who felt the same way about books. It was almost more of a requirement than a handicap.

The City Hall was nice enough on the outside, but on the inside it was like a ghost town. A long bank of teller windows stretched from one end of the building to the other. The wooden counters had long ago lost their varnish from countless bored elbows. Amanda didn't know where all those elbows had come from or where they had gone — there was never anyone here.

Amanda stepped up to one window and peered around before ringing the bell for attention. She immediately wished she hadn't because, almost before her hand had lifted up off the bell, she caught sight of Mr. Snodgrass behind the counter. He was so old, shriveled, and tweedy that he blended right into the creaky wood and stacks of dusty papers.

"I'm right here," Snodgrass snapped. "Do you think that bell is a toy? Or were you just ringing for one of your slaves? Will it please Her Majesty to dine on plucked pheasant today, or would you just like me to get down on all fours and start cleaning the floor with my tongue?"

"Sorry, Mr. Snodgrass. I didn't see you there. I called earlier about doing some research?"

"Had to have a reply right away, didn't you. Couldn't write like any decent person, oh no. You had to talk right then and there."

"Sorry. Did I interrupt something?"

"Only my life! I don't have much of it left, but here, by all means take what dwindling seconds I have. I'll probably only squander them breathing in and out. I'm sure you'll find a better use for them, like texting on your telephone."

"I did try and email, but I think your website was down."

"Email!" Snodgrass screeched. "Where do you think you are — the CIA? The Pentagon? Want me to get cancer from all those dings and dongs and beeps and whistles and" — Mr. Snodgrass scrunched up his face and hissed — "prurient voyeurism."

Amanda patiently pushed an envelope across the counter. "You said I couldn't see the archives unless I had permission."

"Yes, and I also said you couldn't have it," Snodgrass crowed triumphantly.

"But the mayor said I could," Amanda said, indicating the envelope again.

Snodgrass was finally obliged to look at the letter, but not without snarling, "Don't take that tone with *me*."

"I'm not taking a tone, I'm just telling you what happened," she said, taking a tone.

"Come on then. But don't expect me to help you find anything. I hope you know how to use a microform reader."

"Of course I do."

"And if I come back there and catch you in the middle of any kind of prurience," he said, shaking a finger at her, "I'll eject you and your juices off the premises."

Despite Snodgrass' insistence that the Gold Rush era was in a different cabinet, Amanda said she knew what she was looking for and made a bee-line for the 1970s. Snodgrass threw his hands up in disgust and left her to work.

Amanda regarded the cabinet with undisguised glee. The answer was in here somewhere, she knew that much. The town's mysterious benefactor, the statue of Spivey Spillane, and the man who loved their town so much he never came back again... She knew there was something in it that everyone had overlooked. Someone knew something about that treasure, she was sure of it.

She tugged on the handle. The cabinet shook, but the drawers were locked tight.

"Mr. Snodgrass?" she asked.

"Told you," Snodgrass crowed. "You're here for the Gold Rush, you can get whatever you like. But only Mayor Franklin has the key to the 1970s cabinet. Did your good friend 'Frank' forget to fill you in? Maybe he smelled a rat — a dirty, prurient, teenage rat."

Amanda flipped open her phone and found the mayor's number. Snodgrass snorted and went back to the front room, leaving Amanda with the mayor on the line.

"Mr. Franklin? It's Amanda Spillane. I'm in the archives but there's a filing cabinet that seems to be locked."

"What do you want in there?" asked the mayor. Amanda wasn't sure, but something in his voice seemed to waver.

"I keep thinking Lawrence Leverett found something in the '70s. There's got to be something in that cabinet about why he commissioned a statue of Spivey Spillane."

"There's nothing in the 1970s that you need to worry about," he said. "We already know why Leverett donated that statue, the man was a great philanthropist who loved this town. Now you can have access to all the Gold Rush records you like, but the 1970s archives are strictly off limits."

"But —"

"No buts!" the mayor insisted. "I'm sorry, but it's council policy. The records in that cabinet are protected because they relate to people who are still alive. It would be grossly negligent for me to let you into those archives. I could be impeached for less."

"Fine," said Amanda. "I'm sorry I asked."

"Don't be upset, you have to understand the position I'm in. I'd gladly let you do your research, but what can I say? My hands are tied."

His voice had the tone of a vindictive dundridge who was all too happy to have his hands tied as long as it meant no-one else could get what they wanted either. With some surprise, Amanda found herself picturing a smile creeping across Franklin's turkey-jowls. She hung up the phone and sighed. This whole exercise had been for nothing.

In the other room she could hear Snodgrass sniping at someone again. Amanda was all ready to tune it out when she realized she knew that voice — it was Mr. Allan. She crept up to the doorway and tried to hear what was going on.

"This isn't my fault," Mr. Allan insisted.

"Whose fault is it, then?" Snodgrass replied. "Batman's? That's the problem with you young people — no sense of personal responsibility."

"It was an accident. I tripped over a bearded lady and the candy Batman just happened to land in the unfortunate lady's bosom."

"You see that envelope and you just keep on a-pushin', don't you?"

A woman's scream tore through the building.

"Miss Beagle!" cried Mr. Allan.

"What are you doing?" she wailed. "You're stalking me."

Her footsteps began clattering away into the distance.

"Please, no, I just want to explain. This is all just a misunderstanding."

Mr. Allan's voice faded off in the direction of the women's toilets. Snodgrass chased after him in a desperate attempt to prevent any more prurience.

Amanda exhaled slowly and stared at her shoes. Today could not have been a bigger wash-out.

Night crept over Skunks Dance like a bad smell after a party when you've cleaned everything but you know that somewhere, somehow, a stray glob of chicken liver pâté is slowly going rancid. Amanda lay on her bed with the window open, hoping she could relax a bit in the warm evening. It wasn't working. She kept going over everything that had happened, and each thought just made her cringe harder. She furrowed her brow and rubbed her palm against her forehead, trying to smooth out the memories that wouldn't go away.

She heard something rustle in the trees outside, and she eyed the window suddenly. She cast a glance back to her bedroom door. It was shut tight and the lights were off in the hall. Her parents were probably asleep, but they might just be reading in bed. Or they might wake up if she made too much noise — her dad was a very light sleeper. But if she crept out through the window, she could get out without waking anyone. No-one had to know.

The idea tickled her. Tonight she just wanted something — anything — that she could have to herself.

She slipped her shoes on and carefully inched the window further open, trying not to make any sudden creaking noises, until the gap was wide enough to squeeze through. Her room was on the second floor, and as she looked out into the night she could see the lower part of the roof outlined beneath her bedroom window. She put one foot through, feeling for a stable spot among the roof tiles. Then, with an easy push, she was free.

The night felt fantastic. Her room stared back at her, flooded with light, cramped and hot. The evening was dark and dangerous — it was the taste of liberty.

Already the worries from the day were melting off her. Amanda focused on lowering herself to the top of the fence between her house and the neighbor's, and then from there it was just a short hop to the ground. She landed hard, but relished the ache in her feet. Every step she took filled her with a sense of freedom and power. She had been tired before, but she had cashed in her nerves for energy and she was on top of the world.

The road was splashed with yellow from the sodium street lamps. Bright points of light shone from the neighbors' yards where LED lights stood guard along the garden paths. Above her the moon hung lightly in the sky.

Amanda heard footsteps ahead of her on the street, and she ducked behind a garden fence in a neighbor's yard. She was a little irked at having her reverie interrupted, but as long as she stayed hidden then the night was still her secret. She refused to share it.

The footsteps came closer, crackling on fallen leaves and twigs, until they passed by the garden where Amanda crouched. She peered over the fence at the receding figure and, with a clench of her stomach, recognized it.

It was Jet.

He was wearing dark clothes and trying not to make any noise as he went. He kept casting his eyes to and fro, looking at the house numbers as if he wasn't quite sure where he was heading.

He paused cautiously in front of Amanda's house, checking to make sure the lights were off and no-one could see him. Evidently he'd found what he was looking for. With a quick glance around him, he took a rock out of his pocket and pulled his arm back to throw it as hard as he could.

"Jet!" Amanda hissed.

Startled, he awkwardly tried to disguise the fact that he'd been about to throw a rock. He just about managed to keep ahold of the projectile and hide it behind his back.

"What rock?" he asked, unsure what was going on.

"What are you *doing*?" Amanda demanded, stepping out from behind the fence.

"*Amanda?*"

"Are you throwing rocks at my house?"

"You can talk. I'm just returning the favor."

"I never meant to throw that rock, I swear. And before you say anything, I had nothing to do with that law suit. My boss made me deliver those papers…"

While Amanda continued to talk, Jet's eyes wandered slowly down. Although Amanda dressed like a puritan, Jet was amazed to find the top button of her blouse had come undone.

"Are you a B-cup or do you go as far as a C?" he asked.

Amanda flushed and fumbled with the top of her blouse. "You said you'd leave me alone. You said we'd never have to talk to each other again."

"Yeah well that was before you served papers on my dad."

"That's not fair."

"Well, what am I supposed to think? You like bird-baths and doilies and fungus. And have you *seen* your hands? They're all grabby, like hand-feet."

"I do *not* have hand-feet!"

"Fine, foot-hands, whatever you want to call 'em." Jet watched her fume for a moment, but cut her off before she could say anything. "Look, all I'm saying is you're a terrible person. I don't mean it in a bad way, but whenever you're around the hairs stand up on the back of my neck. It's like a 'fight or flight' mechanism."

"I don't suppose you've considered flight," she said between gritted teeth.

"No. But I've been considering Spivey Spillane for a while."

"What *about* Spivey Spillane?"

"Well you guys have been looking for that lost treasure for a million years without finding it. I'm just willing to bet I can get there first."

Amanda turned an unflattering shade of turnip. "Do you know something about Spivey Spillane's gold?" she choked.

"Maybe I do and maybe I don't," said Jet in a voice designed to totally madden Amanda. He pulled the Spillane Bible out of his pocket and held it up so she could have a good long look at it. Jet's mouth twisted into a smug smile. This would show her.

Amanda burst out laughing. Jet frowned — the woman had to be hysterical or something. She was laughing out of sheer panic. Maybe something had broken inside her tiny brain and now all she was good for was sitting in a rocking chair and collecting cats.

"Oh my God," Amanda gasped as she fought for breath. "That is the funniest thing I've seen all day."

"I have Spivey Spillane's Bible!" Jet insisted. "It's full of secret notes and maps and directions. I'm going to find that treasure before you do."

"I know it's Spivey Spillane's Bible, I have like a million of those things. You didn't think you had the only one, did you? I've got so many I use them as draft excluders."

"This has hand-written notes on the inside!" Jet said.

"Oh I know. My favorite one is, '*Matercula tua tam corpulenta ut eam Hannibal trans Alpes equitare voluerit.*' That means, 'Your mom is so fat Hannibal wanted to ride her across the Alps.' Jet, they're all insults. There's nothing in that Bible that can help you find the treasure."

Now Jet turned a funny color.

"What about the bits in Spanish?"

"What bits in Spanish?" asked Amanda, holding onto her smile with a struggle. None of her Bibles had bits in Spanish. It was a Latin Bible.

"The notes in the margin. Harvey Spackle can read them and reckons they're from the early 1800s."

Amanda took a step towards him. "Let me see."

70

"No, I don't think I will."

"Please? I really want to see those notes, Jet."

"Well tough. I'm going to find that treasure and there's nothing you can do about it."

Jet began to walk away, but caught himself before he got further than Amanda's house. He made a short detour to her mailbox where he conspicuously placed the rock he'd been going to throw, waggled his fingers at Amanda, and sauntered off into the night.

Amanda stormed up to the mailbox, tore the rock out of it, and threw it at Jet's receding figure as hard as she could. It skittered off into the darkness. She hadn't even been close. Amanda couldn't believe Jet was about to beat her at her own game. It couldn't happen. She tried to reassure herself. The boy was practically a special needs student. He could never crack this thing before she did.

But the thought niggled — what if he'd lucked into something? Was it possible there was one real Bible among all the fakes? Because if he stood any chance of finding Spivey Spillane's treasure, she was going to stop him. She promised herself that — she would never let that scumbag beat her to the gold.

Chapter 9

Spillane didn't know whether to keep the phony Bibles or just leave them where they were. Knowing Alabama Sam, one of them might just say something designed to drive Spillane completely insane — or something vitally important. It would be just like him to dangle a real clue right under his nose among a hundred red herrings. Spillane resigned himself to his fate and began gathering the phony Bibles in his arms. By the time he staggered out onto the street, the Bibles towered up over his head. He could only see where he was going by peering around the side of the teetering stack. He had already stepped in horse droppings twice and taken an unwelcome detour through the dynamite store when he felt a tapping on his shoulder.

As Spillane turned around the Bibles toppled over and scattered onto the dusty road. The pages flickered open sadly in the open air and began to curl under the intense sun. Spillane looked back to see who had derailed him. It was a dusty-looking man with unkempt hair and a skewed necktie. The buttons had been torn off his vest and his coat had a tear along the shoulder seam. In one hand he kept an unhealthy grip on a parchment envelope. Spillane squinted at him. Was he wearing lipstick?

"Mister," said the man, "I'm gonna do some asking and you're gonna do some answering."

"No!" screamed Spillane. "Whatever it is, no. I've just about had enough o' you Californians buttin' in and never mindin' yer own business. I told you about a hundred times already, I'm the real Spivey

Spillane. There ain't no other Spivey Spillane unless you're referrin' to a mean-eyed Bible-thief who's got nothin' better to do with himself than blight an innocent farmer from Tennessee."

"Well ain't that just dandy, on account of it's you I been looking for. I'm the postmaster of Skunks Dance and I got a message for a Mr. Spivey Spillane. Wanna hear how I came by such a thing?"

"No!"

The postmaster reached out to adjust his hat before he realized he didn't have one. He crossed his arms instead and eyed Spillane as if it was his fault. "Well that's too bad. I'm gonna tell you anyhow. You see I was in my office minding my own dang business when one of you cowboys hit me on the back of the head and stuffed this letter into my unconscious hand. By the time I come to he was gone and so was my wallet. I just thank my lucky stars he didn't get up to any other nonsense while I was unconscious."

Spillane tactfully decided not to mention the lipstick.

The postmaster held out the letter. "It's for you."

Spillane flinched at the sight of it. He knew this *modus operandi*. That letter could only be from Alabama Sam, and Alabama Sam could only mean trouble.

"Who's it from?" he asked warily.

"Well," said the postmaster, tilting his head upwards in contemplation, "that I don't rightly know. The feller who walloped me on the back of the cranium didn't bother to introduce himself. Some might call that bad manners, but I prefer to think of it as enigmatic. Yeah, come to think of it, he was a real enigmatic son of a bitch. Now are you going to take this here missive and tell me what this is all about, or am I gonna have to get all enigmatic up in your business?" he asked, pulling up his sleeves.

Spillane reached out cautiously. "I'll take the letter," he said. "But any more'n that and you're on your own. I got my own troubles."

"Well whoop-dee-doo, ain't that a coincidence. Did you get beaned on the back of the noggin for the sake of a letter? 'Cause I did."

Spillane opened the letter slowly. There was no telling what Alabama Sam had in store for him this time.

His eyes scanned the letter in confusion. It was written in an unfamiliar hand and signed only with an X.

Spillane looked back at the postmaster. "Where's Dreadnought Hospital?"

The postmaster's face broke into a smile that gave Spillane a chill.

"If you're going to Dreadnought Hospital, you really do got your own troubles. There ain't no power in Heaven or Earth can help you there."

The town of Dreadnought was a few hours' ride from Skunks Dance. It was slightly bigger and, though it had fallen into disrepute, it had been around for longer than the gold rush town. After asking around Spillane had found out that the town's real name was Santa Sofia, but had become almost universally known as Dreadnaught. He was beginning to think the nickname had been intended ironically. As he rode into town he realized the buildings were boarded up and the stores were closed down. There were scattered signs that people still lived here — the occasional whinny from nearby stables, or the creaking of floorboards as the townsfolk pressed their eyes against the doors to see who had ridden into town — but aside from those eerie remainders of humanity the place looked like a plague had swept through it.

Spillane rode through the center of town and over to the outskirts on the far side. The buildings thinned out and soon he was almost in unsettled land. The only thing on the horizon was one big, black building.

Dreadnought Hospital loomed against the sky like the last rotting tooth in a mouth full of gums. A cracked bell lay on its side in the belfry — the only thing keeping it from falling through the roof was a mountain of garbage and filth that had been left there, jamming the bell in place. The setting sun cast a glow across the hospital, intermingling fiery embers with the wretched wood and wrought iron railings. A sign on the front gate hung crooked, flaky, and faded, the words "Dreadnought Hospital" barely visible in the dying light. In the distance a scream echoed across the grounds. Spillane heard the noise again and again until something muffled it and the grounds abruptly fell silent.

In a more optimistic time someone had put up a sign on the lawn that said "Keep Off the Grass." Spillane looked around now and saw only brown, desiccated grass entombed in the rock-hard earth. Even the rose bushes had died a long time ago. Now they were twisted, unfriendly cages with thorns jutting from every branch.

Spillane dismounted and looked for a post to tie up his horse. As he cast his eyes around, a colony of bats took flight from the belfry and suddenly the sky above them was filled with black leather wings. The horse tore itself out of Spillane's grip and bolted.

"Son of a bitch…" Spillane mumbled.

But he was too tired to be angry. His horse bolting away from him was just the latest in a long line of indignities. He had come this far. He may as well see what horrors lay in store for him next. They could hardly be worse than what he had already endured.

Spillane was surprised to find the front door open. It creaked as he stepped inside, but aside from that the hospital seemed unnaturally quiet. Then, as his ears adjusted to the silence, he heard frightened shuffling noises from upstairs and, in off-moments, the sound of someone crying.

Without warning a wild-haired old woman swept into the room on dusty skirts. She moved quickly for her age. When Spillane caught her eye he saw no hint of life — just the dull reflection of her surroundings. Spillane decided she must be the head nurse here, but only because he couldn't think of anyone else who would willingly stay in a place like this. Aside from that one glance she didn't acknowledge that Spillane was there.

"I'm here to see the patient in room 373," he said, trying to catch the woman's attention.

The old woman stopped in her tracks and looked at Spillane. For a moment the spark of something that might once have been curiosity glinted in her eyes, then died. She nodded and strode off towards the stairs. They ascended together, Spillane trying to keep up with the nurse's quick feet.

"You the family?" she barked.

"No, ma'am. Just an interested party."

"We get those from time to time," she said. "They don't stay long."

They reached what must be the very top floor and stepped onto the landing. Spillane took a moment to catch his breath. By now the light had completely gone and the house was shrouded in night. The nurse lit a candle and led Spillane down a long corridor until the slope of the roof brought the ceiling in so low he had to hunch over. The last door at the end of the hall was marked "373 — By Special Admittance Only."

The nurse unlocked the door with a heavy iron key and handed Spillane the candle. She was about to disappear when Spillane stopped her.

"What do I do when I want to leave?" he asked.

The old woman looked back at him as if the answer was obvious.

"Scream."

Chapter 10

"Jet, you're carrying a spade. Try and see reason."

"It's not a spade!" Jet huffed. "I'm not building sand castles. This is a shovel, like the army probably use."

Mrs. Ashwood, standing on her hands, crossed her legs in consternation. "I'm a simple woman, Jet, and I call a spade a spade. Your father and I are worried about you."

Jet's dad was more upright, but toyed nervously with his mustache the same way he did before a big show.

"But I've cracked it!" Jet said. "I know where Spivey Spillane's treasure is buried. It's not a Gold Rush treasure at all, it's even older than that. It's all in this old Bible. Harvey Spackle says it's in Latin."

"Where did you learn Latin?" asked Gina.

"The moon," said Jet.

"Don't talk stupid, they speak Spaceman on the moon. 'Roger roger, my warp thrusters are interfering with the waffle maker. Breakfast is gonna be late. A-hurp-durp-durp.' Everyone knows that."

"It's in Spanish too," said Jet, pointing at the page. "Someone's gone through and made notes. Whoever it was figured it all out. The treasure was hidden there by the Spanish before the Revolutionary War. It's worth more than anyone ever suspected. And *I* did it! I figured it out!"

"It's not the treasure we're worried about," said Mr. Allan. "Don't get me wrong, I'm glad you're putting your high-school Spanish to use, but you've become obsessed by material wealth. We wouldn't be good parents unless we told you how serious a mistake that is. Marx has a lot of things to say about valuing money over people. It's a warped and fetishistic point of view. You'll head straight for a nervous breakdown, and you know where you'll wind up then? Dreadnought."

"You remember what happened to Winnie," said Mrs. Ashwood.

"There you go," said Mr. Allan. "She had an unhealthy obsession with money too, but after the electroshock therapy her wits weren't sharp enough to cut a French cheese. And what about poor Amanda?" he continued. "What has she ever done to deserve all this?"

"Oh you don't have to worry, I'm not in it for the money. I'm in it so Amanda will never feel like a complete human being again. I'm going to take her soul and crush it like a soda can."

Jet bundled the shovel out the door and grabbed his dad's car keys on the way.

"I'm borrowing the car!" he called back through the house. "Stay cool, comrades. I may be gone some time."

The door slammed behind him and Jet's parents exchanged the same look.

Max Allan supposed this was what Jet's teenage rebellion looked like, although frankly he'd been hoping more along the lines of something he'd had too much body mass to do himself, like being a stunt pilot or operating a Dalek. Max suspected this came from Cerise's side of the family — there was certainly no dialectical materialism in his own family tree, but Cerise had a great uncle who was an investment banker, and they had always been vaguely worried those genes would resurface when they least expected it. At this rate Jet was going to be a lawyer or a chief financial officer, or something too ghastly even to contemplate — a politician.

At least, for the time being, Gina had avoided the same fate. Sure she looked up to her older brother, but she was far too independent to obsess over him.

The house fell strangely quiet. The only sounds were his own breathing and the Zen slurps Cerise made as she drank her coffee upside-down.

"Gina?" he called out.

But the house remained still.

The car juddered over the dirt roads as Jet approached the outskirts of Skunks Dance and went up into the hills in the direction of Calaveras Ridge. The shovel slid back and forth in the trunk, but he was barely thinking about how he was going to dig up the treasure and transport it back to town. That was all just trivia. No, he was thinking about exactly what he could do to rub Amanda's nose in it.

As the camera flashes went off and the national journalists thrust microphones towards him, he would say, "I can't figure out how no-one found it sooner. When you look at all the clues, it was all so obvious. Anyone could have done it."

"But no-one did!" a helpful reporter would remark.

"Well," Jet would say smugly, "that's because they're idiots."

"Tell us, miracle wonder-boy," they would ask, "what will you do with all your millions?"

"I'm going to donate it to charity," Jet would say solemnly. And he was going donate a (small) amount of the money to charity, he really was, just so he could say, "You didn't think I was going to *keep* it all, did you? Haha, nooooo. That would be so selfish and greedy. Do I look like a Spillane to you?"

And then what? He could have the statue of Spivey Spillane taken down and replaced with one of him instead, with a big imposing face looking down on the town like Mussolini, and then Amanda would have to pass by it every day of her life and remember how he'd beat her.

He had got as far as the annual town fair that would be held in his honor when Gina, secreted in the back seat, popped her hands over his eyes and yelled, "Guess who."

Jet swore and the car skidded to a halt in a ditch, barely missing a eucalyptus tree and frightening a den of skunks, who sprayed the tires without mercy.

Gina leaned over Jet's shoulder and whispered, "You're not a very good driver, are you? Dad's gonna go mental."

"Gina! You could have killed us. Why —"

"Fun," Gina said before Jet could finish the question.

He hated it when she did that.

"How —"

"Because I'm awesome."

Jet forcibly hauled her out of the car to inspect the damage. He didn't strictly need her help, but he knew if he left her inside she was liable to drive the thing into a nursing home or find out that their Toyota had a hidden ejector seat. Plus he was also kind of hoping the skunks would come back and spray her, just a little bit.

They sprayed him instead.

"Jesus!" he screamed.

"He can't help you now," said Gina. "Are you going to smell like that all day? Because it's making me uncomfortable."

"It's making *you* uncomfortable? How do you think I feel?"

"Who can say? It's just one of those mysteries we'll never know."

Jet grabbed Gina and, despite her kicking and thrashing, managed to wedge her back into the car. As soon as he had locked her in, Jet jumped back into the driver's seat and turned the car around. There was no way he was making this whole expedition with his little sister attached to him like a face-hugger.

Gina sat in the back seat, arms crossed, glaring at Jet in the rear-view mirror.

Then she said, "I'll tell Mom you're the reason her Shetland pony can't have babies."

The car screeched as Jet turned it back to the hills. He was stuck with her, but he swore to himself there was only so many times Gina could play that accidental vasectomy card.

The engine strove against the hilly road, grinding as the tires threw up dust behind them. Soon they had to park the thing in a quiet spot by the side of the road and make the rest of the trip on foot. Jet took out the piece of paper with his notes from the Spillane Bible and followed its directions exactly. It had been all of 150 years, but the trees and rocks and distances had not changed. Ten paces here, oddly shaped rocks there... It matched the Bible exactly. Whoever had made all these notes hadn't left anything to chance.

The further they walked, the darker the sky seemed to get. The trees grew thicker and closer together, the leaves and branches intertwined above their heads and conspired to block out the sun. Jet shivered in the sudden shade, aware that they were quickly losing track of time and distance. He pulled his phone out of his pocket to check the time, grimacing a bit even now at the thought of having to shell out his hard earned pennies for a new model after Spackle had so thoroughly annihilated his last one.

"Come on," said Jet. "We've got to be close by now."

But the instructions grew more and more complicated. Distances that sounded short on paper turned out to take ages. It felt like they'd been hiking through the trees for hours. Jet was beginning to wonder if they'd even be able to follow the instructions in reverse and get back to the car. All those people on the news who they find in the forest after two weeks, dead, and being eaten by ants — they all started like this. The first inkling they had that anything was wrong was, "Do you think we'll make it back before lunch?" Then, "Do you think we'll make it back before dinner?" Soon, "Do you think we'll make it back?" And finally, "Then it's agreed, we eat Gary first."

Jet wasn't sure where the ruins started. The first he knew was that the ground had become more even, and when he looked down he realized the rocks he'd been walking on were cobblestones. They were crumbling and encrusted with layers of dirt, but they were there. The further they walked, the higher the stones piled until they were walking past decaying walls and hallways.

Gina's eyes were filled with awe. "Was there a castle here?" she asked.

Jet shrugged. "Probably a fort or something. It's a Spanish treasure. They built forts, right?"

"They built inquisitions!" said Gina. "This was where they tortured heretics. 'Bring me the thumbscrews. I can make him talk.'"

"I don't know. We should be careful. We don't know how stable the ruins are."

As Jet spoke he stepped on a loose cobblestone. Something in the walls creaked, heavy with the weight of centuries, groaning and grinding ominously. A loud twang reverberated through the ground.

Jet's heart leaped out of his chest — but nothing happened.

"What was that?" he breathed.

Gina only stared in shock. It was the first time Jet had seen her lost for words.

Jet looked down and saw the stone he'd stepped on move back into place. He gently pressed it with his foot and heard it click again. There was another twang — and silence.

"Look!" said Gina, pointing to where a dozen ancient arrows had buried themselves into the wall years ago.

The arrows were all in a row at regular intervals, except for one in the middle, which seemed to be missing.

"Jet, doesn't the statue in the plaza have an arrow in its leg...?"

She trailed off, realizing the answer to her own question. Jet went pale. Spivey Spillane had been here 150 years before them, and he found out the hard way that the ruins were booby-trapped. It was only thanks to Spillane blundering into the trap first that Jet and Gina weren't face-down on the ground and skewered like pin-cushions.

"I want to go home," said Gina, suddenly shivering. "I don't like it here."

"We can't go back now. We're almost there. Here," he said, unzipping his hoodie and handing it to her. "This'll keep you warm."

Gina put the hoodie on and the long sleeves flopped around, but she did look a lot cozier. She wrinkled her nose playfully at Jet.

"Just be careful, all right?" he said, wrapping his arm around her shoulders in a half-hug. "There might be traps that haven't been set off yet. You know, collapsing ceilings, giant boulders..."

"Pits of snakes?" Gina asked.

Jet nodded. "Pits of snakes," he murmured. "Come on. We'll be all right. How does the *Indiana Jones* music go?"

"Dun dah dah dahhhhh," quavered Gina, before trailing off. She shivered inside the hoodie and wrapped her arms around herself. The breeze rustled through the trees, and the movements of the world seemed to spiral about her in slow motion.

"Jet," she said. "I don't think it's snakes we have to worry about."

Jet followed Gina's gaze and saw the walls of the ruin were encrusted with layers of knotted spider webs. They weren't like any kind of spider web he saw in movies — those delicate, geometric spirals that lure their prey by gentle persuasion, or the thick cotton props that might as well have been sprayed onto the sets. These were random, angry, uncaring webs, coating bricks and branches like a layer of dust just waiting out the ages until the next unsuspecting passer-by came along. Now that he saw the webs, Jet also began to make out other shapes crouching in the dark crevices between stones and under leaves. A spindly black leg here, the egg-laden bulge of an abdomen there, and just occasionally the curve of an eight-eyed head. They clicked gently to themselves, and waited.

"Are they friendly?" Gina asked.

Jet shook his head and whispered, "I think they're black widows."

One of those black widows scurried cautiously up to Jet's shoe and stood there, poised and waiting. Without warning it struck, biting into the rubber sole and jumping back again. Jet shivered and kicked the thing away.

Gina scrambled for something in her pocket.

Jet pulled her towards him, whispering, "Try not to make any sudden movements."

"I've got that pepper spray Mom gave me," she said, and pulled out a small black cannister. "Do you think this will kill black widows?"

"Heck, if Mom gave it to you it'll probably kill people. Give it here."

Gina whisked it out of Jet's reach. "Nu-uh. It's my pepper spray and I don't wanna get bit any more than you. Don't worry, big brother, Gina Allan-Ashwood is on the case."

Gina started to murmur the *James Bond* theme to herself while holding the pepper spray at arm's length like a gun.

"All right," Jet sighed, "just be careful."

With a shriek Gina was gone.

Jet's heart pounded against his ribs. He dropped his shovel and dashed over to where Gina had slipped out of sight. There he discovered an enormous the hole in the ground. It was almost invisible in this light. He peered carefully over the edge.

"Gina?" he shouted. "Where are you?"

"I'm okay," she said uncertainly. "I don't think it's far down. I just can't see anything."

"Are there any... snakes?"

"I can't see anything! Why would you say there's snakes? Do you think there's snakes? What am I going to do if there's snakes?"

"I'm sorry, just keep calm and try to stay still. I'm sure there's no snakes — it's night-time. They only come out in the day, right?"

"Except the deadly Night Cobra in *Fantastic Firecat*," Gina giggled nervously.

Jet smiled despite himself. "And he's afraid of light, right? Well here we go…" He reached for his phone and shone some light down into the pit. But as he leaned over to get a better view, the ground began to crumble underneath his feet. The hole gaped beneath him as its edges collapsed inwards. Jet skidded on the cobblestones and fell tail-bone-first into the ruined cavern.

"Oh my God!" he screamed, rolling over in the dark. "I think I fractured my spine! What —"

"You fell in," Gina said.

"Don't *do* that," Jet hissed. He stood up and rubbed his tail-bone. It felt a bit better now he'd stretched. "Why did —"

"You were too heavy. All those cafeteria lunches," she said, and Jet couldn't help smiling again.

He hunted around in the dark and the rubble, searching for where his phone had landed. His hands touched only rock and grit. A sweat sprung up on his brow. He might never find it in all this mess. He and Gina might be stuck down here until morning. His phone *had* to be here somewhere.

As he got more and more desperate he started throwing chunks of rock out of the way until finally he caught a glint of moonlight reflected off a glass surface. His phone had actually landed underneath some of the collapsing rubble. Jet retrieved it and inspected the damage. It was a wee bit dented, but basically okay. He cursed the smug look on the genius' face when he'd said he didn't want the insurance policy — it was almost like he'd *known* this would happen, the bastard.

Jet turned the screen back on and illuminated the cavern. It seemed to be an underground room in the old fort. Now the roof was crumbling, it was more than easy to fall into one of these tunnels. He was surprised the whole building hadn't collapsed in on itself.

Gina stared up at Jet in horror.

"What?" he said. "Have I got something on my face?"

"No," Gina said a little too quickly.

"Is —"

"Fine!" said Gina. "It's all just peachy-keen."

Jet brought the phone slowly up to his face. As the light fell across his features, he could just about make out the shape of a fat black shadow crouching next to his nose.

Before Jet could even scream, Gina fired the pepper spray directly into his face. The spider dug in, but as Jet screamed and thrashed he managed to fling the thing off into the darkness. His phone followed it, and as it hit the ground the light suddenly went out.

"Are you all right?" Gina asked.

"I can't see! It bit me and I can't see! We've got to find a hospital."

"But it's too far to climb," said Gina.

"Find the phone and call someone," said Jet, desperately trying to keep his breathing regular. "Is there a way out of here?"

Gina picked the phone off the ground and tried to turn it back on, but it didn't respond.

"Uh, Jet? What kinda insurance plan you got on this thing?"

"I didn't get one," he snapped.

"Well, I hate to break it to you, Orville, but this ain't gonna fly."

"Help me find a wall," said Jet, trying to keep the panic from rising up in his throat. His eyes were streaming and his whole face burned.

With one arm on Gina's shoulder he felt his way through the darkness until they found a wall they could follow. Gina had lost all sense of the dimensions of the chamber but she had the feeling they were getting deeper and deeper underground. She decided not to tell Jet.

At last they thought they could see something — a faint gleam in the distance. A way out? It seemed to shine unnaturally in the darkness like... Gina reached her hand out in the direction of the light and felt her heart sink. It wasn't a light at all. It was only a stray glimmer of moonlight reflecting off a metal sconce. They'd come hard up against the far wall.

"It's getting colder," said Jet. "Are we —"

"No," said Gina. "It's a dead end."

Jet shivered from more than just the chill. He could feel his face starting to go numb.

"Let's just retrace our steps," he said.

Gina was ready to lead him back the way they came, but before she could move she heard a deep, rusty groaning sound. A portcullis slammed shut, trapping them against the wall.

"No!" cried Gina. "We're trapped here now."

Jet could hear she was close to tears.

"We'll find a way out," he said. "Don't worry. Busted phones still give out a signal, right? They can follow that. They'll come find us soon."

Neither one of them felt very convinced.

Gina's foot collided with a stray object on the ground. It skittered across the stones until it came to a halt against the portcullis. She could just about make out a shape. She knelt down and felt the object cautiously. It was dry, and a little cool to the touch. Her fingers followed its contours. Some edges were smooth, others were rough, and then… were those *teeth*? She dropped the thing with a yelp.

It was a human skull. Something had swiped it clean off its body.

A heavy clank echoed through the tunnel.

Gina tackled Jet and brought him crashing to the ground. A second later something sliced through the air above their heads.

They had just found out what beheaded Spivey Spillane.

It was all too much for Gina. Jet was wounded and they were trapped underground miles from the nearest hospital. Even if they did manage to get out, Gina couldn't drive them back.

"Jet, how —"

"I don't know," he said slowly. "But we'll find a way."

Jet's head felt heavier and heavier. The swelling was making it difficult to speak.

Chapter 11

The cell at Dreadnought Hospital used to have windows. It used to have a lot of things — light, happiness, wallpaper... They were all gone now. The cell was dark, the walls flaky with plaster, and the floors furry with mold and shaved hair.

In the middle of it all sat a man.

At first Spillane could only make out his outline, but as he drew closer he saw the grimy straitjacket that had, by some visionary, been extended into a pair of straitpants. Nobody was taking any chances with this man. He was quite mad.

He was facing towards the black windows, so still that Spillane wasn't even sure the man was breathing. Slowly Spillane walked around him until he could make out the figure's face. He couldn't suppress a shiver.

"Who are you?" Spillane asked. "I have a letter," he said, holding out the message he'd received from the postmaster.

The man said nothing, but slowly the muscles in his face began to move. They twisted themselves up into knots, leaving his teeth bare, his face contorted, his eyes trapped inside a horrible mask. It was the first indication Spillane had that the man was even alive.

"Welcome, Mr. Spillane," said a voice from the corner of the room.

Spillane jumped out of his skin. They were not alone.

A man stepped out of the shadows wearing an immaculate white suit. The red carnation in his buttonhole was the only color in the room that wasn't permeated with misery. Despite the low, slanted ceiling, he'd found the one corner of the room where he could stand without hunching awkwardly. It took a second before Spillane realized it was his landlord, Aurelio Nunes.

"What're you doin' here?" Spillane breathed.

With a deft flick Nunes produced a letter similar to the one Spillane had received.

"I believe you and I have a common acquaintance. It's one we share with this poor, wretched creature," he said, indicating the madman. "He was once Gregory Stone."

Spillane grunted. "So?"

Nunes chuckled throatily and lit the end of a cigar. The heavy, fruity smoke wafted through the cell, if anything improving the smell of the rotting walls.

"You are a naïf, Mr. Spillane. That is a quality I respect, and regret that I no longer possess. So, I expect, does Mr. Stone. A meeting with Joe Rattlesnake tends to disabuse one of any higher notions."

"Joe Rattlesnake?" Spillane asked.

"Or, as you know him, Alabama Sam. You may be surprised to learn you are not the only person Rattlesnake has confounded. Mr. Stone and I also have a debt that we fully intend to repay. But I didn't come all this way to warn you off Rattlesnake. No — I propose we join forces to bring the scoundrel to justice."

"He's mine," snarled Spillane.

"Oh, you are very welcome to try on your own. But before you do, I suggest you take a good look at Mr. Stone here," he said, indicating the madman again. "He too encountered the unparalleled 'Alabama Sam.' "

A scurrying noise echoed from within the walls. A frenzied look came over Stone's face. He rolled over onto his front and began inching towards the wall using only his teeth, then waited. An enormous rat poked its head out into the cell. With a speed that shocked Spillane, Stone swooped at the rat. The next thing Spillane knew, the madman had the rat in his mouth and was biting down hard on its head. Its skull burst like a grape.

"Rattlesnake is no ordinary man," said Nunes. "Rather, he is an elemental ghoul — an immovable object, an unstoppable force. No one of us can outwit him alone. But together, you and I can corner him and crush him."

Nunes ground his cigar out on the wall, fingers clenched with a rage Spillane understood all too well.

"If you didn't send me this letter…" said Spillane slowly.

Nunes smiled wanly. "You are slow, but you get there in the end Mr. Spillane. I think our foe would like to pit himself against both of us at once. He has issued us a challenge."

"Then we're doin' just what he wants," said Spillane. He turned towards the door. "You go your way, mister. I'll go mine."

"Mr. Spillane, you don't fully understand what you are dealing with. Do you see our friend there on the floor, covered in rat blood and giggling like a schoolgirl?"

Spillane nodded.

"The first time *he* ever met Alabama Sam was last Saturday morning at the Skunks Dance Rainbows for Orphans charity fête. This time last week he was bank manager."

Stone gaped at Spillane with a blood-soaked chin and empty, glassy eyes.

The blood ran cold in Spillane's veins. "All right," he said. "Let's you and me have a talk."

The Belle and Bullet-Hole Saloon was a friendlier place than its name suggested. It was not one of the more popular bars in Skunks Dance, but that also meant you were less likely to get shot over a game of poker or have your mother's integrity called into question. It was, however, ideally positioned to sell refreshments to the patrons of Ambassador Ming's Garden of Terrestrial Delights. These gentlemen (and the occasional lady) could usually be seen, sweaty and ruffled, pouring a beer over their head and asking for salted nuts.

The tip jar at the Belle was a skull with the cranium sawn off. Spillane looked at it askance before the barman caught his raised eyebrow.

"That," said the barman, "is the last feller who didn't leave a tip."

By now its eye sockets were crammed with silver. Spillane ordered his whiskeys and was sure to leave some coins behind.

Nunes had already taken a seat at a table towards the back of the saloon under the shadow of the stairs. He smoked laconically, letting clouds sneak up from under the staircase and billow upwards towards the guest rooms. Spillane was sweating uncomfortably in the airless room. Despite wearing a three-piece suit, Nunes never appeared to perspire.

Spillane plonked himself down at the table, sloshing whiskey over the rims of the shot-glasses.

"I'm most obliged," said Nunes, raising his glass to Spillane.

Spillane raised his own uncertainly in return.

"All right," said Spillane. "What's your business with Alabama Sam?"

Nunes smiled condescendingly, and Spillane found himself getting annoyed at Nunes' breezy attitude.

"My dear Mr. Spillane, everyone from St. Louis to Sacramento has business with Alabama Sam. The man is a prolific confidence trickster. And the one thing worse than a con-man, Mr. Spillane, is a con-man with a sense of humor. Our Alabama Sam fancies himself a comedian."

Spillane grunted. "I know what you mean. He's got everyone in this town thinkin' I got some kinda one-man show…"

"A show you will have to perform, of course."

Nunes took a sip of whiskey and enjoyed watching Spillane splutter.

"No, don't be so quick to reject the idea," said Nunes. "We are here to trap Alabama Sam in a web of his own intrigue. We cannot do so without the help of these townsfolk. They may be stupider than a dead herring, but the more of them we have on our side the more powerful we will be. For that is the one thing Alabama Sam will never understand — human solidarity. The man is criminally deranged, and will never comprehend why one human being would help another. That is a weakness we shall exploit to our advantage."

"So what?"

"I'll be waiting in the audience, Mr. Spillane. Do you seriously think Alabama Sam will pass up the chance to watch you humiliate yourself on stage? It is the one move he will not expect you to make, and the one move he will not be able to resist witnessing himself."

Nunes pulled a poster out of his pocket and examined the words through a pince-nez.

"What did you say the production was called? *Heliogabalus' Pursuit of the Sugar Plum Faeries?*"

Spillane gawped at the poster. It spelled out the name of the play in garish block letters, and had a picture that seemed to depict Spillane wearing a ballet costume and doing a splits.

"What's that?" demanded Spillane. "Where did you get it?"

Nunes waved the poster at him. "This little guarantee of good times has been plastered all over the town. The charming Mrs. Delaney has been most diligent in preparing for your one-man show. It's rather sweet, really — she must have been looking forward to it for weeks."

"I ain't gettin' on a stage and makin' a damn fool outta myself!" he spluttered. "I'm gonna look like the biggest half-wit in the West. An' what's this about?" he said, pointing to the illustration. "My legs ain't never done nothin' like that. They're gonna have to wheel me outta there."

Nunes crossed his arms skeptically. "Mr. Spillane, there really is no other way. This bait is guaranteed to lure Sam out of hiding. Without it he will dispose of you at his convenience and the most your family will have to remember you by is your toenail clippings. The only thing I fail to comprehend is why he's still in this podunk little town. If I were him, I would have vanished into the ether a long time ago. I can't imagine what he is hanging around for."

Spillane pursed his lips.

"You might think you're mighty clever with your poster and your plans, but you can't take me in as easy as you think. You learn a thing or two on a farm, mister. One of those things is how to lay a trap, an' if you can lay 'em, you can spot 'em. You'd like me and Sam to fight it out so you don't have to dirty your lily-white hands."

"Spillane, if you could spot a trap you would never have come to Skunks Dance in the first place. Alabama Sam isn't trying to get rid of you. You're not his arch nemesis. You are his plaything. You're what Sam likes to do for fun. You're not frustrated at every turn because you're a danger to him, you're frustrated at every turn because Sam loves to taunt a dog with a fresh bone and then kick it, and for some reason you keep coming back. To catch Alabama Sam you need to be smarter than a dog, Mr. Spillane, and you need to be smarter than a man — you need to be smarter than Alabama Sam, and that's a greater proposition all together. That is why you need me."

Spillane slumped forward in his chair. His eyes ached, and he rubbed them with grubby hands.

"What do you want me to do?"

Chapter 12

"*What* do you want me to do?" asked Bentley.

"I don't have time to explain everything," said Amanda over the phone. "I need you to distract Jettison so I can pinch his Bible and get to Spivey Spillane's treasure before he does."

"Who is this?" he asked disingenuously.

"Ben!" she hissed.

"All right, all right. Where are you?"

"I'm across the street from Jet's place."

"All right, I'll be there in a few minutes."

"No!" she said, but Bentley had already hung up.

It was lucky for Amanda that the Allan-Ashwoods had a eucalyptus tree across the road from their house. It was easy to reach the branches, and its leaves hung in just the right way to shield anyone hiding there with a pair of binoculars and a cellphone. The only downside, as far as Amanda could see, was that the bark was tearing holes in her stockings.

Her phone started vibrating in her pocket.

She attempted to fish the phone out of her pocket without falling out of the tree. She flipped the phone open and said, "Ben?"

"Amanda?" said a girl's voice. "It's Nina."

"Oh! Helllooooo," she said, trying to sound like she wasn't in a tree.

"Where are you?" Nina asked.

"Nothing. I mean, nowhere. You know, not *nowhere*. Just hanging out. Chilling out. Chilling and hanging out."

"Whatever. Hey listen, are you doing anything on Saturday?"

"No," said Amanda, determined that if she could ignore her racing pulse that meant she wouldn't sweat. She could hardly believe Nina was calling *her*. They'd barely even hung out.

"Wanna go see *Afterglow* at the mall? There's a session at one so we can get lunch first."

"I'd love to!" she said.

"Yeah, that's great. Hey listen I gotta go. See you then."

Amanda flipped the phone shut and let it rest in the palm of her hand. Her skin tingled. She'd never been sure about Nina. In fact she'd been 99% sure Nina was into boys, but *Afterglow* was undeniably a date movie. Why else would Nina ask her out? They never even talked unless they happened to be with the same group of people.

Sometimes, when they were sitting near each other in class or during an exam, Amanda would stare at Nina when she wasn't looking. She had amazingly smooth skin. Her hair was so long and straight, and it seemed to fall effortlessly behind her ears, except for every now and then when a stray strand would tickle across her face and she'd tuck it away with one hand, smiling. Sometimes Amanda would try and say something funny, though Nina never laughed, just looked away a bit awkwardly. Maybe Nina had finally noticed her, or realized that boys weren't her thing. Whatever. It didn't matter. All she knew was that every time she saw Nina, Amanda felt lighter on her feet — smarter, more interesting — happier to be alive.

She smiled to herself. Saturday seemed so far away, but the wait would be a pleasure. She wondered if she should buy a lottery ticket while she was on a roll. The only thing left to do was beat Jet to that treasure, and she had a good feeling about that too. All the cards were coming up Spillane.

Footsteps interrupted her reverie, and Amanda bunched up tight against the branch to make herself less conspicuous. The footsteps rustled the twigs and leaves on the ground below her, circling the tree a few times before Amanda spied Bentley's sunny hair. He sat down carefully by the trunk and Amanda watched him for a moment, trying to figure out what he was thinking.

"Psst!"

Bentley looked up.

"You're in a tree," he said.

"I know where I am!" Amanda hissed.

"Are you a peeping Tom now? What do you call a female pervert? A peeping Tina?"

"You need to keep your voice down, someone will hear you."

"Is that it there?" asked Bentley, indicating Jet's house. He grinned mischievously. "I *knew* you had a crush on him."

"Why does everyone think I have a crush on Jet?" she asked.

Bentley rubbed his chin and said, "You're spying on him from a tree. Why would anyone think you have a crush on him? That's a stumper. Can I phone a friend?"

"Okay, first of all, if this is a game show, I'm totally the contestant and you're the friend. I called *you*, remember? I need your help."

Bentley considered whether he had anything better to do than watch Amanda's speedy decline into insanity, decided he didn't, and started to climb the tree trunk uncertainly.

"If I get any sap on these pants, I'm going to send you a bill for the dry cleaning. That goes for any other suspicious fluids I find in your vicinity too."

"It's not *my* fluids you need to worry about — I'm going to set you up on a date with Jet."

"You want to set me up on a date with your boyfriend?" Bentley asked. "This is perverse. Tell me more."

"I knew you'd like that. But don't get too excited — it's all part of the plan. I need to get Jet out of the house while I sneak into his bedroom. He has something of mine that I'm very keen to get back. So, I set you up on a date so you can lure him out of his web of lies."

Bentley smiled wistfully. "As long as you're granting wishes, can I also get a secret underwater base? And are you all out of death rays, or should I just ask for a pony?"

"He won't know it's you," said Amanda. "I'm a girl."

Bentley snickered and said, "Well, there's some debate about that. Still, at this angle, one good breeze and I'll be able to see for myself."

Amanda glanced back at him on the branch and pulled her skirt down protectively. "You better not be perving on me from down there."

"It'll take more than your moldy knickers to lure me over to the dark side of *that* force."

"*I'll* call Jet, put on a voice he won't recognize, and get him out on a date. Only when he gets there, it'll be you. You hold him up for as long as you can. I get in and out of the house before he gets back. I get what I want, and I get to humiliate Jet to boot. He has been asking for this for such a long time."

"Thanks a bundle," said Bentley. "It's so nice to be everyone's favorite humiliation date. Remind me to warm up the tar and feathers before I go."

"I know, I know, but listen, I'll cut you a deal — I'll go to the prom with you."

Bentley crossed his arms as best he could without falling out of the tree.

"Well," said Amanda, "do you *have* a boyfriend?"

"No…"

"Is any girl going to choose you over an actual date?" she asked.

"No…"

"So, you either go alone and have a stark premonition of your lonely and loveless future, or you go with me and have a pretty girl on your arm."

Bentley suppressed a smile and raised an eyebrow at her.

"Don't push it," said Amanda. "What do you say? Prom date for baiting Jet?"

Bentley sighed. "Okay," he said, "but only because you were a Girl Scout, and I respect the good research your people have done in the field of cookies."

"Ben, I could kiss you! Thank you, thank you," gushed Amanda, pulling out the cellphone again and bringing up Jet's number. She hit the call button and waited. They could just about hear the phone ring in the house across the street. "Hello, Mrs. Ashwood," said Amanda. "Is Jet home?" Amanda's eyes grew wide. "Do you know where he is? Seriously? Never mind. Thanks very much."

She turned to Bentley and said, "He's already gone! Plan's off, thanks for the memories, I'm going in!"

She jumped off the branch, landed awkwardly, and before Bentley could get a word in she was hobbling across the street.

Jet was, as far as Amanda could tell, a man-child. The first thing she saw as she hoisted herself through the window of his bedroom were walls plastered with posters of heavy metal bands like Venom of Vengeance, Apocalyptic Goat Hemorrhage, and Sweet Adeline. She could only assume that last one was supposed to be ironic. These metal bands all played music that sounded like someone throwing up onto an untuned electric guitar, but then Amanda suspected she'd sing badly too if someone had pierced her ears with a hole-punch.

Mixed in with the metal posters were hundreds of old comic books, some even dating back to the 1940s. This, Amanda had to concede, was actually kind of cool. Each was kept in its own plastic sleeve and stored in order on a bookshelf. Jet actually had more bookshelves than she did, though, in her opinion, no actual books.

Amanda jumped when she heard footsteps in the hall. She froze and tried to hold her breath. If anyone came in now they'd catch her in the act. But the footsteps went by, and Amanda's heart slowly returned to a moderate gallop.

A scuffling noise at the window made her jump again, but as she spun around she realized it was Bentley hauling himself up over the window-sill. Amanda hurried to give him a hand.

"What are you doing? I told you, the plan's off."

"Moral support," he said a little too loudly.

Although she knew that a risk shared was a risk doubled, she had to admit it was kind of nice having Bentley in on this with her. Then at least if they were caught, she had someone to face the music with.

"What did you say you're looking for again?"

"You can stick around, but you have to *be quiet!* If you don't keep it down I'm going to tell your parents you were alone in a bedroom with a girl."

Bentley chuckled and said, "It's too late to go giving them false hope now."

Then Amanda's eye caught the corner of something on Jet's desk. It was buried under a huge stack of comics, papers, and pencil-shavings, but it was there. Amanda didn't even stop to ponder the fact that Jet had been drawing comics of his own and that the illustrations weren't as bad as she'd have expected. She just brushed everything to one side and seized the thick, leather-bound Bible. It was open at Revelation 13 — the number of the beast.

The margin was crammed with notes written in an ancient hand. Amanda had seen it all before. She had a dozen similar Bibles at her own house, all of them dating from the time of Spivey Spillane — but none of them had writing like this. These notes were different. With a gasp Amanda realized that this was the genuine article.

A second hand had also been writing in the margins. It had circled the original notes, underlined them, and started to decode them. No way Jet was smart enough to do this — besides, it wasn't his handwriting. Someone else had been here after Spivey Spillane. The writing style looked mid-century. Amanda's heart fluttered. She *knew* Lawrence Leverett had been on to something. If these notes were his, then maybe he really had found something in Skunks Dance.

"It's a Vigenère cipher," said Bentley.

"A what?" Amanda breathed.

"It's a polyalphabetic cipher. Look, it uses a repeating keyword to encrypt a message. The keyword here is… 'NERÓN' — Spanish word for Nero. Clever bastards. In the 1840s this would have been totally unbreakable."

Unbreakable for the 1840s, maybe, but little more than a brain-teaser to anyone in the 1970s. Sure enough Leverett had scrawled his own decipherment in the margins. The message, however, was in Spanish.

"It's a good thing I came top of the year in Spanish," said Bentley.

"And it's a good thing I came second," said Amanda. "Can you back off a bit? I need some light."

"Hey, I helped you get this far!" Bentley protested.

"All right," whispered Amanda, "just keep your voice down. Check the door, you can come with me to find the treasure."

"If someone else hasn't gotten it first," said Bentley.

"What are you talking about?"

"Whoever deciphered that message knew where the treasure was buried. He had full instructions. Chances are by the time you get there, the treasure will be long gone."

Amanda swallowed hard and prayed he wasn't right. Hell — he was always right. Amanda's fingers clutched the book with sweaty rage. She hadn't come this far just to find out Leverett had made off with the treasure and was sunning himself silly in a villa somewhere in Italy.

"Just watch the door, will you? I thought I heard someone coming."

Bentley went over to put his ear up against the door while Amanda slipped quietly out the window.

"Is the coast clear?" Amanda called up.

"Yes!" Bentley shouted without thinking.

He grimaced and cursed himself for apparently forgetting how to whisper. He could already hear footsteps coming up the hall. It was too late to follow Amanda out the window.

The door swung open and Mrs. Ashwood came up short at the sight of Bentley attempting to look casual in the middle of Jet's room.

"Oh!" she said. "I thought Jet was out. Ohhhh," she said with a wink. "I didn't realize that was an excuse to sneak a boy into his room. Well let me know if you want any cookies or sandwiches. And be safe! There's protection in the medicine cabinet. Just ahhh, don't look in the bottom drawer under the sink. Unless you want to. In which case there are fresh batteries in the utility drawer, and make sure you wipe it down before you put it back. Have fun!"

Mrs. Ashwood shut the door and Bentley stood there, stunned, in the middle of Jet's room, wondering what the hell just happened and whether he'd somehow been given the wrong parents.

The light was failing by the time Amanda found Jet's car up on Calaveras Ridge. She'd come all the way on her bike, pushing herself hard over the rocky dirt roads and sending up clouds of dust that stuck to her sweaty skin.

She skidded to a halt by the car and leaned her bike up against it. It seemed deserted. Amanda put her hand on the hood and tried to feel how warm it was. She didn't know much about cars, but it didn't feel like anyone had driven it for a few hours at least. The light was fading fast, and Amanda could just barely peer in through the car windows. There was no sign of Jet.

With a sigh Amanda pulled the Bible out of her bag and squinted to see the writing. If she didn't hurry she wouldn't even be able to read the directions. She set out into the forest as quickly as she could without losing her way. The trees closed in around her until it was so dark she had to shine her phone to illuminate the pages of the Bible. She charged forward, slowing down only to avoid tripping over or startling anything poisonous. It was probably a good thing it was too dark for her to see the spiders gathering around her in the trees.

The ground gave way to cobblestones. Her feet surprised her when she felt the paving below — it was too dark to make out any more than the shadows of the ruins. With flatter ground, Amanda found she could increase her pace. Who knew how far along Jet had come. He might be digging up the treasure right now. Her only consolation was that his car was still here, so he must still be here too. Amanda wouldn't let him win. She wasn't going to lose sight of the treasure now. Her whole life had been building up to this.

Amanda's foot came down unevenly on the edge of something and, with a brief shriek, she twisted and fell. The night spun around her as she tumbled into the cavern. Her phone went skittering off into the dark. The Bible slipped out of her hands, fell down after her, and struck her squarely on the head.

She hauled herself up and groaned as she felt her aches and bruises. Her foot seemed okay, and although her leg was sore she didn't think anything was sprained or fractured. She'd done all right considering she just fell through an invisible hole in the night. She took a moment to pocket the Bible and find her phone again.

"Who's there?" called a voice.

It was far off in the cavern somewhere, and strangely high pitched. If Amanda didn't know better, she'd have sworn it was a child's voice.

"Hello?" Amanda called. "Is that you, Jet?"

"He's here!" said Gina, breaking down into sobs.

Amanda felt her way towards the voice, trying not to walk into any walls or any more pits.

"What's wrong?" asked Amanda.

"He's hurt. I think he's going to die."

"Wait there, I'm coming. Just keep talking. You're Jet's sister, aren't you?"

"Gina," she said.

"Gina, I'm Amanda."

"Jet's girlfriend?"

"I am *not* Jet's girlfriend," said Amanda through her teeth.

She continued to make her way through the dark asking Gina about what happened and how they found themselves here. As far as Amanda could tell something had happened to Jet but it wasn't clear whether he was hurt by the fall or by something else. Gina was strangely quiet on the subject, and Amanda didn't want to push her for details in case she started crying. The most important thing now was to find them and get to a hospital as soon as possible.

Gina's voice was so close now, Amanda thought she must be almost on top of them. Amanda's hands brushed something in front of her. Suddenly she felt Gina's hand reach out for hers. It was such a surprise that Amanda shrieked and jumped back before she was able to calm herself again and inch back towards them.

"There's a metal gate," said Gina, wiggling her fingers through the grille. "I can't lift it on my own."

"Hang on," said Amanda. "I have an idea. I just need to find something to lever it up. When you and Jet came down here, did you see anything I could use? Like a branch or something?"

"No," Gina whispered. "Please hurry! Jet's breathing funny."

"Oh gosh," said Amanda. "Here goes, then."

She set her phone down, grabbed the portcullis and heaved it upwards as hard as she could. It was heavy and the rust bit into her hands, but it was also ancient. The rusted locking mechanism must have been stripped when the portcullis came down, because as Amanda heaved she felt the mechanism give way with a snap and a grinding sound. The portcullis slowly lifted and inch, then two.

"I can't hold this much longer," gasped Amanda. "Can you crawl out?"

"I can squeeze under," said Gina, "but Jet's too big."

Amanda grunted. The only way she'd be able to get more leverage was to lie on the ground and try to push it up from underneath. She slowly lowered the portcullis back down, then positioned herself on the ground next to it. She pushed up. It felt easier this time, but it jammed at the same height as before. She managed to bring her legs to bear on the metal, and now she was pushing with both arms and legs.

The cobblestones felt cold and wet against her back. Amanda could feel the damp moss and mud soaking through the back of her shirt. She couldn't help give a shiver.

She groaned and pushed harder, finally forcing the portcullis high enough to crawl under, but she panicked as she realized she'd pushed herself too far. She felt her arms and legs begin to give way. If she didn't get away now, that gate was going to come crashing down on top of her. It was all she could do to roll out from underneath it as it slammed onto the ground, barely missing where she'd been.

A cold horror crawled over Amanda's skin as she realized she'd rolled into the cage and was now trapped with Gina and Jet. Amanda dived into her pocket for her phone before remembering she'd put it down — on the other side of the portcullis. Its soft light was just about strong enough to let her make out Gina's silhouette. Amanda slumped in despair.

"Did you bring any food?" asked Gina. "I had some animal crackers in my pocket, but we ate them last night."

"No," Amanda whispered. "I didn't think I'd be here that long."

"You don't do this very often, do you?" Gina said, trying to make a joke but not making anyone laugh. She held up the skull of Spivey Spillane and moved its jaw like a puppet. "Amanda, you are a very disappointing granddaughter."

Amanda spied the skull through the gloom and shrieked.

"It's pretty dead," said Gina with a sniff.

"I know that. But… ew."

"We reckon it's Spivey Spillane. He got found without a head, didn't he? He must have come looking for the treasure and got trapped too."

"That's Spivey Spillane?" Amanda demanded. "You've been playing patty-cake with the skull of my great-great-great grandfather?"

Amanda was ready to shout the place down, but she stopped herself before she did.

"Wait a minute," she said. "The rest of the body floated down the river, right?" Amanda pressed her ear to the ground and said, "Listen!"

Gina did the same.

"It's the river," said Amanda. "It runs right under here. When Spivey got trapped, something took off his head… and his body must have fallen into a trapdoor or something. That's how he made it back to town. The whole thing's probably rusted over, but it must still be here. We just have to trigger it."

Gina and Amanda began inspecting the floor inch by inch, trying to find a cobblestone that moved or a latch that might be stuck. Amanda made her way to the far corner when she heard the floor creak ominously.

"Here!" she said. "I've got —"

But she didn't get much further than that before the entire floor collapsed underneath them, dumping them out into the river before springing back to reset the trap. Gina and Amanda suddenly found themselves fighting to stay above water that ran wickedly fast through whites and rapids.

"Where's Jet?" Gina called out.

Amanda tried to glance around her, but the light had gone a long time ago and the water was forcing her under. She could hardly see a thing. With precious seconds ticking by, Amanda ducked underwater and tried to make out Jet's body. The water was thick with bubbles and the current jerked her head to and fro.

Finally she spotted a dark shape a few yards ahead of her being carried by the rapids. It could have been Jet — it was impossible to tell. Amanda dived again and swam over, hauling Jet's limp body up into the air as best she could while the current carried them homeward.

Chapter 13

Sewing a tutu always looked so much easier when other people did it, but for some reason Spivey Spillane was finding this sewing machine a lot more confounding than he'd expected. He couldn't keep a steady rhythm on the crank, the stitching was all crooked, and the fluffy pink netting was so fine that it just kept ripping and tangling. The heat in the house was stifling. Spillane's eyes were bloodshot. The sweat was running down his face. His hands and fingers felt like a collection of sausages tied to a stale muffin.

Finally he threw his hands up in the air, anywhere, so long as they didn't have to touch that devil's tutu again. "This is woman's work!"

Nunes strolled over to him and regarded his efforts dispassionately.

"That would be true, my friend, if all we were doing was sewing," said Nunes. "But we are the architects of a terrible vengeance, and that work lies solely in the domain of men."

"You ain't met my grandmammy. If she heard you say that she'd bury you in the cornfield afore you could spit."

"All this is necessary, Mr. Spillane, I assure you. How else are we to lure the elusive Alabama Sam into the open, how else are we to ensnare him in our trap? Now keep sewing, I am puzzling out a fiendishly daring couplet."

So while Spillane swore at the sewing machine, Nunes paced up and down the room with a slip of paper in one hand and a long, white quill in the other. Occasionally he would stop in front of the inkwell to dip the quill and scratch something down onto the paper. More usually Spillane would look over his shoulder and see Nunes brushing the feather against his chin, eyes far off in thought, mouth twisted cruelly in iambic vengeance.

"It's a whisker cattywampus," said Spillane, holding up the deformed tutu, "but I reckon it'll do."

Nunes murmured, "I suppose it will have to. How are you coming along with the slippers?"

"I ain't started yet. But what am I gonna do for a shirt and pants?"

"My dear Mr. Spillane, you don't expect to perform an interpretive dance in shirt and pants, do you? No, to do justice to the topic of Heliogabalus you must allow your physicality to achieve its ultimate expression. That can only be done in a pink tutu — and nothing else."

Spillane threw the tutu on the ground and shouted, "What the hell does it matter, anyhow? I ain't supposed to do a one-man show. It's supposed to be a trap to catch that fink, that thief, that no-good, traitorous —"

Nunes' normally placid face turned dark for the first time. He slammed his sheaf of papers on the table and shouted, "Don't you think I know that? You are not the only one who has been hoodwinked here. If we intend to catch that man, we need to be every bit as cunning as he is. You'll never catch him with your cack-handed tactics. This show needs to be real. Don't you understand? You need to make it look genuine. Only then will our quarry make himself known." He stopped to breathe and smooth down his hair. "Take heed and follow my advice. We will catch him yet."

Spillane had to concede the point, but he didn't have to like it.

"What have you wrote so far then? It don't have to be perfect. This skirt sure ain't."

Nunes let a wry smile play across his face.

"You do not know me so well yet, Mr. Spillane, but at heart I am an artist. Your tutu may be the slipshod product of a man with the manual dexterity of a flaccid buttock, but my play shall be a masterpiece. Every couplet must be a bold indictment of the Emperor Heliogabalus, every quatrain a soul-stirring dive into the emotions of that royal tumult. Who are these sugar plum faeries? Why does he pursue them so? And what part does the color lavender play in this dizzying maelstrom of passion and forbidden eroticism?"

"Ero... *what*?"

"Shhh! I can feel another quatrain coming on. 'Her Grecian bosom heaved with maiden joy, And lust that put to shame the Queen of Troy, As Caesar sighed a sultry, sullen breath, He wished that she were turn'd into a boy.' Yessss."

"That's indecent!" said Spillane. "I can't get up in front of a bunch of God-abidin' men and women and say things like that. I'll get arrested for makin' an affray."

But try as he might, he couldn't get Nunes' attention. The man was too deep in his work.

Spillane turned back to the sewing machine. His hands had been resting too long and were beginning to feel stiff. He wasn't sure he could work up the enthusiasm to make a pair of ballet slippers. He wasn't even sure if he wanted to. It was a miracle he even knew what year it was.

Alabama Sam hadn't made a move for days now. No-one in town seemed to know anything about the man except this Nunes, but every second Spillane spent with Nunes felt like another mile away from Sam. All this time was being wasted, while Alabama Sam got on with the real work of digging up the treasure.

It struck Spillane that he hadn't even seen Alabama Sam in Skunks Dance. He hadn't seen him in months. The specter of Alabama Sam had been looming over him for so long, thwarting his every move, frustrating him at every turn, it was hard to believe he hadn't been locking horns with the man himself every day since he fled Tennessee. But it really was just those few days on the farm, he realized, so many months ago. Then Sam vanished into the air like a ghost. Spillane was beginning to wonder if he existed at all.

Maybe Sam did exist. Maybe he didn't. Spillane sighed and held his head in his hands — maybe he should just go home and forget the whole thing. He'd come so close to quitting before, but something always pulled him back. Every time he thought of going home, he wondered how maddeningly close he was to the truth. If he turned back now, he'd never know what he left behind. He'd never know what was just around the corner. Spillane gripped the tutu between clenched fingers.

He knew he couldn't quit this filthy business.

A crowd was gathering in the First Skunks Dance Baptist Church. It was a bit of a spare place that hardly looked lived in yet. The walls were painted a color of white that had not had time to age. A gallery ran down either side of the church, while at the front was the sanctuary where the altar usually stood. In preparation for the play they had removed the altar and the wall hangings, giving them a makeshift stage. The pews buzzed with keen viewers taking their seats and speculating about the great one-man play which had promised to give them such unlikely acrobatics. With the reputation Spillane had earned in town, not a single resident of Skunks Dance was going to miss the big show. Already the church was packed to capacity and people were starting to cram into the aisles. A restless murmur was rising.

Spillane eyed the crowd nervously from the sacristy, which he and Nunes were using as the wings. This room made him anxious — this was the same place Sam had ambushed him with those phony Bibles. The closet still stood behind him, and even now Spillane couldn't shake the feeling that Sam could spring out of it at any moment and take him by surprise. But he didn't. It was just him and Nunes.

He glanced down and spun to and fro, desperately trying to find something worth admiring in his insane ensemble. The tutu barely covered his privates. The only other item Spillane wore were the "ballet slippers," though these were more just pink cloth bags that Spillane had wedged his feet into and tied at the top with string. His legs and chest were bare, but looked fine as far as Spillane could tell — strong and manly. He flexed his arm in anticipation of planting a fist in Sam's face. He felt tough. Then he caught sight of the tutu again and his face fell.

"I feel like a girl," said Spillane.

"Good," snapped Nunes. "So did Heliogabalus. You are getting into character quite nicely."

"What do you mean? Who *was* this Heliogabalus anyway?"

Nunes stroked his beard hedonistically and exhaled a luxuriant sigh.

"Ahhh, Heliogabalus, the one and only Marcus Aurelius Antoninus Augustus!"

"Was any o' that speechifyin' supposed to make sense?" Spillane asked.

Nunes scoffed. "You lack a classical education, my friend. Heliogabalus was a Roman emperor, a mere boy and beardless youth who came to power at the age of 14. His reign was scarred by scandal and disgrace. He blasphemed against Rome's dearly held gods and prostituted himself in the imperial palace. He offered a fortune to the man who could equip him with female lady-parts. And then the Praetorian Guard turned on him. He tried to hide in a trunk, but the guards found him, dragged him out, and cut him down. He was 18 years old."

Spillane stood by with mouth agape.

"You want me to play a sex pervert? That's un-Christian."

"Mr. Spillane, half of Christendom are sex perverts. If you got rid of them all, you would be left with just Jesus and his chief eunuch, and I've had my suspicions about those two for a while now. Just think of *Heliogabalus* as a parable about how if you're going to prostitute yourself, you probably shouldn't do it in your own palace."

"You're not helpin' me here," said Spillane.

"Neither are you!" said Nunes. "I labored like Heracles on this one-man play and all you can do is nitpick. I didn't choose the topic, if you will remember. Joe Rattlesnake did that. This is exactly the pickle he wanted you in and it's the one you'll give him. Now take this script, grasp it firmly between your thumb and forefinger, and put on the most convincing performance you have ever given."

With those words Nunes propelled Spillane out onto the stage. The crowd fell silent. Every eyeball was glued to Spillane, every mouth twisted in disbelief, every ear cocked to hear whatever words this bizarre vision would spout.

Spillane shuffled the script and found the start of page one. He cleared his throat and held the pages before him.

"I beg you, sing to me, o muse of light, To light my fiery verse into the night, I tell of noble Caesar, blond and shy, His Bud of Boyhood tender, sweet, and tight."

Ripples of disapproval were already coursing through the audience. Spillane coughed and tried to find his place in the script, but the tide of outrage distracted him from the page. The longer he waited the worse it got, sweat dripping from his temples and running down his bare sides, until at last salvation came.

A woman with an enormous peach-colored bustle leaped onto the stage. Her crimson lips seemed poised and confident, ready to deliver a victorious blow. The fact that she must have been in her 40s did nothing to diminish her swagger.

"That's no kind of entertainment for the folks of Skunks Dance, Mr. Spillane. I don't care how you do things back in Louisiana —"

"Tennessee," he said.

She slapped him hard.

"Then shame on you, Mr. Spillane. A gentleman of Tennessee should know better than to go exhibiting himself in a ballet skirt in front of normal people. Heavens above, you're liable to spread all sorts of perversions, parading yourself around like that. And as the folks of Skunks Dance are well aware, perversions are *my* department."

She winked and the crowd laughed nervously. Spillane couldn't believe it, but this woman seemed to be softening them up.

"Now then, Mr. Spillane, what say you and me step backstage for a moment." She leaned in and whispered in his ear, "Then maybe you can show me some of those perversions up close."

Spillane yelped as he felt the woman's hand reach under the tutu and grab his bottom. The audience laughed again and fell into confused clapping. She chased Spillane into the wings and left the crowd to their own devices. Spillane could hear their dissatisfied murmurs.

He turned on the woman and demanded, "What in the hell d'you call that?"

"Saving you a great deal of embarrassment," she said.

"No! I mean grabbin' my ass."

A broad smile crossed the woman's face as she said, "Honey, I call that getting acquainted."

"Keep your hands off a me, painted Jezebel."

"Jezebel!" she cooed. "You're lucky you're pretty, boyo — I don't let just anyone flirt with me like that. Jacqueline Hyde," she said, holding out her hand. "But my friends call me Jackie."

"I'm gonna bet an awful lotta people call you Jackie. Now get outta here. This is my last chance to catch Alabama Sam."

A scuffling noise came from the opposite side of the stage. When Spillane peered from the wings he caught sight a silhouette disappearing into the shadows.

"That's him!" shouted Spillane, and started sprinting after the specter.

He launched himself over the altar and followed the rapidly disappearing footsteps. His quarry ducked and dodged into the rectory with Spillane hot on his tail. Spillane bolted through the musty rooms until they reached the far door, then burst out into the night, hot and muggy. The shadow darted across the graveyard. Spillane leaped over a headstone and came crashing down on the man. He'd been holding onto a baseball bat which went flying. Spillane heaved him over, pinned him to the ground, and punched him in the face.

The boy was too stunned to try and escape. Spillane looked down in horror. Even by the moonlight it was obvious this was not Alabama Sam.

"Who are you?" he demanded.

The boy squirmed, half from the punch, and half from the view up Spillane's tutu. "Don't hurt me. I'm just doing what the man said."

"What man?"

"I don't know. Some feller in a white suit, he told me to clonk you on the back of the head a bit, that's all. He said if I did good he'd give me a dime."

"Nunes?" Spillane wondered. "But why would he…?"

Jackie wandered up behind them with the baseball bat slung over her shoulder. "If I were you I'd let that boy go. He's obviously not Alabama Sam."

"Then who is?"

"I haven't the faintest idea," said Jackie. "But I'll bet your Mr. Nunes is closer to finding him now that he's got you out of the way for a night. You really do ask to be bamboozled, don't you Mr. Spillane?"

"Bamboozled?" he repeated. He wasn't sure what it meant, but it didn't sound good. "Nobody bamboozles me!"

Jackie gazed down at him and remarked, "You're wearing a tutu."

Spillane got to his feet unsteadily. The boy fled into the night.

"Look," said Jackie. "I've been hearing about you all over town. You're Skunks Dance's number one source of entertainment these days. You're even fixing to become bigger than the gold rush itself. Don't you think you're out of your depth? You'll never catch that man. He's been running circles around you since you got here. Even his other victims are smarter than you."

Spillane shook his head. "I don't care. I ain't gonna let him go now, not after everythin' that's happened. Him and me got a score to settle."

"Is that all?"

Spillane glowered at her. "No. But that's as much as you're gonna find out."

Jackie leveled the bat at Spillane, but he only raised an eyebrow at her.

"Now you're gonna wallop me too?"

"Would you say this is about chest height?" she asked, tensing up to swing the bat.

"What?"

"Duck, Mr. Spillane. Just about… NOW."

A chill crept up his spine and he dropped to the ground.

Just then a gunshot echoed through the night. As Jackie swung she batted the bullet out of the air. Spillane felt splinters of wood sprinkle down around his ears. A twinge of gunpowder and burnt wood hung in the atmosphere.

"What the hell was that?" Spillane shrieked.

"It was a gunshot, you idiot. Run!"

Jackie and Spillane both sprinted into the darkness, taking as many corners as possible and zig-zagging across the town. It was hard to see where they were going. Once or twice Spillane stumbled and nearly fell, but he managed to keep his footing enough to keep up with Jackie. Despite her enormous petticoats she was actually going faster than he was.

They paused for breath behind the cover of a large oak. Spillane cocked his ears and listened for the sound of a pursuer. He couldn't hear footsteps, but every rustle and snap made his heart jump.

Jackie brought the bat down to eye level and examined the bullet embedded in it.

"Not a bad piece of work, eh?" she asked.

"How did you…?"

"He was aiming for your chest," said Jackie. "And although you will insist on parading it all around town, it's not *that* big a target."

Spillane realized he was still shirtless and wrapped his arms around his chest.

"Listen, lady, let's get one thing straight. There ain't nothing gonna happen betweenst us no matter how much you grab my ass and look at my chest and show off your bosoms…"

Spillane trailed off as his eyes traveled down Jackie's body and he began to regret being so hasty. He was in California, after all. God would never have to know.

Jackie snorted. "Please keep it in your tutu, Mr. Spillane. I have absolutely no interest in molesting you. Sex is too much like snow — you never know how many inches you're going to get. Although," she said, glancing at the skimpy tutu, "I dare say I could make an accurate weather prediction from here."

"A lotta people like snow," said Spillane, trying to cover both his chest and his tutu at the same time.

"They don't live in California, do they?" said Jackie. "But you'll be buried here unless we can catch your elusive Alabama Sam. Judging by his handiwork, I'd say the cat has become tired of playing with the string and decided to put a bullet through it."

"Cats don't have guns," said Spillane.

"No," said Jackie, smiling and pulling a pistol out of her bustle. "But cougars do."

Spillane stared at the gun in surprise. He felt suspended in that moment for ages, not knowing what to do next. He couldn't take his eyes off the barrel, which wavered in the air before him like a cobra about to strike. His chest felt tight. It was becoming hard to breathe. For a moment he was certain Jackie was going to shoot him. This didn't seem like the end — but that didn't count for much.

"Are you going to kill me?"

"Mr. Spillane!" she said. "I'm going to do better than that. I'm going to protect you."

He finally exhaled, and the tension he'd been carrying began to dissipate. Now he just felt exhausted. "Can I go home now?" he mumbled. "I could use a whiskey or nine."

As he made to move away, Jackie laid a hand on his shoulder and stopped him in his tracks.

"You go home now, Mr. Spillane, and you're going to spend the night in a pine box. Now that Alabama Sam wants you dead, he's going to do it. All this time, all the humiliation you've endured and the setbacks he's put you through, that was him being friendly. If he wants you dead now, I can tell you this for nothing — you're going to die."

The night started spinning around Spillane as if the ground were being yanked out from under him. If the Devil had a country, it had to be California.

When he spoke he could hardly force his voice out his throat.

"What am I going to do?" he gasped.

"Get in that tree," said Jackie.

After everything that had happened already, climbing a tree seemed reasonable enough. The lowest branches were still high up, so Spillane leaped and grabbed the nearest branch. From there he hauled himself up and vanished into the branches.

Jackie cocked one eyebrow as she glimpsed up Spillane's skirt. "Well glory be," she murmured to herself. "And I thought all the low-hanging fruit was out of season."

With an elegant flourish too fast for the eye to follow, Jackie hoisted herself up into the branches.

Being in the tree made Spillane feel a whole lot safer. He realized Jackie knew what she was doing — they were bound to be safe here until morning at least. The leaves were thick enough to block the view, and they would hear Sam approaching long before he saw them. Now the only thing ahead of them was the long night.

The bark dug into Spillane's thighs and the trunk of the tree kneaded his spine.

"Can I ask you a question?" he said. "How d'you know it was Alabama Sam holdin' that gun?"

"Easy — I'm the one who sold it to him."

"And that bein' the case, why is my life worth savin'?"

116

"Because I'm one of the cowboys and Alabama Sam is one of the Injuns."

And that seemed reasonable enough.

He shut his eyes and tried to rest, but the night wore on forever. Every time he started to sleep his head would nod or he'd feel himself slipping off the branch, and suddenly he was awake again. Even if he'd been in bed he didn't know how well he'd have slept. His head was full of tutus and one-man plays and the creeping fear that somewhere Alabama Sam was watching them, monkey-fingers clasped around the trigger of a gun, taking aim into the trees. Spillane shivered.

By the time it began to get light he could feel his eyelids swollen and glued to his eyeballs, his mouth tasted like the floor of the saloon, and he didn't even dare to think about what his bottom looked like after all this time sitting on the rough bark. He looked over and was amazed to see Jackie sleeping soundly. It was no wonder. Her bustle and numerous underskirts were giving her plenty of padding. And here he was still in his tutu, shivering in the early morning chill. This day would get a whole lot better once he could get home.

"Jackie?" he whispered.

"Yes?" she said without opening her eyes.

"When can I go back to my room?"

She yawned and stretched, waving her gun around in the air carelessly.

"I suppose now is as good a time as any. I doubt he'll strike during the day, and if he does there won't be much you can do about it. But he'll surface again tonight, you may count on it. He won't suffer you to live long."

"What'll I do?"

"Well *I* need to go to work," she said. "What you get up to now is your own affair."

Spillane nodded and dropped down out of the tree. His legs had fallen asleep so badly that he collapsed onto the ground and squirmed in pain. Jackie fluttered down elegantly and stood over him, ready for action.

"Just one thing," Spillane croaked. "Thank you."

Jackie smiled and strode off without a word.

After a few minutes Spillane hauled himself to his feet and began to trudge home. There were not enough hours in the day for all the sleep he had in mind.

He opened the door of the house and paused for a moment, listening for any sign that Nunes might be here. The house was quiet. The only sound that reached Spillane's ears was the panting of his own sour breath. He could only hope that Nunes really was out. He didn't think he had the energy to confront him, not after the night he'd had.

With singular determination he scuffled across the dusty floorboards towards his room. The door was exactly as he had left it. Had Sam been here? He couldn't tell. Everything was quiet. The whole town was still asleep.

Cautiously Spillane lay his hand on the doorknob — and felt nothing. He let the door creak open.

His heart stopped.

It was Alabama Sam.

Chapter 14

Amanda and Gina hadn't realized how long they'd been underground. By the time they managed to haul Jet up onto the riverbank, the black sky was beginning to brighten a little with the pre-dawn glow. The trees rustled darkly, their leaves making invisible movements in the half-light, while the last of the nocturnal creatures scuttled through the grass and went to sleep in their burrows. Somewhere a bird began to cry, and after a minute a few more joined it. The sleep deprivation, the hunger, and the tumble through the rapids made the world teeter around Amanda like a spinning top about to fall. Gina wasn't looking well either, but the dip in the river seemed to have perked her up a bit.

Jet was conscious enough to cough and splutter, but Amanda couldn't allow herself time to relax. Jet needed urgent help if he was going to live. His whole face had swollen up so much that he could give the Elephant Man a run for his money. Strangely Amanda didn't feel the panic. When the adrenaline kicked in she knew what she had to do next — and Jet wasn't going to like it.

"I'm going to have to suck the spider venom out of the bite," she said.

"Oh my God, that is so gross," said Gina. "You might have to *kiss* him too."

"I'm not going to kiss him," said Amanda. "This is a medical procedure and it might just save his life. Where did the spider bite him?"

Gina pointed at the puffy skin under Jet's eyes and said, "It was on his nose."

Amanda delicately prodded Jet's face looking for the telltale puncture marks. But as much as she prodded, she couldn't figure out where the spider had bitten him. It had to be around here somewhere.

"It's hard to believe all this mess came from a spider bite. His eyes are red and everything."

Gina feigned a little cough. "That might be from where I, you know, pepper-sprayed him."

"You pepper-sprayed him?"

Gina nodded.

Amanda sat back on her haunches, glanced down at Jet's face, and slapped him hard. Jet spluttered into life.

"You massive idiot! You complete and utter retard! You had me worried sick and you weren't even bitten."

"I was too!" he shouted. "My face looks like the ass-end of a parade balloon. I couldn't breathe."

"It's from the pepper spray," she said. "You're having a reaction to the capsicum. How the hell did you think you were bitten by a spider?"

Jet felt his face with his fingertips. Everywhere he felt was sore, but he couldn't find anywhere that was more sore than anywhere else. There didn't seem to be a wound anywhere.

"I'm going to live," he cried. "I'm invincible!"

Amanda slapped him again. "Get up and shut up. We need to find that treasure."

Jet made to slap her back, but Gina said, "You can't hit a girl."

"That's sexism," Jet replied. "This is complete discrimination. I have a dream that one day men will be able to hit women whenever…" He stopped himself mid-sentence. "I'm on a bad road here, aren't I?"

Gina nodded.

"But it started so well," said Jet.

Gina shook her head solemnly. "It really didn't."

"Let's start walking," Amanda sighed. "I want to get to some higher ground so we can figure out where we are and maybe find something to eat. Then we need to get back to that fortress, only this time we're going to avoid any spiders and pits and pepper sprays. Got it?"

Jet grumbled. There was no sympathy for the wounded. It wasn't fair. And he had water in his shoes. And his pants were itchy.

This hadn't worked out the way he'd expected. Somehow the Spillane girl had caught up with him, and now he was stuck with her, stranded amid endless miles of forest that felt worlds away from home. He didn't even care if there *was* a treasure. All he knew was this sucked.

They had been carried a fair way down the river. The walk back was long and climbed steeply to get back to the high fortress. Soon they could make out crumbling stonework towering above them. Although it looked so close, the perspective upward gave them dizzy spells. Once or twice Jet glanced up and lost his footing, slipping on dewy leaves or stumbling over a tree root. His stomach growled ominously.

Amanda clearly heard it and cast a look back at him. "Okay, we may as well take a break. You guys wait here."

"Sieg heil," said Jet, clicking his heels together and doing a Nazi salute.

Amanda ignored him and said, "*I'll* go see if I can find anything to eat."

"What is there to eat? We're in the middle of nowhere."

Amanda snapped, "You might not like me but you could at least give me some credit. I was a Girl Scout you know. I'm not completely useless, unlike some people. If you were capable of acting like a decent human being for five consecutive seconds, none of this would have happened. Now shush up while I go save your worthless life, *again*."

Gina gazed at Jet wide-eyed. "Duuuuude," she said. "You got schooled."

Jet crossed his arms and sat up against a tree. Amanda disappeared into the foliage while he and Gina waited. The minutes wore on and the length of the night began to catch up with him. He glanced over at Gina and saw she was already curling up and going to sleep. It couldn't hurt to close his eyes for a few minutes. Amanda would be back soon enough.

Ants were crawling up Jet's arm looking for shade from the sun. It had to be at least 100 °. Jet scratched his arm absent-mindedly before feeling the incredible cramp in his back from sleeping against a tree for the last few hours.

He looked around their little group and saw Gina still fast asleep. Amanda must have returned while he was unconscious because she was also lying down in a shady spot.

Jet touched his face again and realized that, although it was still tender, the swelling had mostly gone down now. His eyes were still a bit watery, but he was almost feeling human again. His stomach cramped and he realized how hungry he was. He hadn't eaten in forever.

Amanda's expedition had apparently been successful. Next to her was a small pile of daisies and raw asparagus. Jet grimaced, but he was hungry enough to eat just about anything. He reached over to grab a few stalks without waking Amanda up.

The asparagus was pretty much as disgusting as it was when cooked, only now it was crunchy too. But Jet couldn't complain. He was grateful to have anything to eat at all. To his surprise the daisies were all right — better than the asparagus at least. There wasn't nearly enough food here to stop him being hungry, but at least it took the edge off. He was feeling better already.

"What are you doing?" mumbled Amanda, cracking open her eyes. "Are you eating flowers?"

"What do you mean? Isn't this food?"

"The asparagus is! I just picked the daisies because I thought they were pretty. Who eats flowers? Who does that?"

Gina began to giggle, and Jet realized she'd woken up while they were talking. He smiled and bit the head off another daisy, making Gina burst out in another fit of giggles. He'd forgotten how much he liked that sound.

"Come on, Jean Genie," he said to her. "There's some asparagus left. And if you're really good, I'll let you have some of my flowers."

Gina hated veggies, but she didn't complain. She even tried a flower, and when she'd stopped laughing she had to admit they weren't all that bad.

Now they were awake and slightly better fed, they decided to get moving. The sooner they made it back to the ruins, the better. It had to be afternoon already and they knew the light wouldn't last forever. The last thing they wanted was to be out here another night.

It was obvious this part of the forest hadn't been traveled in many years. If there had ever been any old paths, they were completely over-grown now. They would never find a direct path up the hill. Some-times they had to force their way through bushes or push aside heavy branches. Other times they had to scale precarious rocks or walk the long way around them. It took at least another two hours to get back to the fortress.

When they arrived at the outskirts of the ruins they all agreed to watch their footing very carefully. They tip-toed past the arrow trap just in case there was a similar surprise that hadn't been set off yet. Nearby they found the hole they had all fallen into, still yawning and inviting them into the wretched cavern below. They side-stepped it, making very sure to keep well clear of the crumbling edge.

"Do you still have the directions?" Gina asked.

"I'm lucky I'm still alive," said Jet. "I don't have anything. I think it was up ahead, though — we should keep going."

"You think," Amanda snorted, pulling the damp Bible from her pocket. "*I* still have the directions. We're supposed to turn right up ahead. We're pretty close now. Keep your eyes peeled. Spivey Spillane may have left a marker or something, like a wooden post or a flag..."

"Yup," said Jet. "I think I found it."

He pointed up ahead to where the ground gave way to a crater. Its edges were smoothed over by decades of rain and it was full of silt and leaves, but it was clear that something had been dug up. Next to the pit was a collection of rusty picks and shovels. Someone had got here a long time before them.

Jet viciously kicked a shovel into the pit.

"I was afraid of this," said Amanda. "We were only ever going to find the treasure gone, or the body of Lawrence Leverett in one of those traps. I'm still not sure which one's worse."

"Now who the hell is Lawrence Leverett?"

"Are you serious? You just blundered into this, didn't you? Couldn't leave it up to the experts."

"The experts hadn't done all that well on their own."

Amanda scowled with bad grace. She crouched over by the aban-doned tools. She plucked through them, setting the decaying shovels to one side as she looked for anything that might help them.

"Why did he leave all his stuff?" Gina asked.

"If you found the treasure, you'd want something to carry it back in. He probably used a bag or a wheelbarrow to bring the tools up this far, then ditched them when he found the gold. It must have weighed a ton — but that amount of money would motivate anyone. Ahhh!"

Amanda broke off and lifted up the splintered handle of a pick. A brittle, yellow piece of paper was wrapped around the handle with a rubber band. The band had dried out a long time ago and crumbled away, but the paper was still in tact — and just about readable.

"Gimme that," said Jet, snatching the paper away from Amanda.

"Careful!" she said. "You're going to rip it."

Jet unfolded the paper and examined the faded writing. It had been written on one of the old manual typewriters. He'd seen enough of them at Harvey Spackle's house.

"It's a receipt," he said. "It's for all this junk."

"Does it have a name?" asked Amanda.

Jet scrutinized the writing. "It's a bit faded, but I think it says 'Everett.'"

"*Leverett*, you dingus," said Amanda. "He's the guy who donated the statue of Spivey Spillane. You only walk past it every day of your life. Didn't you ever stop to read the inscription? He donated that statue, then no-one ever heard from him again." She breathed in like she was about to speak, but then stopped and furrowed her brow.

"What?" asked Jet.

"Just let me think for a minute. If you found a fortune, what would you do?"

"Spend it," said Jet.

"What if someone else knew you had it?"

"So hide it, I guess, and lie low until I could get it back. *Then* spend it."

"That could explain why no-one ever heard from him again. He hid the gold, then one way or another his friend caught up with him and he never got the chance to spend it."

Jet threw up his hands. "It's probably long gone now. He could have hidden it anywhere."

"Then why would he give Skunks Dance a statue?" she asked. "It was built without a head… And someone put a head on it right after it was dedicated…"

"Again with the statue!" said Jet. "Who cares? It's not like he hid the money in there."

There was a pause for a moment while everyone turned it over in their heads.

"You know I think I could use a good shower," Amanda said slowly. "I might head back into town."

"Woah woah, what's the big hurry?" said Jet. "We're going back too."

"No need," said Amanda. "I'll make my own way back, I don't want to hold you up."

Without warning Jet grabbed Gina and started running back to the car. Gina yelped as Jet dragged along her by the arm.

Amanda chased after them. Jet laughed breathlessly as he put more and more distance between them and Amanda. He could hear her outraged cries behind him, and for the first time in days he felt himself flush with joy. This was more like it — *this* he understood.

Branches struck them in the face as they sprinted back across the ruins and through the forest. Gina would never have been able to keep up with Jet if he didn't have a death grip on her hand. He was dragging her along behind him, her feet barely even touching the ground.

Jet burst onto the roadside and slammed into his car. He fumbled for the keys. For a heart-stopping moment he thought he might have lost them in the river, but after a moment he found them at the bottom of a soggy pocket. He jammed them into the lock, shoved Gina into the car, and shut the door behind him just as Amanda caught up with them.

Amanda banged on the window, shouting, "Don't you dare drive away without me, Jet."

"We don't want to hold you up!" he crowed. "I'll let you make your own way back."

Jet revved the engine and tore away, leaving Amanda in the dust. She glanced around and found her bike. When Jet looked back through the rear-view mirror, he caught sight of Amanda pedaling for all she was worth — in the other direction.

"Where's she going?" asked Gina.

Jet swore. "She must know another way back. It doesn't matter. A car is still faster than a bike no matter what road you take."

"I'm-a tell Mom you cursed," said Gina.

"I'll give you a quarter of the money," said Jet.

"Half!"

"A third, and you're lucky to get that much. You're only tagging along, remember?"

Jet flicked on the headlights. It was hard to believe how much time they'd spent in that forest, but it was getting dark already. It had been almost three days since they left. His parents were probably worried — if not about him then about Gina. His stomach growled again but this time it was easy enough to ignore. He stepped on the accelerator.

The car tore through traffic as they entered the outskirts of Skunks Dance.

Jet swore again and thumped the steering wheel in frustration. He grabbed the wheel and swung it round, taking them on a sudden detour.

"Now *we're* going the wrong way," said Gina.

"I left the shovel up at the fort," said Jet. "But there's still a pick in the shed. We're going to need it."

They screeched to a halt on the curb and Jet leaped out of the car. He pushed his way round the side of the house and found his parents having late-night cocktails in the back yard.

"Thank God you're here," said his dad. "We can't find Gina any-where."

"She's with me," Jet blurted.

"Someone's had a fun time," said his mom with a wink. "I caught one of your experiments looking for you yesterday in your bedroom — and you told me you weren't interested in that kind of thing. You should know I —"

Jet ran past her and shouted, "Sorry, Mom! I'm in a hurry."

He practically tore the door off the shed, grabbed the pick, and jetted back to the car. As they tore away from the curb, Jet prayed that his parents wouldn't kill him too badly when all this was over.

They sped into the heart of Skunks Dance — the plaza where the statue of Spivey Spillane had watched over the townspeople every day for 40 years. The plaza was deserted at this hour. Jet didn't bother parking, he just skidded up onto the pavement and screeched to a halt.

He ran up to the statue, only to see Amanda Spillane sprinting up from the other direction. She was gasping for breath as if she'd run all the way from the ridge. She looked like she'd fallen out of a tree.

"What happened to you?" said Jet. "You're soaking."

"I came by river," she panted. "Bike doesn't matter, buy new one. Buy ten. Money is mine."

"We'll see about that," said Jet through gritted teeth.

He tightened his grip on the pick and swung it directly at Spivey Spillane's head. A loud clang echoed through the town. Jet's arms stung from the impact, but that didn't stop him hauling the ax out of the metal and swinging again.

This time there was an almighty crack. The head sheared clean off the body, leaving Jet panting and trembling.

Jet, Gina, and Amanda peered over at the decapitated head.

"What's *that*?" asked Gina, pointing at the head.

Something had splattered on the ground. There was an awful stench. Even Jet had to cover his mouth and nose — he'd never smelled anything so vile, even when he'd been sprayed by the skunks.

They moved over to the head slowly and bent down. That's when they saw a spinal column protruding from the neck of the statue.

Amanda choked back as her stomach began to heave. She just about made it to a bush in time.

Jet was too absorbed by the grisly sight in front of him to try and block out the sound of Amanda hurling into the bushes. After a moment he heard her spit and sniff back tears.

"I guess we know what happened to Lawrence Leverett," she sobbed.

Jet looked down at the bones and the slime dripping out of the head.

Someone had put Leverett inside the statue. Jet could only hope it had happened *after* he'd been killed.

Chapter 15

There was no mistaking Alabama Sam. His hair was greasy and his face was carelessly strewn with grime, as they were when Spillane first met him. He stank of rancid sweat. Sam's features were stony and his harrowing eyes burrowed into Spillane's soul.

Spillane took a step towards him. His footfall echoed painfully on the wooden floor.

"What in the hell are you doin'?" he breathed.

Sam was holding onto a rafter by one hand. His fingers trembled, slipping slowly on the splintering wood. Around his neck was a rope tied to the same rafter. Sam's expression quavered into what could have been a smile for just for a second.

And then he let go.

The rope snapped taut and there was a sickening crack. Sam hung in the air, gently twisting to and fro, blank eyes still meeting Spillane's gaze in a ghastly showdown that, Spillane couldn't help thinking, Sam had somehow won.

Spillane stared into Sam's face and forced himself to swallow the lump in his throat. The air was heavy and stagnant. The rafter creaked ominously.

The silence broke with the sound of a pistol being cocked. Spillane jumped. He saw a man in the door. He wanted to run, but his feet would not move.

The sheriff leaned forward into the room and casually waved his pistol at Spillane.

"Now ain't that a purdy sight," drawled the sheriff.

Suddenly feeling a chill, Spillane realized he was still only wearing the tutu from last night. Aside from that he was practically naked.

"Now're you gonna tell me how you come to have the body of that there gentleman swingin' from your rafters?" asked the sheriff. "Or why I shouldn't shoot you here an' now?"

"It's him," Spillane croaked. "He's finally dead."

A wry smile crept over the sheriff's face. "Looks like all your Christmases have come at once, don't it?"

Spillane's joy slowly drained from his body. He'd known it was too good to be true. He shook his head. "No. No, I… He hung himself, just now."

The sheriff took a step into the room. "That was a mighty fine play last night, son, but your kinda theater don't fly in this town. What we got here is the body of the man you wanted dead more'n anythin' else in the world. And now you're lookin' down the barrel of my brand of justice."

"I didn't…" Spillane mumbled. "I wouldn't…"

"Wouldn't! In my experience the jail-houses are full o' folks who wouldn't. But even if you wouldn't, Mr. Spillane, I'm willin' to bet that when it came down to just you an' him, you figured out you *could*."

"I been out all night. I *couldn't* have killed Alabama Sam."

"Oh, 'out!'" scoffed the sheriff, stepping towards Spillane ominously. "That's a new one. You an' the other murderers who was 'out' all night are gonna have a lot to talk about."

Spillane and the sheriff spun around as a new voice startled them both. Someone was standing in the doorway. Spillane was amazed to see the silhouette of a panama hat and the cherry of a slowly burning cigar.

"Mr. Sheriff, you have the wrong man. Spivey Spillane cannot possibly have committed this murder, as he was with me the entire night." Nunes stepped into the room and offered his hand to the sheriff. "I am Aurelio Nunes, sir, Mr. Spillane's landlord, playwright, and forever in debt to the high quality of service provided by lawmen such as yourself."

"Is that right?" barked the sheriff. "Only I have it on good authority that you two were seen partin' ways after your little exhibition down at the Lord's house."

Nunes lowered his head. "Your skills of detection are, indeed, second to none, sheriff. Mr. Spillane and I did part ways briefly in order to divide our efforts. Mr. Spillane fetched some necessary coal for the stove while I returned home to prepare the sweetmeats. We have, if you'll care to examine the state of my kitchen, been cooking all night."

The sheriff squinted at Nunes without lowering his pistol.

"Show me," he said.

Nunes gladly led the sheriff into the kitchen, where a bewildering array of ingredients were laid out around a coal stove.

"As it happens," said Nunes, "Mr. Spillane and I were in the middle of a most delicate stage of the process when he felt the need to return to his room for a squirt of goat's milk. However, having seen the unsavory contents of that room, I am now inclined to believe the recipe could do without it. Mr. Spillane, would you be so kind as to lacquer the soufflé wand for me?"

Spillane stared at Nunes in confusion for a moment before stumbling around and eventually laying hands on something that looked like a spoon.

"That is not a soufflé wand!" Nunes snarled. "Does that look anything like a soufflé wand? What you have, in fact, begun to manhandle is a Hungarian melon baller. *This* is a soufflé wand," he said, waving a dubious utensil in Spillane's face. "Now do you see this soufflé wand? Do you?"

Spillane nodded.

"Well *lacquer it.*"

Spillane stared at the wand. The sweat was standing out on his brow.

The sheriff was watching keenly. "Well?" he demanded. "What are you waiting for? Lacquer it."

Spillane breathed some condensation onto the wand and began to polish it on his tutu.

"Very good," said Nunes. "Now you must bring the syllabub goblets to an autumnal chill. Do you think you can manage that?"

Nunes handed Spillane the goblets. Spillane took them uncertainly over to the ice box and chilled them for a few moments before bringing them back to Nunes. As soon as he picked one up Nunes shrieked and dropped it to the ground where it shattered into a hundred pieces.

"Autumnal, I said! Good God, man, that was positively wintry — if I were inclined to hyperbole I would almost go so far as to say it was Carthaginian. Did I ask for a Carthaginian chill?"

"No," mumbled Spillane.

"What's that?" demanded Nunes.

"No!"

The sheriff stepped in and said, "Very well, Mr. Nunes, I believe you. No-one could make up this kind of hoodoo. However if I find any evidence of wrongdoings and shady dealings, the both of you are gonna find yourselves the same way I found Alabama Sam — at the end of a rope.

"My deputy'll be along presently to collect the body," he added. "Try not to use it in any o' yer 'one-man plays.'"

Nunes smiled as the sheriff took his leave. When he finally disappeared down the road, Nunes held his hat to his chest and said, "There goes a good man. It is a pity he is such a fool. America has produced many fine specimens in her first 70 years, but alas that poor bumbler is not amongst them."

He turned back to Spillane, who immediately punched Nunes in the face.

His cigar went flying. Nunes reeled backwards, but not so fast that Spillane couldn't catch him by the lapels and slam him into the wall.

"You done me a service, but no-one speaks to me like that, you finicky-footed pantywaist. You understand?"

Nunes raised a sardonic eyebrow at Spillane. "Well, it seems like the frontier spirit has finally found a home in you, Mr. Spillane."

"I've had just about a bellyful o' this state. If there's a place in Hell for all the traitors and hornswogglers and, and... *wand-laquerers*, it's here in California."

He let Nunes go and the feline man promptly landed back on his feet.

"Now Alabama Sam's dead," said Spillane, "I got me some work to do."

"Not so fast, Mr. Spillane," crowed Nunes. "A little bird has told me a very interesting thing."

"I don't care about you or your lil' bird."

"The bird *I* have told me Alabama Sam was looking for a rare and precious thing buried somewhere in the hills…"

He trailed off and cocked an eyebrow at Spillane. Spillane's face turned dark. Nunes only smirked and beckoned Spillane to sit down. Spillane's bones ached and his head was throbbing fit to burst. He sighed and took a seat, wondering what fresh hell he'd found himself in now.

Chapter 16

"Is he dead?" asked Gina.

"No, he's about to dance the Whangdoodle," said Jet. He suddenly seemed to remember Gina and forcefully steered her away from the body. "Don't look. There's nothing you want to see." He leaned over to Amanda, who was still kneeling by the bushes and trying to hold down her stomach. "What are we going to do?"

Amanda grabbed Jet by the shirt and hauled herself up.

"We have to go to the police."

"We can't do that," hissed Jet. "They'll think we know something we don't. How did we know the body was in the statue?"

"We didn't," Amanda protested.

"Exactly — so why did we knock its block off? They're going to trace this back to the treasure and, if that money is still around somewhere, it's going to be evidence."

"He's *dead*, Jet. This isn't like setting a car on fire. We can't just put the head back on and hope no-one notices. We have to report this at the station."

"What if the gold's inside there with the body?" piped Gina.

Both Jet and Amanda turned to look at the girl. Gina idly scraped her shoe against the ground and eyed the statue.

"*No*," said Amanda.

Jet mumbled, "Well… we could just look."

Amanda found herself inching towards the remains with Jet and wondering how she had agreed to this so quickly. She tried to hold onto the thought that Leverett was dead now no matter what happened next. There was nothing gross about picking up his head, pouring out the brains, and looking for lost treasure.

"Who's gonna pick it up?" whispered Gina with more than a hint of eagerness in her voice.

Jet made to pick up the head, but Amanda stopped him short. Her family had been looking for this treasure for generations. She wasn't going to let Jet weasel into the picture at this stage of the game.

She leaned over gently, trying to hold her breath and not think too closely about what she was doing. Her fingers touched the bronze. It was warm and slick. She shuddered and carefully lifted the head off the ground with her fingertips.

It slipped in her fingers, sending another splash of liquefied Leverett onto the sidewalk. Amanda shrieked and dropped the head. It hit the ground with a clonk, heavy metal grinding into the cement. The putrefied remains came pouring out, with the exception of the skull which remained firmly sealed inside its bronze mask. That didn't stop a few vertebrae from crumbling loose and skittering across the concrete.

"Well?" said Jet. "What's in there?"

"A dead body!" Amanda shouted.

"Maybe it's in the rest of the statue," said Gina.

This time Amanda and Jet agreed that no-one was going to go fishing around in the statue's torso looking for nuggets of gold.

Amanda's heart was pounding and she could feel her pulse in her temples. She suddenly felt faint. A tugging in her stomach reminded her how long it had been since she'd eaten a proper meal. She doubted she could keep anything down now.

Her head snapped up — "Shhh," she hissed.

"What?" asked Jet, but Amanda only shushed him more insistently.

Long, leisurely footsteps were approaching from across the plaza. They were accompanied by an indefinable sound, like someone tapping an umbrella or a cane against the ground — click-tap, click-tap, click-tap.

Those footsteps contained the unmistakable bliss of ignorance. As soon as they reached the statue, they would run terrified and fetch the police. God only knew what would happen then. All Jet and Amanda knew was that the inevitable was happening, and it was happening now — they were about to be found out.

Amanda froze to the spot.

"What are we going to do?" she choked.

Jet grabbed her by the shoulders and looked her in the eyes.

"Amanda, I'm going to let you in on a secret. I have an age-old strategy for getting out of tricky situations. It takes a little bit of confidence and a little bit of flair. I've done it a hundred times, and if you follow me very carefully, we're going to be just fine."

"Hurry up!" she hissed, glancing behind her in the direction of the approaching footsteps. By the time she turned back Jet was halfway across the plaza.

"Son of a…" she said to herself. She had just enough time to grab Gina and run. Then, seconds later, they were gone.

Amanda's legs were burning. Her stomach still pirouetted in her abdomen and she could taste the stomach acid that seemed to coat her back teeth with a gritty film. She ran, forcing herself onwards through the warm night and the darkened streets of Skunks Dance, gasping for air, desperate to be somewhere — anywhere — safe. Even with the blood throbbing in her ears she caught the sound of the leaves gently rustling in the trees, and of cicadas measuring out the night with chirrups and clicks. It was unfair how the rest of the world could go on like nothing had happened.

She and Jet had split up in town, and now Amanda was bearing down on the quiet street where she lived. With the last ounce of strength in her body she hobbled into the driveway. She finally let herself pause for breath. Her feet felt like the heavy metal legs of the statue. They weighed so much Amanda wondered if she'd be anchored there forever. She forced one foot ahead of the other as if tacking against an invisible wind.

She shoved a trembling hand into her pocket looking for her keys. Her fingers tangled in the humid fabric and for a second she considered forgetting the whole thing and collapsing right here. She gritted her teeth and forced her hand further down. Finally she grabbed the keys and pulled them free, turning her pocket inside-out in the process.

The key didn't seem to want to find its home in the lock, and Amanda had to try it several times before she finally rammed it home and twisted it. The bolt slid back. With a little gasp that surprised her, she pushed the door open and entered the house.

It was dark. Amanda had expected to be able to smell the last traces of dinner dissipating through the carpets and curtains, but the house just smelled warm and musty. It was evident that no-one had been home in hours.

Amanda was too tired to eat. The only thing she could bring herself to do was climb the stairs and collapse into bed. She shut her eyes and within seconds she was asleep.

The sound of her parents' car pulling into the driveway was not enough to wake her. She was dead to the world. Let it spin on without her for a while — she had earned her blackout. But when her father helped her mother out of the car — click-tap, click-tap, click-tap — Amanda's eyes snapped open.

The room spun around her but she sat bolt upright like a vampire in her coffin. She grabbed onto the windowsill and peered down onto the driveway. Her mother's leg was in a cast. When her crutches hit the cement, they made a tapping noise.

How much did she know?

The night didn't seem so warm now. The sweat had evaporated off Amanda's skin and left her chilly. She was scared. She crawled underneath her sheets with her clothes still on and wrapped herself up tight, desperate to forget everything that had happened. She thought she would never sleep with all the worries running through her head, but she was unconscious again before she could even finish that thought.

And while she slept, she did not forget the tapping of her mother's crutches. She dreamed of footsteps in the dark.

There were not enough eggs in the world. The kitchen counter was strewn with empty shells, shredded orange peel, coagulating globs of bacon fat, and a scatter of coffee grounds. The roof of Amanda's mouth still burned from her first cup of coffee, but if it didn't matter then, it sure as hell didn't matter now.

After gorging herself she was almost ready to feel human again, provided she didn't explode first. She took another sip of coffee and felt it burble in her stomach. She didn't want to face the music and somehow, at the back of her head, she thought that if she kept eating breakfast maybe she wouldn't have to.

As it happened, the music faced her.

Click-tap, click-tap, click-tap.

"You will not believe what's happened," said Amanda's mom as she made her way into the kitchen.

"What happened?" she asked disingenuously.

She braced herself for anything. She'd had enough time to work out her story. She had not been in the plaza. There was no body. She'd never heard of Skunks Dance. And above all, there was no statue.

"There's no statue!" said Mrs. Spillane.

Amanda wasn't quite sure if she'd heard correctly.

"No statue at all!" Mrs. Spillane continued. "I asked Marjorie Banks, she's always up there early to get her odds and ends, and she said it wasn't there when she got there at six."

"What do you mean?" asked Amanda. "It's...?"

"Gone," said Mrs. Spillane. "Someone's stolen the thing right out of the plaza. Can you believe it? Who'd have thought it?"

"What happened to it?" asked Amanda slowly.

Her mom gave her a funny look — puzzled, maybe even a bit suspicious. One eyebrow seemed to arch of its own accord. "What makes you think I know?" she asked.

Amanda stood at the kitchen counter, protectively holding her coffee in front of her as if that was going to do anything. She felt like the guy from *Rear Window* defending himself with a camera flash.

Mrs. Spillane hobbled out of the room on her crutches, click-tap, click-tap.

"Mom..." called Amanda.

She heard her mother pause in the hallway before she tapped her way back into the kitchen.

"Yes?" said Mrs. Spillane, suddenly cheerful again. Her heavily pancaked makeup gave her a ghoulish air. She was only a lipstick smear away from being a Batman villain.

"Are you okay?"

"Never better. Why?"

"Your leg…" said Amanda.

"Oh, this old thing!" said Mrs. Spillane as if noticing her cast and crutches for the first time. "I twisted it — coming off the escalator at the mall yesterday. Silly old goat. Sometimes I don't even realize what I'm doing. I'm a menace. There's no telling who could get hurt if I'd knocked someone over, or I'd been driving…"

She trailed off as she followed the train of her own thoughts. Amanda held the coffee in a death-grip, staring at her mother, waiting for her next words and hoping they would make all this horror go away. Her mother couldn't have threatened her. Could she? What else could she mean? Why had she been at the plaza last night?

Then Mrs. Spillane seemed to snap back to reality. "Anyway. Listen to me go on. You've got better things to be doing, I'm sure. Strange about that statue though. Who'd want to steal a statue?"

Someone with something to hide, thought Amanda.

Now she wished she hadn't spent so long sleeping and having breakfast. There was too much to do. She had to get into town and find out what had happened to that statue.

After an emergency shower she huffed out into the garden, hoping she could still walk despite how much she'd eaten and how sore she felt. She set a brisk pace towards the shops, every bone aching and every muscle protesting.

The plaza was packed with people gawking at where the statue used to be. Its plinth stood bare and empty. All that was left at the base were some rusty iron bolts and shattered cement. The statue had been stolen clean off its base.

Something funny was hanging in the air too. Amanda tried to make out the scent but the crowd of on-lookers made it hard to smell more than mid-morning dog and old ladies' Eau de Toilette. Underneath it all was… grease? Motor oil? And the vaguest hint that something nasty had gone off. The memory triggered a gurgling in Amanda's stomach and she had to hold onto her tummy to stop herself heaving breakfast right back up again.

Mercifully she couldn't see any trace of where last night's body had spilled its guts. Whoever had stolen the statue had done a very thorough job of cleaning things up.

A hand landed on Amanda's shoulder and she jumped out of her skin.

"Jet!" she snapped. "Don't do that."

"Nice job with the statue," he whispered. "Real professional. Stroke of genius, really. I'd been going to suggest it myself but I couldn't figure out where we could rent a pick-up truck at that hour. Also, I kind of wanted cake. I kind of still do, but then that's my secret — I always want cake."

Amanda just looked at him like he was mad.

"So?" he asked. "Where did you put it?"

"*I* didn't move it."

Jet scratched his butt. "So who'd steal a statue with a dead body inside it? I mean the only person who'd want it is the…" Jet trailed off and felt Amanda's eyes glaring into him.

"The murderer," said Amanda. "Jet, I'm scared. Whoever took the statue must have seen us there."

"That noise…" said Jet.

Amanda bit her tongue. The sharp pain made her eyes water. It was beginning to make a horrible kind of sense. Her mother was walking with crutches, making the same noise she'd heard last night. But she couldn't tell Jet. Her mother wouldn't murder anyone. She couldn't have. But it had all happened so long ago. And what about her dad? He'd been driving the car, and her mom couldn't have done it alone. Her head was spinning.

"I've got to go," she blurted out. "I'll see you later."

"Wait!" he called out. "You can't just go."

Amanda raced home, gritting her teeth the whole way and wishing she still had her bike. She ran hard and the blood pounded in her ears.

What could she possibly say? She couldn't ask her mother directly. Who knew what this was about or who else was mixed up in it. It wouldn't be safe. But then if her mother had already seen her with the statue the night before, she would already know that Amanda had discovered the body.

Amanda cut across the street. Next thing she knew a car was honking loud, its tires skidding against the road.

Amanda came up short and stumbled onto the asphalt. The grit bit into her hands and knees as the car jerked to a stop only a foot away from her.

She picked herself up. Her legs felt like pipe cleaners and she was trembling all over. She could see bloody red gashes, but she couldn't feel them yet — just that numb inkling of a burn that she knew would flare into an excruciating pain.

She stumbled against the car and for a moment she leaned against the hood.

"Amanda!"

She looked up — her father was standing at the car door, her mother in the passenger seat. Amanda felt her trembling worsen as she realized it was her parents' car.

"What do you think you're doing?" demanded Mr. Spillane. "You could have been killed."

Amanda bolted as best she could, knees nearly giving way beneath her, but at least she was getting away.

She darted over the curb and onto her front lawn. She hobbled into the house, slamming the door behind her and panting as she drew the deadbolt.

She leaned against the door for a moment and tried to catch her breath. Her ears strained to catch any sounds from outside. A car approached and Amanda's heart seized up in her chest, but it passed by as if nothing in the world were the matter. She let out a sob and dragged herself up to her bedroom where she shut herself in and curled up on her bed.

The house was silent.

Chapter 17

Old Bill lay decked out on the side of the road, luxuriating as well as he could in the dust and the dirt. He tried to find an angle of shade, but he still had to squint against the burning sun. His bottle of whiskey was warm now. He relished the burn as he took another swig. It was the only feeling he had left. Except for resentment. Yeah. Come to think of it, there was an awful lot of that.

A shadow fell over him, and for a brief moment the tramp felt grateful for something. But he knew his luck too well. When he gazed up at the figure standing over him he caught the silhouette of a ten-gallon hat and the glint of a sheriff's star.

"Now Bill," said the sheriff. "Ain't we talked about this?"

"Good day to yer, Clancy. You wouldn't arrest a fellow for enjoyin' a lick o' the great outdoors, would ya?" He glanced down the street and saw a tumbleweed being vigorously chased by a rat. "Seems a shame to waste all the sights an' sounds Skunks Dance gots to offer on a beautiful day."

"Is that liquor?" demanded the sheriff.

Old Bill regarded his bottle and said, "No. It's sarsaparilla."

"Public drunkenness," said the sheriff, gleefully jotting notes in the pad that never seemed to leave his hand. "And vagrancy in the third degree."

"Now sheriff, you know right well I gots a shop just here," said Bill, indicating the boarded up building behind him.

"*Had* a shop, Bill. You had a shop afore you steered her aground."

Bill clutched his heart. "You sure know how to hurt a man, Clancy. Yep, that gets me right here in the ol' ticker."

"You can just tick right off outta town," said the sheriff. "I don't even want one town drunk an' that position's already filled."

Bill scowled at another tramp down the street, also camped out in the ruins of his own business. And in between them — the gun store of one Jacqueline Hyde.

"Arrest her, why don't you?" Bill slurred. "She rides inta town like she owns the place, scares all my customers away. She's the reason I don't gots a bed to sleep in. I used to be a gynecologist and even I hate her!"

The sheriff's voice softened for a moment. "Did she ever come see you? When you was still in business?"

"Yes!" he cried. "It was like looking into the sun!"

"Move along now, Bill. Ain't got no room in this town for no drunken gyn… gyn… lady-inspector. If I see you vagrant in a public thoroughfare agin, I'm gonna have to take you in."

"It ain't fair, Clancy!" he sobbed. "You know it ain't."

"There now, Bill. You'll get to inspect lady parts agin someday."

The sheriff strolled away in the direction of Main Street while Old Bill lay homeless, destitute, and rapidly losing track of the world as it careened around him. New footsteps began to make their way into the street, and for a moment Bill was afraid it was the sheriff coming to make an example of him. But no — now he looked it was somebody new. That newcomer in town, the one everyone was talking about after his obscene one-man show down at the church last night. Bill couldn't help but crack a wry, cankered grin in his direction.

Spillane shifted nervously in his boots and wondered why that tramp was giving him the hairy eyeball. It was possible, he realized, that the previous night's performance had made him a target for all kinds of Californian perverted types. As if he didn't have enough to deal with.

"I don't wear lady clothes," Spillane blurted. He cringed as soon as he said it. He was beginning to sound just as crazy as everyone else.

But the tramp just stared back at Spillane dumbly for a second before keeling forward into the dirt. His bottle of whiskey rolled onto the ground. Spillane stopped it with his foot, picked it up, and took a fortifying swig. If there was one thing Skunks Dance had taught him, it was that you never knew if you were going to live to see the next drink. He drained the bottle and tossed it to one side where it shattered in the street.

Spillane raised his eyes to the storefront before him. It had a painted sign outside that read:

JACQUELINE HYDE
THE GIRL WITH THE GUNS

Spillane glanced once to the left and once to the right — on either side was a trail of human wreckage. Stores were boarded up, trash collected in the gutters, and now Spillane could make out yet another drunk giving him a greasy look.

"Oh don't mind them!" called Jackie's voice from the doorway. "I try to warn people, but moths never can stay away from a flame."

"Some people oughta have more sense," grumbled Spillane.

"And yet here you are again," Jackie said with a grin. "I told you — no-one learns." She beckoned him inside. "Right this way, my fluttery little friend. Step into the light."

Spillane sighed inwardly and, knowing Ma Spillane would never approve, decided to tell her he'd been ungainfully employed this entire time.

He followed Jackie inside.

The place was cavernous. The walls were stacked high with an enormous variety of firearms — hunting rifles, six-shooters, even a few true vintage pieces that didn't looked like they'd been used since the war.

Jackie followed his admiring gaze and said, "They don't call me the girl with the guns for nothing."

"They oughta call you 'danger in a dress.'"

"They do. They ought to call you 'trouble in a tutu.'"

"They do, now," said Spillane dejectedly.

Jackie picked up one of the muskets Spillane had been looking at. "This one's an old British piece. No bore on these sweethearts. They shoot like a distressed pig. Probably why the British lost, although," she said, stroking the barrel of the musket, "I daresay my old granny may have had something to do with it too."

"Yours an' mine both," said Spillane.

But now his attention was drawn to an extraordinary gadget in one corner. It looked like a pistol, or at least something that used to be a pistol. Now the barrel was severely bent.

"Someone's been manhandlin' the merchandise," he chuckled.

Jackie scoffed. "You ought to know me better by now. The only manhandling that goes on in my store is done by me. No, that's a little device of my own invention. I call it the sidewinder — it goes around corners."

"That's impossible," said Spillane.

"Of course it is," she replied. "That's why I win."

Spillane rubbed his eyes. This was all getting too much for him.

"I need a drink," he moaned.

Jackie plucked a high-feathered hat from behind the counter and said, "That's the smartest thing I've ever heard you say. To the saloon!"

Jackie's store turned out to be only a few streets away from the Belle and Bullet-Hole. Despite the desolation that seemed to spread outwards from Jackie's store, the saloon still did a respectable trade.

As soon as she marched through the doors, the barman threw up his hands and said, "If it isn't Jackie Hyde! Come in, come in, what can I get for my best customer?"

"Two whiskeys," she said, removing her hat with a flourish.

"What about your friend?"

"He'll have two whiskeys too."

"First round's on the house!" the barman roared at Spillane. "If Jackie can wear a dress and be fantastic, then so can you."

Spillane nodded for a moment before he realized what the bartender was implying. "Hey! F'yer information I was in character."

"Hold your horses, friend, I ain't judgin' no-one. This is after all the land o' the free, and they don't come no freer'n Jackie."

Jackie smirked and said, "You better watch it, fellah. You could ruin a lady's reputation with that kind of talk."

The barman laid the shots down on the bar. "All I mean t'say, Miss Hyde, is any friend o' yours is a friend o' mine."

"Well let's not rush to say 'friend,'" said Jackie. "I see our Mr. Spillane as more of a lost puppy. I don't mind being kind to the strays, but I never take them in. Sooner or later they always wind up in the pound."

Spillane downed his first shot under Jackie's amused eye, winced, and said, "Smooth as a schoolmarm's leg."

"Mr. Spillane, are you trying to impress me?"

Spillane produced his lucky deck of cards and murmured, "How's about you and me settle down to a nice game o' chance?"

With a steely eye on Spillane, Jackie picked up her shot-glasses and somehow managed to drink both of them at the same time. Before Spillane could even wrap his head around how she'd done it, she had slammed the empty glasses back on the bar.

"Boyo," she said, "you really are lookin' for trouble."

Chapter 18

Jet rubbed his forehead and wondered if he was just a masochist for getting himself into this mess. He'd had so many chances to leave Amanda alone, but he just had to kick that hornets' nest. What was worse, there was no way back now. He could almost hear Steve telling him, "Dig up, stupid."

He kept turning it over and over in his head. Leverett found Spillane's gold, then built that statue. There was no reason to build the statue unless he was trying to hide the treasure — from someone who wanted to kill him. Evidently he'd been too late. The murderer found him and killed him. So where was the treasure? And who had the expertise to seal up a dead body inside bronze?

"Cheer up!" said Mrs. Ashwood. "Whatever it is, it can't be that bad."

Jet shifted on the couch and stuffed a pillow over his face.

"Someone's trying to kill me," he murmured.

"That's exactly what I've been trying to tell you for the past 17 years. It's the soda companies. Do you have any idea how bad that stuff is for you? High fructose corn syrup is poison."

"It's not the soda companies."

"Big tobacco?" she demanded. "Tell me you haven't started smoking. If I've told you once I've told you a thousand times, that stuff is evil. Now if you wanted something to relieve a bit of tension you should have come to me. I have a very reliable weed dealer who I can hook you up with, *if* you do all your chores."

"Mom!"

"All right, all right, all I'm saying is it's not my fault the bathroom is a disgrace."

Jet pulled his phone out of his pocket. It was an old one he'd had to fish out of a box full of disused gadgets and electronics, but seeing as it wasn't in twelve pieces at the bottom of the river, it seemed to have the final advantage. He didn't particularly want to be browsing Reddit, but it was the easiest way to ignore his mother. His mom pulled out a sliding tiles puzzle and aggressively pretended to text with it.

Jet caught her out of the corner of his eye and groaned, "Mom!"

"Well if you're going to ignore me I can ignore you just as easily."

Jet jumped as the telephone in the kitchen began to ring. He rolled off the couch and went to pick it up — anything for a distraction.

As soon as he lifted the handset Amanda whispered, "Jet, come with me to the archives."

Jet winced and stared at the handset in disbelief. "What, you're calling me on a *landline*? Are you from 1996?"

"I didn't have your cell," she said.

"How did you even get this number? Weren't all these things disconnected after 9/11?"

"Jet, we have to go. The only way we're going to find out what's going on is if we find out who sculpted that statue. I can't say any more right now. They may be listening."

Now Jet thought he could hear something in Amanda's voice. She might actually be upset.

"Who's listening?" he asked

"There's a murderer at large, Jettison. The Case of the Body in the Statue isn't going to solve itself."

"Are you trying to sound like Nancy Drew?" he scoffed.

Jet smiled as his jibe seemed to draw out some of the Amanda Spillane he was used to.

"Pseudo-feminist claptrap!" she said. "*And* it's badly written. I might have known you read Nancy Drew."

"I do *not* read Nancy Drew!"

"So put down the Nancy Drew book you're not reading and come to the City Hall," she said. "And don't tell anyone where you're going.

This is serious business."

Jet sighed and replaced the handset. Amanda would not have been his first choice of co-conspirator in a murder investigation. But then he was 99% sure Skunks Dance didn't have any lingerie models, so in a pinch he supposed he had to settle.

Jet's car gave an asthmatic cough as it pulled up outside City Hall into a convenient handicap space. The thing juddered to a halt and hissed as it cooled down, settling like an old, blind dog lying down to die.

Jet looked around, but couldn't see anything. He'd half expected to find Amanda's bike locked to the rack, but then remembered that the thing was probably making friends with his cellphone in the river. He didn't think it was like Amanda to be late, but then there was no sign of her here. He almost caught himself beginning to worry that something had happened to her. That murderer would probably be doing the world a favor.

As Jet stood by his car looking around, he heard a sharp hiss coming from the bushes by the wall. He wandered over with a grin plastered all over his face to discover Amanda squatting in the dirt and wood chippings.

"This really isn't your best angle," said Jet.

"Get down!" Amanda hissed.

"This is no time for a dance break," he said, stepping over into the foliage and crouching down beside Amanda. That's when he caught sight of her bleeding hands and arms. It took him another moment to realize, but it also looked like she'd been crying.

"Holy crap, what happened to you?"

"I had a difference of opinion with a car," she said humorlessly. "I agreed to disagree, and it agreed to beat the snot out of me. Can we stay focused on the statue?"

"You're the boss."

"I am not the boss. Just listen, okay? Here's what I think. We don't know how many people are in on this, but it has to be at least two." She seemed to have trouble getting the next words out. "And I think one of them is my mom."

"Sweet, dotty old Mrs. Spillane? You're joking. We've all seen her at the shops on a Saturday morning wearing too much makeup and buying tins of peanut butter and anchovies."

Amanda chose to ignore that remark. "I woke up last night when Mom and Dad pulled into the driveway — and my mom was walking on *crutches*."

"So what?" said Jet.

"So! The sound we heard last night — I think it was my mom."

"Oh my God… Then *she* killed Lawrence Leverett."

"She would have been like 19, she can't have. Can she? I don't know," Amanda sighed, rubbing her face. Jet noticed she avoided aggravating the cuts on her hands, which were beginning to scab. "All I know is, my mom is the one who moved that body last night."

Click-tap, click-tap, click-tap —

"Oh my God, she found us!" hissed Amanda. "She tried to kill me, Jet. Don't let her hurt you."

Jet peered cautiously through the bushes. The parking lot looked empty. But there — he spotted a movement through the leaves. He could just about make out Mayor Franklin strolling up the City Hall steps, clicking a retractable pen anxiously. Click-tap.

Jet groaned. "It must have been the mayor. Unless it really was your mom."

"What are you saying about my mother? The woman's a saint. Clearly Franklin did it. But how does he fit in to all this? Nobody loves this town more than he does."

"You must be joking," Jet scoffed. "He's a professional shyster. Next thing you'll be telling me he couldn't have done it because politicians are all so honest and trustworthy."

They peered out from the bushes and spotted Franklin through the windows. First he spent a few moments chatting to Mr. Snodgrass, or at least as many moments as Snodgrass would let him. Then he set up camp in his office. He seemed to have settled in for the long-haul.

Jet turned to Amanda.

"Well we can't go in now."

"No… You should have heard his voice last time he caught me snooping around the records from the '70s." She groaned to herself.

152

"No wonder he was so tetchy about it. He's trying to keep the whole thing under wraps. Well he's done a pretty good job. We'll never get to those archives now."

"I have an idea!"

There was an awkward silence until Amanda snapped, "Are you gonna tell me, or are you just gonna sit there until I hold a light-bulb over your head?"

"You've never quite got the hang of other people, have you?" Jet asked. "If there's anyone who knows about that statue, it's gotta be Harvey. Plus he's like a thousand years old, he was probably there when they built the thing."

"Harvey?" she asked wonderingly. "You mean Mr. Spackle?"

"How do you know Harvey?" Jet demanded.

But Amanda didn't respond. She was chasing a lost thought, and for the first time that afternoon she broke into a grin. "Of course! That's brilliant. Mr. Spackle knows everything about Skunks Dance."

Jet smiled back and held up a hand for a high five.

Amanda slapped his hand victoriously. "Good thinking, 99!"

"What did you just say?"

"Never mind," she mumbled. "Just... high five!"

She held her hand up again until Jet slapped it slightly less enthusiastically than the first time.

Harvey Spackle's house was on the quiet side of town, and yet he'd managed to position himself right next to the grade school in a way that terrified the children and annoyed the hell out of Spackle. But then everything seemed to annoy the hell out of Spackle, so it was impossible to say if this was anything special. The only social contact he seemed to have with the outside world was on the occasional election day when he set up a small garage sale filled with an infinite supply of junk — Super 8 projectors, Polaroid cameras, reel-to-reel tape decks, and, to the excitement of young Jet, a hoard of vintage comic books. Jet latched onto Spackle at that moment and nothing Spackle could shout at him seemed to deter the young teenager. Jet's pet theory was that Spackle secretly enjoyed having someone who would stop by and be shouted at, although it was impossible to say if this was true.

Jet didn't like to imagine how Spackle and Amanda might know each other. She was probably just some annoying kid who Spackle couldn't get rid of. She definitely had the whiff of a desperate hanger-on.

"How do you know Mr. Spackle anyway?" asked Amanda.

Jet spluttered. "How do *I* know him? We go back years. He taught me everything I know about British comics. How do *you* know him?"

"He's the only other historian in Skunks Dance apart from Mr. Snodgrass. My dad's known him forever."

"Yeah well just try not to get in the way. He and I have a special kind of banter. To an outsider it probably just looks like personal abuse, but you don't know him as well as I do. Don't cramp our style, is all I'm saying."

"I wouldn't dream of it," Amanda said with a roll of her eyes.

It was quiet again for a moment before Amanda glanced at Jet from under her eyebrows and said, "You really love those comics, don't you?"

"I guess. They're pretty cool."

"I've got kind of a confession. You know when I said your comic was in my car when you set it on fire?"

"Exploded," said Jet. "It was really more of an explosion."

"Right. Only it wasn't — in the car, I mean. It's at home in my desk."

Jet broke into a hesitant grin. "You still have my *Fantastic Firecat*? You animal…" he said admiringly. "I never thought you had it in you."

Amanda caught herself in a guilty smile. "I hate you too."

They pulled up to the curb outside Spackle's house. The run-down bungalow looked especially antisocial today. The trees that hung over the driveway were filled with orb spiders that shook angrily in their webs. They had never bothered him before, but now Jet couldn't help shuddering at the sight.

Amanda stepped onto the porch. The ancient wooden boards, long stripped of all their paint and integrity, groaned beneath her foot. She started as Jet clamped a hand onto her shoulder and hissed, "Be quiet! He hates noise."

She clawed Jet's hand away from her arm and said, "I know that. D'you think I did that on purpose? Oh yeah, let's go over to Boo

Radley's house and make as much noise as possible."

Jet's phone began to ring.

He swore, fumbling with it desperately until he dropped the thing onto the cement. The screen cracked, and Jet hissed, "God damn it, that's the third one!" But despite the damage it continued to ring blaringly.

"Curse you Apple and your quality products," he mumbled as he snatched it off the ground in a panic to silence the blasted thing. He immediately managed to slice his finger open on the cracked glass and dropped the treacherous machine onto the ground again.

That's when they heard the footsteps. And a noise.

Click-tap, click-tap, click-tap…

Jet grabbed Amanda and hauled her round the side of the house. The phone remained on the ground, ringing out their guilt.

Harvey Spackle emerged from the other side of the house. Jet, crouching around the corner, was just about able to see him through the latticework that covered the crawl space. In Spackle's hand was a machine, clicking like a Geiger counter, its antenna pointing squarely at the ringing phone. The clicking got stronger as it homed in.

Spackle caught sight of the detested object and, with nothing more than a grunt that could sustain a family of four through a harsh Soviet winter, he crushed the thing under his heel.

The phone stopped ringing once and for all.

Spackle picked up the phone off the crazy paving and held it up to his specs. The sunlight danced off the lenses, as if angry to encounter a creature so thoroughly of the night. Spackle sniffed the trace of blood Jet had left on the jagged glass and then, with a darting motion like a snake tasting the air, Spackle's tongue whipped out of his mouth and licked up the blood.

Amanda looked like she was going to be sick.

Spackle smacked his lips, as if savoring an unmentionable vintage of wine.

"B positive," he muttered, before lumbering back around the side of the house and discarding the phone over the neighbor's fence with a sturdy throw. Then he was gone — disappeared back into his house.

"That was incredible!" said Amanda. "Was he right?"

"I dunno. Who knows their blood type?" Jet glanced over to Amanda and saw the answer written on her face. "Oh that's just typical. I bet you're a little miss regular down at the blood drive. Of course you realize what this means. It could have been Spackle who stole that statue. *And* he was old enough to murder Leverett in the '70s."

"Are you sure it was the same noise?" Amanda asked.

Jet cast his mind back to the previous evening, but it was all a blur. He'd been so tired and hungry, and by the time they'd got to the statue he'd been running on pure adrenaline. He realized that he couldn't be sure.

"It could be anyone," Jet groaned. "It's like everyone in this town makes the same stupid noise."

Just as they paused to take stock, a girl came down the sidewalk on her tricycle. One or two lonely beads rattled along the spokes as she went by — click-tap, click-tap, click-tap.

Jet slumped against the side of Spackle's house and swore quietly to himself.

Chapter 19

Jackie Hyde was sweating hard. She knitted her brow. This just wasn't ladylike. She wasn't supposed to sweat. She wasn't supposed to feel like the squalid air of the saloon was catching in her throat. And she wasn't supposed to lose at cards. She was far too good a player for that, and besides, she was cheating like the dickens. And yet if Spivey Spillane won one more hand she was going to have to start stripping to cover her debts. Not that she generally minded that, but hiding the cards got mighty uncomfortable when you didn't have any sleeves.

"Mr. Spillane," she grunted, "if I didn't have such a trusting nature I'd suspect you were cheating at this game."

"And if I wasn't disinclined to speak ill of a lady, I'd suspect you like it."

Spillane attempted to take a smug puff on his cigar but choked on the smoke, giving Jackie enough time to pull an Ace out of her garters. The illicit card was in her hand before Spillane knew what was happening. She grinned to herself. Spillane might think he had a few tricks, but no-one beat Jacqueline Hyde in a game of chance.

She tried not to gloat as she laid her hand out on the table.

"Full house," she said. "Kings full of Aces."

"Well now, ain't that a hell of a thing," murmured Spillane. He lay down his hand. "Aces full of Kings."

Jackie's jaw hung open. "How did you…? I was *watching* you. You never had time to do that."

"Things ain't always what they seem."

157

Spillane took a much more confident puff of his cigar. "Vile things," he said, "but ain't nothin' better for creatin' a distraction."

"Where do you hide the cards?" she asked.

"Miss Hyde, at this rate you're gonna walk outta here with *all* my secrets."

"Another hand," she said. "This time no smoking."

"Some other time. Right this minute I got me a problem by the name o' Alabama Sam."

Jackie cocked an eyebrow at him, unsure whether or not she had been played. All she knew was this cowboy had just become a whole lot more interesting. She was going to have to keep an eye on him — unlikely as it seemed, he might actually be smarter than he looked.

"Perhaps you don't know this, but Alabama Sam is dead," she said. "Word on the street is, you're the one who did it. Not that I blame you. The man was clearly gunning for you, it was either you or him." She paused and regarded Spillane askance. "To be honest I'm more than a little bit surprised it was him. No offense, Mr. Spillane, you may be a rattlesnake at cards but you're a chihuahua in a gunfight. And you can take that to the bank — I've known 'em all, and I've picked up more than a few tricks in my time. If I hadn't been there last night you'd have been buried in that tutu."

Spillane shook his head. "It's worse'n that. Since I started on his trail I called Alabama Sam everythin' in the book — a sidewinder, a carpetbagger, a two-faced no-good thievin' son of a bitch. But I was wrong. He was so much worse."

Spillane was shaking now, fist clamped so hard around his shot-glass that Jackie was afraid it might shatter. His eyes were red and watering, his face was flushed, and the tips of his ears burned.

"Miss Hyde, I'm beginnin' to think Alabama Sam was the Devil himself."

Jackie burst out laughing. It was a throaty noise, sometimes bitter but with a sublime aloofness. Spillane's face creased inwards. He did not like being laughed at.

"You do have an imagination," said Jackie. "But when you've been in the West as long as me, you stop believing all the tall tales you get told in saloons. I only believe what I can touch and what I can shoot at, and I defy you to show me anything that isn't one or the other."

"I ain't stupid, Jackie. I may be a lotta things, but I ain't stupid. I know what I saw. You want an impossible man? Then get ready to meet Alabama Sam."

With Jackie Hyde in town, the undertaker was one of the few people in Skunks Dance who managed to keep himself gainfully employed. Mr. Cardovan could usually be found in his office, straight-backed and high-collared, immaculately groomed, sitting alert and ready for the day's first corpse. Other times he would have his sleeves rolled up as he labored over embalming a body, with an apron to prevent unsightly splashes and a mustache-guard to hold the tips of his whiskers away from open wounds. It was said of Mr. Cardovan that he had the best sense of humor in town, but that he had never let anyone see it.

Today found him less than alert. He lay slumped over a volume of Poe open on his desk at "The Murders in the Rue Morgue." Despite the heat Cardovan was still wearing a three-piece suit. He was napping soundly. The celebration of Spillane's theatrical debut had left him exhilarated, exhausted, and more than a little hung over.

As Mr. Cardovan dozed, the flies began to collect lazily around an object propping open the door. It was Alabama Sam, rope marks still burning livid around his neck.

Spillane and Jackie stepped past the body cautiously. Spillane, for one, didn't trust the man an inch. He knew that even in death Alabama Sam was the most dangerous man in these United States. He had practically proved that already. The man had been dead for less than a day and already Spillane was one wrong step away from being hanged.

"Sorry to bother you, Mr. Cardovan," said Jackie.

Cardovan shot upright in his chair, awake in an instant like a snake that never closes its eyes. He glanced at Spillane momentarily before his gaze settled on Jackie.

"Miss Hyde!" he cried, relaxing enough to rub his eyes. "You should know you're always welcome in here. Do you have anything for me today?"

Jackie shook her head.

Cardovan's eyes indicated the body propped up against the door.

"I don't suppose that there's your handiwork?"

Jackie put a hand on her hip and said, "Now Mr. Cardovan, you can't go blaming me for every stray corpse in this town. I may like my men hung, but ah... not like Alabama Sam."

"I ain't making no judgments," said Cardovan with open hands. "The only thing that concerns me is running this here place of business. Skunks Dance ain't San Francisco, but that ain't no reason we can't have standards."

"Then what," interrupted Spillane, "is your man here doin' holdin' the door open?"

Cardovan eyed Spillane for a moment before remarking, "Mr. Spillane, isn't it? The honor is all mine, sir. I spend all day painting life back into the faces of the dead, but I never seen a better rouge than the one in your cheeks last night. What brand do you use?"

"The *body*, Cardovan," said Spillane through gritted teeth.

"That old thing? Well, sir, that man is dead and ain't nobody gonna pay for a casket. So, if nobody claims him by tomorrow, he's going straight into the nearest ditch with a Hail Mary and a whisper of quicklime. Until then, he may as well hold the door open. No sense in wasting good labor — idle hands and all that.

"I don't suppose you, Mr. Spillane, are here to give this man a Christian burial?"

Spillane spat at the corpse.

"I thought not somehow," said Cardovan.

"I'm just here to make sure he's dead," said Spillane.

Cardovan snorted. "I've spent 30 years in this profession, and I can promise you the dead are not in the habit of coming back to life."

A kind of mania overtook Spillane's eyes. "In 30 years of this profession, you ain't never buried a man like this. I called Alabama Sam everythin' in the book, but I was wrong. I'm beginning to think that Alabama Sam was the Devil him—"

Spillane cut himself short as he caught sight of Jackie mouthing along to the words of his "Devil himself" speech.

His face flushed again. He could feel himself losing control of his body, his fists clenching of their own accord, the blood rushing to his head where it pounded at his skull. All this time and all these games, and all he'd ever wanted to do was punch someone in the face.

He stormed over to the body of Alabama Sam and laid one on him. His fist slammed into the dead man's head, connecting with the overripe skin and sending the body toppling to the ground. All of Spillane's pent-up rage, frustration, and humiliation came out in one ugly volley. He screamed abuse at the body, leaping up and down on top of the happy corpse. Yes, happy. Even in death Alabama Sam mocked him with a rictus etched indelibly onto his face. All of Spillane's blows and insults could not dislodge that smile.

Finally Spillane stopped — panting, sweaty, but satisfied at last that he'd exhausted everything he had in him.

"Mr. Spillane," said Cardovan dryly, "please do not damage the merchandise."

"I'm done here," said Spillane. "He's all yours."

"What was all that in aid of?" Jackie demanded as they exited the undertaker's office.

"Just makin' sure, is all," Spillane replied.

"Listen, no man on Earth can be as bad as you seem to think Alabama Sam was. Now there's still a killer out there somewhere, and in case you've forgotten it's our job to find him or the next man that swings in this town is going to be you."

"He killed *himself,* Jackie."

She stopped walking and stood on the street, face screwed up in confusion. "*What?*" she breathed.

"He hung himself, right in font o' me. I saw the light go outta the man's eyes. He knew I was here, and he knew I was gonna go down for his murder. That man killed himself outta sheer, cold-blooded spite."

Chapter 20

Amanda's bedroom door had clicked open sometime during the night. It had a habit of doing this because the latch didn't sit right in the door frame — even a little breeze would make the door creak gently open. Usually this didn't bother Amanda. She could sleep right through it. But last night, when she heard that little click and creak, her eyes snapped open.

Someone was at the door.

She lay in bed, stiff as a board, sweating into her night shirt, waiting to see what would happen next. But whenever she peered over in the dark — subtly, so it looked like she was only turning over in bed — there was no-one there.

With a muffled groan she realized it was daytime. She'd been awake half the night. She was already beat, and the day's work was still ahead of her.

Amanda stepped out onto the landing, being careful not to make any noise. From here she could hear people moving about in the kitchen downstairs. The coffee machine was percolating. The dishes were clattering together as her father unloaded the dishwasher. She could even hear her mother trying to scramble eggs, clucking to herself as she cooked up something that resembled Rosemary's afterbirth.

Amanda ducked into the bathroom and showered quickly. She didn't want to have to spend any more time here than she had to, but she was also dreading leaving — because she would have to go downstairs and past her parents. She considered using her escape route and making her way across the roof, but she dismissed the idea. She knew what she had to do, and her parents had to think she was out.

As soon as she was ready, she tripped down the stairs and past the living room. She caught her father sitting in the armchair holding the newspaper open in front of him, peering at it suspiciously through his glasses.

"Bye, Dad!" she called. "I'm going out."

He peered at her now, taking a moment to figure out what she'd just said. "Oh," he said. "All right. Have fun."

Amanda stepped outside and closed the front door behind her. Finally she exhaled. "Have fun?" What kind of a thing to say was that? Did he know?

She started walking before her dad started to get curious about what she was up to. She had a few hours to kill, but she would come back soon enough. In the meantime she wandered in the direction of the plaza. It was warm out and the air was stagnant, but Amanda walked with a nervous energy despite the heat. She was keen to get some distance between her and her parents as quickly as possible. As the house fell out of view a few blocks behind her, Amanda began to relax. The walking helped keep her mind off things, even just temporarily, and the sweat felt good on her face.

She arrived at the plaza to find the morning shoppers getting their groceries, and decided to grab something for breakfast in a café. She made the mistake of sitting outside, thinking the fresh air might be relaxing, but now that she was surrounded by people again her paranoia began to return. Every footstep, every bird call, every snatch of conversation made her anxious. Everywhere around her she heard people talking about the statue. Amanda almost put down her cappuccino — the last thing she needed was something to get her all hyper — but she knew she had to stay alert. There was a killer on the loose.

Anything could happen.

A phone rang, and Amanda instinctively reached for her phone before she realized she'd lost hers up at the ridge. Crap. She leaned back in her chair and decided she may as well get a new one while she had nothing better to do.

It was hours before Amanda snuck back home. She stayed in the shadows, trying to walk in the cover of leaves and fences so as not to attract attention. Her parents mustn't know that she was back.

The lights in the garage were off, like she knew they would be. Her father was taking a break for lunch. He would be at least another 20 minutes in the kitchen getting himself a sandwich and a beer and listening to a Bob Dylan record on the turntable. It was the kind of ritual Amanda had always thought was rather sad and middle-aged. Sometimes she thought that if she heard Bob's obscenely untrained voice advertising postcards at the hanging one more time she might just snap the LP over her knee. This time, though, she was actually grateful to hear the discordant whine coming from the house.

With one eye on the house she cracked open the door to the garage and slipped inside.

She didn't dare turn on the lights, and she really wished she'd brought a flashlight with her, but she couldn't waste time going back now. She'd have to make do with the dusty glow coming in through the windows. And besides, she knew her way around these filing cabinets like the back of her hand. It didn't take long to uncover the file her father had compiled a long time ago on Lawrence Leverett.

The pages were very familiar. They had that rich, oily feel that old paper gets, as if it knew its contents had been loved and cared for. Amanda knew where every smudge was, and every mis-strike of the typewriter. God knew she'd browsed through these pages recently enough, so she didn't know what she expected to find now. Maybe suspecting her parents were involved somehow would throw a different light on it. But had she really hoped her father would leave a page lying around conveniently marked "Secret Plans"?

The lights flicked on.

Amanda jumped out of her skin and whirled to face the door.

Her father was standing there with a half-eaten sandwich in his hand and a bit of lettuce hanging menacingly from the side of his mouth. He finished chewing and said, "Amanda? What are you doing in the dark?"

"I couldn't find the lights," she mumbled.

"They haven't *moved*," said Mr. Spillane. "I almost thought you'd snuck a boy in here."

Amanda giggled nervously.

"At any rate," said her father, "I thought you were at the pictures. Weren't you seeing a film today?"

"Oh shhhugar…"

The blood rushed from Amanda's head. How could she not remember? She grabbed her new phone out of her pocket and switched it on. The last hour's worth of texts from Nina rolled in.

meet u at sushi bar ⬤

where r u 😵

She was so screwed. There was no way she could get to the movies in time. The one time she had a chance to go out on a date with Nina and she'd accidentally stood her up.

"What's that face for?" said Mr. Spillane.

"I forgot."

He furrowed his brow in a slightly bewildered way and said, "Come on then, I'll give you a lift."

He stepped out into the driveway and beeped the car open before realizing Amanda hadn't followed him out.

"Come on!" he insisted. "Don't just stand there like an Easter Island statue. Get in the car. You want to get to the mall in time, don't you?"

Amanda stepped slowly towards the car, still holding the Leverett file and trying her best to hide it. Her father held his sandwich in his mouth while he started the engine. She climbed into the passenger seat, but before they'd even pulled out of the driveway her father grabbed the file off her with one hand and extracted his sandwich with the other.

"What's this?" he said. "Are you *still* reading about this junk? How many times have I told you, it's a dead end. I looked into it all years ago. And now with all this statue business, you don't know what kind of crazy people are hanging around. The Leveretts are bad news, Amanda, they always have been. Leave them be."

"But there was one thing…"

"Amanda! Are you listening to me or not? It's a dead end. You're wasting your time. I couldn't find anything and neither have you. Now you're going to leave it alone and that's the end of it."

And with that her father took out a lighter and set fire to the papers. As the flame spread he threw the file out the window, and he threw it with such vigor that he accidentally sent his sandwich with it.

"Now look what you made me do!"

Amanda shrank into the passenger seat and held on for dear life as her father roared out of the driveway and hurled the car around the corners. But even as she wondered whether this might be her last car ride before a shallow grave, Amanda couldn't help remembering what her father had said.

Leveretts. She'd forgotten there were two of them.

Amanda was relieved when her father pulled into the mall parking lot. It seemed she was safe for now. Whatever her parents might have been up to, he couldn't do anything to her with so many people around.

Her father wouldn't let her go, though. He insisted on walking with her into the mall with what Amanda could only interpret as a sinister comment about wanting to buy new razor blades. Next thing she knew he was standing next to her in front of the movies grumbling about the price of popcorn being "murder."

"I haven't seen this since the first time it came out," mused Mr. Spillane, staring at one of the movie posters.

Amanda cast her eyes around the lobby and hoped Nina wasn't going to come round the corner and catch her hanging out with her dad.

"Thanks for the lift," she said. "Didn't you need to go?"

"The dinosaurs were so realistic. You really believed raptors could open doors."

"*Thanks*," said Amanda pointedly. But now her dad's attention had shifted to the poster for *Afterglow* on the wall.

"Is *this* what you're seeing? I don't know about this, it looks a bit racy. I'm going to call Nina's parents. You kids might need a chaperon."

"Dad!"

"Oh don't worry, I won't embarrass you in front of your friends."

Amanda was too old not to recognize that this was dad code for, "I am going to embarrass you in front of your friends, deliberately and repeatedly." Her heart was thudding in her chest. If she could just get rid of him now she might at least still save this date with Nina.

She scanned the lobby again. She spotted Nina at the far end, and for a fraction of a second she was so happy to see her that she forgot all about her dad. And then she saw the gaggle of friends surrounding Nina. Amanda dug her fingernails into her palms, trying not to let her anger show. She didn't know why she thought this was going to be anything special. Of course Nina was going to invite her ten million friends. She wouldn't even talk to Amanda at all if they didn't happen to know some of the same people.

"Hey!" said Amanda, smiling despite the tightness in her throat.

Mr. Spillane waved at them. "Good morning, Nina… Michelle… Or more accurately, good afternoon," he said after a quick glance at his watch.

Everyone smiled without laughing as Mr. Spillane led them towards the box office. Amanda tried to hang at the back of the group, and couldn't avoid noticing Nina do a little impression of Mr. Spillane checking his watch.

Amanda was at least grateful that as they filed into the theater her father went to find a seat on his own. As they sat down, she noticed Nina made sure to sit next to her. Her heart quavered in her chest. Sitting next to Nina was only going to make her embarrassment so much worse, but at the back of her head she couldn't resist the thought that maybe, for some reason, Nina *wanted* to sit next to her.

While her friends were chattering, Amanda cast a glance around and saw her dad sitting a few rows back. He smiled at her. The shadows lent his face a rather sinister overtone.

She turned back to the screen and picked at her popcorn. It tasted stale and chewy.

"So," Nina said, leaning in toward Amanda. "What's up?"

"Huh? Oh, not much I guess."

"Seriously? Because I heard that you've been hanging out with Jet! People are saying you guys are like seeing each other."

Amanda was too sideswiped by this to catch the weird tone in Nina's voice. Instead she just scoffed and said, "Not likely. I don't even want to spend time with him *now*, let alone forever. It's just we've got kind of a… summer project."

Nina nodded, not really listening. "So does he ever like talk about things?"

"What things?"

"I dunno, stuff."

Amanda shrugged. "I guess."

"Has he talked about *me*?" asked Nina.

"Why would he talk about you?"

"Whatever, forget about it," said Nina. "I can't even."

The group fell silent as the previews started, followed by the film. It wasn't all bad, as far as Amanda could tell, but it was impossible to concentrate on the movie with her dad sitting behind her and Nina on her left. Nina's elbow brushed tantalizingly against hers, giving Amanda goosebumps. She could always pass it off as a chill from the air conditioning, but she knew that wasn't true.

Nina withdrew her arm. Amanda's goosebumps went away and her arm was left, heavy and unfeeling, alone on the armrest.

Amanda felt the bites of popcorn start to churn in her stomach. She didn't know if she was going to throw up, but she knew she needed to get out of that movie. She stood up, trying to keep low enough not to catch her father's attention, and pushed her way past Nina.

Something crunched under her foot. Amanda lost her footing and stumbled against the next row. When she looked back she saw she had just put her foot into Nina's massive bag of popcorn, now sadly deceased. The last thing Amanda saw as she scurried out of the theater was Nina glaring at her in outrage.

Amanda paced hyperactively outside the bus stop. She couldn't sit down and keep still, not now, but no matter how much she marched back and forth the bus refused to show up. That left her alone with her thoughts bubbling away inside her head. Just when she thought she couldn't stand it any more, head aching with the weight of it all, she felt her phone buzz.

It was Jet.

Amanda jabbed the answer button and shouted, "Has anyone ever told you that people can be really shit sometimes?"

"Huh. It's like when kids figure out Santa isn't real, or that *The Wizard of Oz* is about a gang of serial killers who murder everyone they meet."

"You know once, just once, you could drop the whole too-cool-for-school crap and actually give a stuff about someone else. The world doesn't revolve around Jettison Allan-Ashwood. Other people exist too, you know."

"I'll believe it when I see it," he drawled. "Are you upset about something?"

"Oh, you managed to figure that out, did you, professor?"

"Hey! If I'm going to pretend to care about your PMS, you could at least pretend to believe it."

"How dare you," she hissed, clutching the phone so tight she thought she might crush it.

The roar of an engine distracted her for a moment, and she looked up just in time to see her bus pull away from the stop.

All the fight suddenly left her. "You know what?" she said, trying not to sound like she was about to cry. "Just forget it."

She hung up the phone, slumped onto the bench, and cradled her head in her hands.

Chapter 21

The night before they burned the body, Spivey Spillane had a bad dream. He felt a tickle in his throat. He reached his fingers down as far as they would go until he felt something brush against his fingertips. He tried to grasp it and pull it out. When he looked down, he found brown, brittle fragments in his hand, like the legs of an insect. Something had crawled down his throat and died. Now its brittle little insect body was stuck in his esophagus.

He tried to yank it out again but only came away with more broken-off legs. The more he pulled, the less there was to hold onto, and he was only forcing the thing further and further down. He could feel it brushing against his Adam's apple, feel the hairy legs and bits of wing sticking into his gullet. The lump was huge now.

And that was when he felt it twitch. It was still alive.

Spillane woke to his room, not suddenly, sitting bolt upright and panting, but slowly, drawn back into a world that he knew didn't want him. His shirt was sticky, and now felt cold against the warm night. This was the room where Alabama Sam had killed himself. Spillane's foggy, half-awake brain began to think suicide didn't seem like such a bad idea.

Spillane felt a tickle in his throat and, with a decisive cough, knew what he had to do.

As soon as the hour was decent he went into town again. This town had taken enough from him. This time it was his turn.

He gathered what money he could scrape together and took it to the gun store of Jackie Hyde. Even the tramps were gone from the street outside now, leaving it a dusty wasteland. The buildings were pitted with the occasional bullet hole where satisfied customers had taken part in some target practice. Jackie regarded him skeptically as he pushed open the door and set off a little jingle of bells.

"Mr. Spillane, you seem to be making a habit of visiting this establishment."

"Yes, ma'am. Is that gonna be a problem?"

"Not for me, anyhow," she replied with a little smile. Spillane couldn't tell whether that smile was coy or threatening, but then everything about Jackie was either coy or threatening and he was damned if he could tell which was which. Probably this was both.

"Lemme put your mind at ease," he said. "Today is strictly for business."

"Now I know you're in the wrong place. I never do anything strictly for business."

Spillane cleared his throat uncomfortably. "I'm sure I wouldn't know anythin' about that. What I meant was I wanna get me a new gun."

Jackie breathed in sharply. "I hope you're not planning anything dumb, on account of I like to see my merchandise put to good use. No point wasting a good gun on a corpse. You may be a fine shot on a farm, but folks in the West are mighty different from cows. If you're intending to pull a gun on someone, you better be damn sure you get him with the first bullet, 'cause you won't get time to use a second."

"Don't worry," said Spillane. "I got a plan."

Jackie cocked an eyebrow at him, then followed his gaze to one particular item of merchandise out on display.

"Well I can't say my momma would approve of that in a fair fight," she said. "But if I only ever did what my momma approved of, I'd still be in Missouri and Buffalo Bill would still be a virgin. Let's get you some bullets and see if you can actually fire her."

"Her?" Spillane asked. "Why're you talkin' about that gun like it's a lady?"

"*All* guns are ladies. And some ladies," she added, "are guns."

Spillane's next stop was to see Mr. Cardovan. As he entered the undertaker's office Spillane noticed that Alabama Sam was looking noticeably greener around the gills than he had yesterday. The vicious beating he had given the body didn't seem to have affected it. If he'd been alive he would have been covered in bruises. This corpse's imperviousness only lent it a sinister air. Of course Alabama Sam didn't bruise. Spillane was surprised the man had even had to blink.

"Good morning," said Mr. Cardovan. "Have you come back for a second look at the merchandise? I was just about to take it out for indecent burial. Or were you perhaps interested in something for yourself?" he asked, measuring Spillane across the shoulders with a tape.

Spillane grabbed the tape out of Cardovan's hands and threw it aside. Cardovan flinched. He was so accustomed to working on the dead that his social skills with the living seemed to have lapsed somewhat. Spillane advanced on him slowly until Cardovan was up against the wall.

"Don't kill me," squeaked Cardovan. "There'd be no-one to bury the body."

"It ain't your body I'm interested in," growled Spillane. "I'm gonna leave here in five minutes and that there body of Alabama Sam is comin' with me."

"Mr. Spillane, surely you jest. This state may only be newly minted, but it has very clear guidelines on the legal disposition of the dead. If I give you that body I could get done for…"

He was cut off by Spillane's hand around his throat.

"Ah. I see you're determined then."

"Think about it this way, Cardovan. I'm savin' you and the taxpayers of California the cost of buryin' this body. Way I see it, I'm doin' you a civic service."

Cardovan nodded uncertainly. "Yes, now that you put it that way, you have certainly set my mind at rest."

Cardovan hadn't even finished his sentence before Spillane was out the door, dragging the body of Alabama Sam behind him in the dust.

That evening Spillane built a makeshift funeral pyre in the town square. It wasn't very tall, but then Sam didn't deserve a dignified kind of a send-off. The main thing was that he burned and he burned good. It was the only way Spillane was ever going to rid himself of the tickle in his throat, that nagging feeling that somewhere Alabama Sam was watching and waiting for the right time to come back. He knew it was insane — but there was no harm in being sure.

He gave the body one last kick for good measure, ducking out of the way as if the corpse might flinch and wake up. But it didn't. It lay there as unmoving and unfeeling as it had been the day before. With a hasty grunt Spillane picked up the detested object and hauled it onto the stack of wood that waited eagerly for the first match. He struck one, reveling for a moment in the blossom of sulfur and phosphorus that illuminated the night, before he flicked it deftly onto the pyre.

He'd expected to feel relieved. He'd expected to feel clean. He was disappointed on both counts. He watched the flames lick higher and wondered why this wasn't as satisfying as it should have been.

An immaculate hand landed on Spillane's shoulder, making him shiver despite the warmth of the fire. He had been dreading this.

He turned around to find Aurelio Nunes, teeth glinting in the firelight.

"Quite the display, Mr. Spillane, quite the display. This is all most impressive. I'm glad to see you give a mortal enemy such a dignified send-off. The Vikings used to burn their dead too. They put the warrior's horse at his head and his dog at his feet, set his ship adrift at sea, and watched it burn."

Spillane turned his back on Nunes and faced the fire once more.

"Alabama Sam worked alone," he mumbled. "There's no-one on Earth knows what was in that head." He paused for a moment before adding, "What happened to them Vikings in the end?"

"In the end? They ran out of dogs and horses."

They both stared at the flames for a few minutes. For Spillane even the smell of burning skin and hair was preferable to what he knew was coming. He had never killed a man before, but he supposed there was a first time for everything.

"I hope you haven't forgotten our little arrangement, Mr. Spillane. Now that our friend Alabama Sam has taken up residence in the Halls of Valhalla, we have other work to attend to."

Spillane slowly reached into his pocket and withdrew the pistol that he had concealed there. The barrel was bent curiously so as to fire around corners. He angled it like Jackie had demonstrated and prepared to shoot the man behind him.

"I ain't forgotten," growled Spillane.

He inched the barrel closer to his side. He could just about feel it in the gap between his elbow and his ribcage.

"We don't have much time to waste. Rumor has already spread her filthy wings and flown across this town with word that a jackpot has been found somewhere in the hills."

Nunes had barely finished speaking when Spillane fired.

The bullet cleared his body, leaving a singe on the sleeve of his shirt and a ringing in his ears. He didn't dare look, not yet.

A chill still made its home at the base of his neck. He realized with a worsening dread that he had not heard the body hit the ground.

"An ingenious invention," purred Nunes in his ear, "and a gallant attempt on my life. But I'm afraid you missed."

Without warning Nunes twisted Spillane's arm behind his back. Spillane grunted and dropped the pistol.

"But perhaps you forget who I am."

"You're the man that's keepin' me outta jail," Spillane gasped.

"Oh Mr. Spillane, I'm so much more than that. I'm the man who killed Alabama Sam."

Chapter 22

Jet squeezed the phone between his hands and growled through his teeth, "Why are girls so *mental?*"

The next thing he knew he had a shooting pain in his shin and an angry sister staring up at him with the face of Gina and the eyes of a Targaryen dragon. She had just kicked him in the leg.

"That wasn't very nice," said Gina. "You should apologize to her."

"You just kicked me and you're not apologizing for that," snapped Jet.

"That's because you're stupid. And I like Amanda. You shouldn't call her names."

"I was being nice. I can call her a lot worse things than mental."

He found now that his other shin was experiencing the same distress as the first one. He didn't know how he'd wound up with such an ungovernable devil-storm for a little sister, but he swore that if she kicked him one more time then the coroner would have to put the parts of her back together with a staple gun and a jeweler's loupe.

She kicked him again.

"Stop doing that!"

"Apologize," she demanded.

"I'm sorry!"

"To Amanda," Gina insisted. "You're supposed to be friends."

"Friends! That'll be the day. We aren't... Oh my God."

The full horror of what Gina had said was just beginning to dawn on him. She was right. Somehow, and totally against his will, he had become friends with Amanda Spillane. Sure, he still hated her, but then he wasn't all that keen on the rest of his friends either, and he was a lot less invested in them. Amanda, on the other hand — he'd been feuding with her for years. He couldn't think of anything else he'd poured so much time into — willingly, at least. And now they were both being stalked by some kind of psycho statue-killer.

For a brief moment he wondered if his mother had been right, and he and Amanda were playing out a sublimated crush. Then he felt the cold, gray grip of death on his spine and he knew that if his mother were ever right about anything, he would kill himself at once and take as many other people with him as he could.

That thought comforted him. Then he imagined the happy scenario where Amanda would wind up marrying a string of closeted gay men who would all leave her heartbroken when they ran away with Canadian lumberjacks and Brazilian Olympic gymnasts. He, on the other hand, would settle down with a girl whose bras had to be custom-made by a squadron of expertly trained tailors. She'd retire from her stellar career in the modeling industry just to be with him on a beach forever. Jet decided then that she would also play bass guitar in his band. Yeah.

Gina knew the distant glaze in her brother's eyes and wondered if he'd got as far as his first platinum record yet. She was just about to kick him again when Jet, who seemed to be developing a sixth sense for this kind of thing, snapped back to reality.

"We're not friends and I'm not apologizing. She's the one who got angry at me. It's all those lady-hormones making her crazy. In a few years she'll settle down as a librarian with 17 cats, but until then she's going to be criminally insane."

"But I'm booored," moaned Gina. "Why are you so bad at mysteries? I wanna do a mystery."

"We're *trying*," snarled Jet.

"You don't even have a mystery-solving van. Or a sexy mystery name. All you've got is a beautiful, charismatic leader," she said, preening herself as if for a portrait.

"Uh-huh, sure," Jet mumbled. "So what's your sexy mystery name?"

"Tempest," she said.

Jet bobbed his head as if to say, "Fair enough."

"Look," he said, "there's nothing we can do until Amanda finds out more about the statue, and she's the only one who can."

"Oh my God," exploded Gina. "Does everyone just get stupid when they go old?"

"I'm not *old*," said Jet defensively. "I'm 17."

"I've seen you in skinny jeans," said Gina. "It was like that time grandpa rode a skateboard."

"Fine, I'm ancient, but I'm not stupid."

"Then why don't you know who made that statue? It was only written on the plaque for like a million years."

"Wait... What plaque?"

"The one on the bottom of the statue!" groaned Gina. "I can read, you know. But that was before the statue got stolen."

Jet had almost been excited for a second. Now he knelt down to face Gina and grabbed hold of her shoulders.

"Listen to me carefully," he said, saying each word slowly as if to let them sink into Gina's head. "Do you remember what it said on the plaque?"

"No. I. Don't," said Gina equally slowly. "I got too much more important stuff to keep in my noggin all day long." She tapped her head meaningfully.

Jet sighed, but he refused to let up. He hadn't tracked down the 1947 bumper edition of *The Caped Avenger* without a *little* bit of ingenuity. An inkling began to cross his mind and he felt the familiar itch of blood pumping in his fingertips.

Jet dashed up to his room while Gina shouted, "What are you doing now?"

"Shut up for a second!"

The laptop was already open on Jet's desk and he'd begun hammering on the keys before it had even connected to the wireless. A few clicks later and he was at Google Street View and zooming in on the photograph of the statue. He already knew the statue faced the street, but he wasn't sure if the resolution would be high enough to let him read the words. Damn Google! If they couldn't take a photo right, they shouldn't be running the Internet.

There! It was blurry, but it was there. If it had been taken a second later it would have been obscured by the lumbering rolls of Jet's grade-school teacher as she trundled from the pharmacy, but the Google van had taken their snapshot just in time. If he zoomed in as far as it would go, squinted, and prayed very very hard to a God he didn't believe in, he could just about make out the words:

COMMISSIONED FROM WINIFRED LEVERETT
DEDICATED SEPTEMBER 23rd 1974
A GIFT FROM LAWRENCE LEVERETT
TO THE PEOPLE OF SKUNKS DANCE

A chill ran down Jet's spine — Winifred Leverett. She must have been married to Lawrence Leverett. It was starting to make a terrible kind of sense. That was how she'd managed to kill him and hide his body inside the statue — she was the *sculptor*. Jet shivered again despite the warmth of the day. So they were looking for a woman.

Then the happy realization washed over him that Spackle must be okay. He never even associated with *people*, let alone women. There was no way the he could be mixed up in this. All of that grunting, clicking, and blood-licking was just normal for him. Jet didn't really stop to think that Spackle was still a creeper. He just broke into a run, thundered down the stairs, and grabbed his bike from the back yard.

"Hey!" said Gina, waving the phone at him. "Aren't you going to call Amanda?"

"Sure I'll call her. I'll call her a bald monkey-ass next time I see her."

The last he saw of Gina as he wheeled his bike out of the yard was her hitting redial and saying, "It's Gina. He's being a stupid-head again. Do people come put your brain in a jar when you become a teenager or what?"

Jet swung himself into the seat as he began to coast down the road. He was just about to take the first corner when he heard Gina at the front door.

"Wait!" she called out. "Amanda says…"

But Jet didn't care what Amanda said. She could leave it to him now. Jet Allan-Ashwood had this covered.

Harvey Spackle's house seemed more inviting now that Jet knew he wasn't a murderer. Well, maybe not inviting exactly. Spackle had never invited anyone in his life, except to sod off, but at least he was only the Aspergery curmudgeon Jet had always known.

When Jet had locked his bike up in the street he tip-toed carefully up the path to Spackle's door. He was sure to avoid Amanda's mistake and stepped over the porch board that tended to creak.

Spackle's doorbell didn't ring the way most doorbells do. Jet had always imagined that rich men, when they could afford their first mansion, installed a doorbell that played "La Cucaracha." Spackle was well-off enough, but this was no mansion and his doorbell was no ordinary bell. He had wired the thing to some kind of electronic dog whistle that was well beyond the frequency of any records Spackle might be digitizing. He claimed it was beyond the range of most humans' hearing, but not beyond the reach of his own discriminating ears. Jet was pretty sure he'd never heard a thing and he suspected the old man was just psyching out his visitors. But it was hard to prove Spackle wrong — he always turned up when Jet pushed the button.

Jet rang the bell. A few minutes later a shadow fell on the other side of the door, which meant Spackle must be peering through the peephole.

Jet had confirmation of this when he heard Spackle mutter, "Ahhh, shit."

"Hey!" said Jet with a wave.

The door opened and Spackle immediately lumbered off into the house with surprising agility. Jet followed, being sure to shut the front door behind him as quietly as possible.

"It's nitrate," Spackle grunted before Jet had even seen what he was doing.

Then Jet saw that Spackle had an old movie reel that was progressing, one frame at a time, through a scanning machine. "Very volatile. One sneeze and the stuff goes up like the Hindenburg. Best part is, you can't extinguish it until it burns itself out."

Spackle snatched up a sample of nitrate film off a table, held a lighter to it, and let it drop into an art deco ashtray. Jet watched it curl and blacken under a yellow flame. He was slightly disappointed. He'd hoped it would be purple.

When the flame fizzled out on its own, Jet turned and found Spackle staring intently into the screen of a high-end computer.

"So —"

"What?" snapped Spackle. "What is it?"

"There's something I wanted to ask about. Do you know anything about Winifred Leverett?"

"Who the hell's that?"

"The woman who sculpted that statue of Spivey Spillane," said Jet.

Spackle turned and gave him what Jet guessed was a smile, but looked more like the expression Disney villains have right before they throw the protagonist into a vat of acid.

"I never thought you had any appreciation for art," said Spackle. "And I was right."

"Do you know her or not? I think she may be involved in something. Like, something criminal."

But Spackle had already begun to lose interest in the conversation and was staring back into his computer. "Always knew she was a woman of many talents," he murmured, "but I can tell you this for nothing. Crime's not one of them. Neither is sculpture, for that matter."

"How do you know?" Jet insisted.

"She was in the loony bin. Stuck there for decades."

"What? What for?"

The last he got out of Spackle was a flicker of his eyes up from the computer screen and the words, "What do you mean, what for? She was freakin' *nuts*."

Jet cycled back home under a cloud. He swerved a few times and was nearly annihilated by someone opening their car door into the street. But as much as he tried to focus on not killing himself, he couldn't help his mind wandering back over the bad decisions he'd made. How much of his carefully woven logic did he have to unpick now? If Winifred wasn't the murderer, then who was? It could even still be Spackle. Jet gripped the handlebars in frustration as he came back to the messy notion that the murderer and the thief might not even be the same person. Winifred might still be the murderer, and someone else might have stolen the statue. But then why didn't they report the body? Who steals a statue with a body inside?

"Jet!"

Jet jammed on the brakes so quickly he nearly flew over the handlebars. He let one foot fall onto the road and looked back to see who had called out.

"Nina?" he asked. "Hey. How's it going?"

She must have been walking by the side of the road — he hadn't even noticed. He was a little cagey about stopping to talk to Nina, but he couldn't ride off now. He kicked out the stand on his bike and left it at the curb.

Jet was worried about what she might want. He'd made it pretty clear that it wasn't going to work out between them. She'd been a bit unstable ever since they broke up and he didn't trust her not to start crying here and now. God, that would be messy. He wondered if he'd have to pretend to care.

"It's all right," she said. "You know your friend Amanda has real problems, right?"

"She's not my friend."

"Well whatever, she's not mine either. So… whatcha been doing this summer?"

"Not much. Did you say you'd seen Amanda?"

"We were just at the movies. That bitch left early and stepped on my popcorn."

Go Amanda! Jet thought. He only wished he'd got the chance to step on Nina's popcorn himself.

"Why did you ask about Amanda?" Nina said. "Is there something going on with her?"

"What?"

"Is that how you like 'em? *Homely?*"

Before he even realized what he was saying, Jet blurted out, "You can't talk about Amanda like that." He clamped his hand over his mouth before mumbling, "Well that came out of nowhere."

"I'm sorry," said Nina softly. "I shouldn't have said that. Listen, do you wanna grab a coffee or something?"

Jet paused, wondering whether he could actually get away with saying no, but he realized he'd paused for too long when Nina insisted, "Jet!"

"All right, let's get a coffee. Jesus, you're in a weird mood."

He and Nina walked his bike to the plaza, where the long arm of Starbucks had established an outlet. The interior looked like someone had spent a lot of money to make it look welcoming, but the corporate board-approved version of welcoming just came off as phony and sterile.

"Is this okay?" asked Nina as Jet locked his bike up at the curb.

Jet shrugged. "I don't care. I always figured coffee is supposed to taste like ass, so I don't know why everyone hates on Starbucks all the time. Have you noticed they always complain about the same thing? 'The beens are too young. The beans are burnt.' "

"The beans *are* burnt," said Nina.

He ushered her into the café. "See this is exactly what I mean. You're one of them. You're a beanie baby — you love to whine about your beans."

Nina plonked herself down at a table and looked at Jet expectantly. Jet sighed and accepted that he was going to have to pay for Nina's coffee. He went up to the counter and a few minutes later returned with two cups.

Nina took a sip and sighed almost happily. "I miss this."

"Yeah, I miss this like I miss Nuremberg."

"Why does everything have to be a joke with you?" she said angrily.

"'S not my fault you're acting funny," Jet mumbled. She glared at him for a moment before he finally said, "Do you even like me?"

"What?"

"Do you like me?" asked Jet. "You're always unhappy with me, I've always done something wrong. If you don't like me then don't hang out with me, but you can't want to hang out and then bitch at me all day long."

"I don't bitch!" she insisted.

"Yes! You do."

"So what are you saying?" Nina asked. "You don't like me?"

Jet spluttered, "I'd be amazed if anyone does. Let's review exhibits A through K — you're dumb, demanding, moody, mean-spirited, jealous, resentful, and selfish. You're the worst. No, I take that back," he added. "You're not the worst, because at least you're not doing it on purpose — it's just who you are."

Nina burst out crying, and Jet suddenly felt the eyes of everyone else in the coffee shop staring at them. "Hey," he said, patting her arm awkwardly. "Don't cry."

"Why shouldn't I? You hate me. And Tristan said he heard Josue call me 'Drama-Llama-Ding-Dong,'" she sobbed.

Jet couldn't hold back a smirk. He wiped it off his face as quickly as he could, but it was too late — she'd already seen it.

"So you do call me that!" she said.

"Why do you *care*? This is my point. You don't even like me, so what do you care? You'll meet someone else."

"What, me? Drama-Llama-Ding-Dong?"

Jet snickered. For some reason it just got funnier the more she said it.

"Well you're pretty," he said. "I always thought you were pretty."

"You're just saying that," she sniffed.

"No, I mean it. I'm a shallow, shallow man. I'd never have gone out with you if I thought you were an ugmo."

"You're very sweet," Nina said, and, horrifyingly, seemed to mean it.

"No, I'm not," said Jet. "You need to find someone who is, someone who'll say really *nice* things about you. Y'know, a liar."

Nina grabbed her purse and left her coffee untouched on the table. "I'm leaving. I don't know why I bother."

"That's what I've been saying!" he said. "I don't know why you do either!"

He watched her storm out, and for a brief second he felt like he should apologize for being so brutal. But he pushed that feeling away — if he called her back now, there was no telling how long he'd be stuck with her. When the door clicked shut behind her before he breathed, "Thank God for that." Then he waited another minute over his coffee until he was sure she was safely a few blocks away before he chucked their coffees, mostly still full, and retrieved his bike.

When Jet finally did make it back home, he was so beat from his confrontation that he just slumped down onto the sofa and shut his eyes. It was still and quiet, but to Jet it felt like the whole house was running circles in his head. He felt bad about what he'd said to Nina, but in all honesty he couldn't think what else he could have said. It had all just come out of him at once, everything he'd wanted to tell her. The air felt chilly on his skin now, and his clothes clung to his body.

Then, uninvited, that niggling sensation began to tickle the back of his brain. He tried to ignore it. He didn't have the energy for this.

But there it was again, and in a moment the bubble shimmied to the surface of his mind and burst.

Where was Gina?

Chapter 23

The funeral pyre still blazed, but the pain in Spillane's arm was more intense than the heat searing his eyebrows. Nunes held Spillane's arm behind his back and began marching him, step by step, towards the inferno where Alabama Sam's body lay burning. The flames licked the hollow sockets of the skull, making it seem like Sam was still watching him, taunting him even now.

"What do you say, Mr. Spillane?"

"You didn't ask a question," Spillane gasped.

"Am I going to have trouble with you?" snarled Nunes. "I have been playing games long enough. Now it is time to get that gold."

"Get it yourself," he spat.

"Mr. Spillane," said Nunes, punctuating his words with twists of Spillane's arm. "There are dangers up at Calaveras Ridge contrived by the Spaniards centuries ago. I should not go into those hills alone. Not without sending a sacrificial lamb ahead of me."

Spillane shuddered as Nunes inched him closer to the fire. One good push and Nunes would propel him into the flames. Was this how he was going to die? A chill ran through his bones while the hairs on his arms burned away, and for a second Spillane was ready to let it all end. Then Nunes twisted his arm again, cruelly, just for the enjoyment of watching Spillane squirm, and the tide inside Spillane began to turn. He had nothing to lose now. The heat filled his body and multiplied inside his skin. He was burning up inside. Sweat soaked into the collar of his shirt and he felt his head, a thousand times bigger than his body, throb with the beating of his heart. His arm was nothing now. He didn't care what happened to him, but he'd be damned if he was going to die at the hands of this dandy.

Spillane yanked himself free, ignoring the pain, and spun to face Nunes. Before the man knew what was happening he had Spillane's fist in his face.

Nunes felt his face as if confused. Spillane watched him, waiting for him to react, but he seemed not to feel any pain. His eyes flickered back towards Spillane.

"I should not have done that if I were you."

Spillane socked him in the other eye, then landed another one on his jaw.

Nunes reeled back a few steps under the blows, but calmly regained his footing and adjusted the sleeves of his suit. "Perhaps you have made the mistake of thinking that I need you," he murmured. "Anyone would do. It took my fancy, appealed to my sense of poetry you might say, that you should be the one to lead me to the gold.

"But I was wrong. It has become clear to me now that you are a liability. Mr. Spillane, you are dead to me."

Like lightning Nunes drew a gun, but Spillane managed to block his arm just as he fired. The bullet knocked his hat off. It had come only an inch from burying itself in his skull.

Spillane grabbed the startled man by the lapels and hoisted him up into the air, hat, gun, torso and all. Nunes writhed like a cut snake. His elbow landed a blow on Spillane's chin and his knee caught him in the gut, but these were nothing to Spillane now. He kept his death-grip on Nunes. His biceps felt like they were going to tear right out of his skin. The veins criss-crossed his arms and his legs felt like concrete pillars buried in the Earth. With a grunt in which he took no satisfaction, Spillane dumped Nunes into the fire. He stepped back from the flames, feeling the sudden cool on his skin where only a moment before had been blinding light and fire.

Then there was nothing. Spillane could see nothing. His arms ached. His fingers were numb. The world slowed down and Spillane lost himself in the glow of that all-consuming fire. It felt like minutes passed. The flames licked happily at Sam's body. Nothing moved.

Then Nunes burst out the other side of the bonfire, immaculate white suit blazing in orange and black, arms reaching for the sky.

That was when a single, bestial shriek tore through the night.

The figure vanished into the darkness. Spillane panted heavily, skin goosebumped and wracked with shivers from the memory of that terrible scream. He kept his eyes glued on the night, never moving from the spot where that orange man had disappeared.

Where had he gone?

Cautiously Spillane put one foot in front of the other. His legs seemed weaker now, like a child learning to walk, but he forced them onwards anyway, slowly, one step at a time.

An itch traveled up his spine as he began to wonder, what now? Was he finally free? It was almost impossible to believe. He had spent so long under the thumb of one invisible torment or another. He didn't feel free. He knew that somehow, somewhere, there could only be more horror to come.

A blood-slicked hand grabbed Spillane's arm and finally wrenched it out of its socket. Now Spillane let out a cry of his own. His arm lay unnaturally at his side. His shoulder stuck out at a sickening angle. Every twitch sent waves of pain through the joint. Spillane dropped to the ground and stared up into the face of his attacker.

Nunes had managed to extinguish himself, though not before suffering terrible burns. His hands and face looked the worst, but even in those disfigured features Spillane thought he saw something familiar. The light from the fire cast haunting shadows across Nunes' face, and the fingers that had dislocated his arm had a strange, monkey-like grabbiness to them. It all made sense now. The moment had finally come.

"Sam," he croaked.

Alabama Sam chuckled hoarsely.

"You still callin' me that?"

"But you're dead," Spillane whined, more to himself than to Sam.

"I've died a hundred times," said Sam. "But this weren't one of 'em."

Spillane's head was reeling. Was it possible this man had lived two lives? Was that him, incinerated on the pyre, and was this him too, standing and gloating?

Sam caught Spillane glancing back at the bonfire and smiled. The effort cracked his face and the crispy skin started to bleed. He looked at his hands now, as if noticing his burns for the first time. He flexed his fingers and winced as the skin split around his knuckles. He shut his eyes in concentration, and for a moment he appeared to swoon. Then his eyes snapped open and fixed themselves on Spillane.

Spillane felt a sinking in his heart.

"Why are you doin' this to me?" he sobbed.

Sam looked at Spillane disbelievingly. "Fun," he said, as if the answer were obvious. "Most men ain't got that special somethin', that genius for the games we play. Like that Dago you found with the Bible all them months ago in Tennessee. Oh he could run, but he didn't last long. They never do. 'Cept for you, that is. You were somethin' else, Spillane, the likes o' which I ain't liable to see agin for a long time. I hope you had as much fun as I did."

"*Fun?*" he groaned.

"I never had better sport than you in my whole life. Every time I thought you was finally gonna give up an' go home, you just kept comin' back fer more. You, my friend, are the gift that never stops givin'. Now I'll ask you one more time. Are you gonna come inta them mountains with me an' git that treasure?"

"You mean... you're gonna split it with me?"

An uncontrollable bout of laughter seized Sam. He shook so violently Spillane thought his brittle skin was going to split right open and peel away from the muscle.

"See what I mean? You're a gem, Spillane. You don't got the first clue what's in them mountains, do you? Lemme tell you a little story about Christians."

"What right d'you got to talk about God?" he spat. "God died the day he made you."

"I ain't talkin' about God, ya dummy. I wouldn't dirty my mouth with his name. I'm talkin' about his friends, the idiots who get together an' sing songs in dusty little buildin's every Sunday. D'you know what a hymn is, Spillane? They ain't no more'n skeeter bites. How small do people look to God? How close d'you reckon he listens to the housewife who wants new curtains or the farmer who wants a better crop? How many times have *you* listened to the prayer of a worm? But them religious types, they reckon they can hold a little sing-song an' move the world around 'em. They band together on account of they think their biggest strength is each other, the *love* they have for their neighbor.

"In ancient Rome, when Nero was throwin' Christians to the lions, d'you know what they did?"

Spillane shook his head.

"Christians used ta push their neighbors in front of 'em an' hope the lions was full up by the time they reached them. There's things no man understands in them hills, my friend. And you, well, you're my neighbor."

Spillane spat at him. "You're no neighbor of mine. From the sorry day you rode into Breakneck, you and me was enemies."

"But I love my enemies, just like any Christian would. Funny how they got it wrong. They pity their enemies when they should be savorin' the fight. Look at you now. Best friend I ever had."

"I'd rather be dead."

Sam's face didn't look amused any more. "Death ain't a luxury I hand out to just anyone. You gotta earn that."

The thunder of hooves interrupted them as the sheriff and his deputy drew up in front of the fire. Spillane tried to prop himself up to see better, but he nudged his bad arm and let out a whimper. Through the haze and the darkness he could only make out the silhouettes of the two riders.

"What in tarnation is goin' on out here?" barked the sheriff. "Folks is sayin' they heard screamin'."

"Sheriff," said Sam, and before Spillane realized what was going on all traces of Sam had vanished from the man's face. Aurelio Nunes pointed a finger at Spillane and said, "This is the man who killed Alabama Sam. He made me lie for him. He said he'd do the same to me if I didn't give him an alibi."

The sheriff eyed Spillane with undisguised glee. "Sonny, I bin waitin' a long time to take you in. You just made your last mistake in my town."

Spillane opened his mouth to protest. That was right before the throbbing in his head seemed to burst into a bright flash and he finally passed out.

Chapter 24

A loud crash cut off the voice at the other end of the phone.

"Hello? Gina?" Amanda said.

But there was no response — just a muffled noise, then the sound of breaking glass. And then, just before all noises stopped completely, the sound of something that sent a shiver up Amanda's spine — click-tap, click-tap, click-tap.

She fumbled to hang up and end the horrible silence that followed. Her mind was racing. She'd only just got home from the disaster at the movies when Gina had called to ask about Jet — he was still MIA. And then that noise — that had sounded an awful lot like… But Gina couldn't be *dead*. Amanda couldn't bring herself to believe that.

The lump in her throat didn't help. That was it. This had got too big for her and Jet. If Gina was in danger then she had to go to the police.

The doorbell rang and Amanda nearly jumped out of her skin. It took a second to calm herself down enough to answer it, but just as she put her hand on the doorknob a creeping suspicion inched up her spine. If the murderer had just gone for Gina, then maybe she was next. They'd all been there that night. None of them was safe.

She went to look before she opened the door, but that was before she remembered that TV show where the murderer shot someone through the peephole. He'd never even seen it coming.

Instead of putting her face right up against the door, she tip-toed over to the next room and peered through the window. If she cocked her head at the right angle, she could just about make out who was standing at the door.

It was no-one she recognized, but with a flood of relief she saw it was a policeman. She breathed out, realizing that she'd been holding her breath. She ran back to the door before the policeman left and hauled it open. Now she could see him properly, she recognized Sergeant Murdock from her last jaunt to the station. He was one of the nice ones. Suddenly it felt like her whole body was smiling.

"Thank God you're here," she said.

"Amanda Spillane?" asked Murdock.

"Yes, I've —"

"You're under arrest."

She was about to demand what for, but before she could utter a word Murdock spun her around, clamped the handcuffs on her, and read her the Miranda rights. As he escorted her to the car with bars on the windows and no handles on the doors, Amanda forgot all about the charge. Murdock's holster was at his hip, and as they marched down the driveway it tapped against his belt, click-tap, click-tap.

Her blood turned cold. Now the murderer had her too.

Amanda squeezed herself into the far corner of her cell. To her chagrin it was the same cell they'd held Jet in only a week ago. It still stank like feces, but at least from this corner she could keep an eye on the door and no-one could sneak up on her from behind.

Every now and then she heard noises from inside the station — the fax, the coffee, sometimes the scraping of chairs or clipped, curt whispers. Every one of them made her flinch and claw at the ground.

If Murdock came for her now, she had no way of defending herself.

She tried to calm herself down. If Murdock had meant to kill her, he could have done it already. He must want something. But she didn't have anything. She didn't even know anything. As far as she could tell, everyone in town was still a suspect. Except, of course, Winifred Leverett. Amanda might be stuck in jail, but she could still spare a scoff for the thought of Jet chasing after *her*. She idly wondered what it was about teenage boys that made them so retarded. Was there like a gene that went off in puberty, or did all the hormones just float up to their brains in a big, foggy cloud? Honestly, she would have been better off teaming up with Spongebob Squarepants.

A clang startled her. The door to the cells swung open, letting a shaft of light from the main office fall across Amanda's cell. Sergeant Murdock stood in the doorway.

"What do you want?" asked Amanda.

Murdock didn't say a word. He just walked up to her cell and slid a tray of food under the bars. If Amanda had been expecting airplane food, she was disappointed. It looked and smelled an awful lot like KFC.

If she was being honest with herself she was starving, but she'd seen enough TV to know never to eat the food. You eat the food now, you wind up upside-down and naked in the killer's dungeon later. She pretended to gag on the smell, and she was impressed with how well she could fake being about to throw up. Who says four years in the Girl Scouts don't teach you anything?

"I'm a vegetarian," she said between retches.

"What do you care?" he demanded. "The chicken's already dead. You're not saving any lives today."

"Take it *away*," she said, shoving the tray back through the bars.

Her stomach gurgled so loud she was sure the sergeant noticed it. There was an awkward silence for a moment before he grinned at her and picked up the tray. Without taking his eyes off her, he picked up a leg and tore a piece with his teeth. He chewed at her deliberately, grease glistening on his lips as he smiled.

"What am I being charged with?" she asked again. "I know the law. You can't keep me in here without charging me with something."

Amanda only hoped that was true. It sounded good.

Murdock waved the half-eaten leg in the air casually. "You know what we want."

"We?"

"What *I* want," he said.

"I don't know anything," said Amanda, folding her arms across her chest.

Murdock's expression turned sour, but he didn't seem too rattled.

"Listen, sweetheart," he said, flinging a greasy, gnawed chicken bone at her. She flinched as it bounced off her and left a streak on her shirt. "I'm not Columbo and you're not Bonnie and Clyde."

Amanda wrinkled her nose as she tried to process that.

"Just tell me where the statue is, and you can go home."

"What statue?" she asked, then wished she had thought of something a little cleverer than that. Murdock just glared at her until she relented. "Oh. The statue of Spivey Spillane. Obviously I don't know where the statue is. I mean where do you think I've hidden it? Under my bed? Behind the sofa? In my *bra?*"

Murdock wiped his hand on his shirt and picked up his radio. "221 from 223. Report on the missing statue. Eyewitness locates the missing statue at 71 San Antonio Boulevard. Check under the bed and behind the sofa." He put down the radio and turned his attention back on Amanda. "I guess that just leaves your bra."

A ding from the front desk interrupted him. Murdock contemptuously slid the tray of fried chicken back into the cell and strode off towards reception.

Amanda sat still, trying to keep her breathing under control. The voices from reception were muffled, but she could just about make out the words.

"What do you mean you can't do anything? My little sister is missing."

"Sir, are you her legal guardian? Then there's nothing I can do about it. Have your parents get in touch with us, then we'll talk."

"Jet?" Amanda shouted.

"What was that?"

"Jet, it's me!"

"We took in your friend," Murdock said reluctantly. "Seems like you kids can't stay out of trouble."

"She didn't do anything," said Jet. "Have you ever *met* her? It's like knowing a really, really annoying Mother Theresa."

"We're holding her here until we locate the town statue. You wouldn't happen to know anything about that, now, would you sir?"

"I've got to talk to her."

196

There was a pause from the hallway. Then Amanda heard a smug, "If you insist."

Amanda gritted her teeth. She could practically *hear* his disgusting grin.

The next shadow in the doorway was Jet's. Amanda breathed a sigh, and finally ran to the bars.

"Jet! You have to get me out of here."

"Amanda?"

"Yes, it's Amanda, who do you think it is?"

"What are you doing in here?"

"Stop joking around! They think I stole that statue."

"You didn't, did you?" he asked a bit too loudly.

"Of course I didn't!" she hissed.

"Why are you whispering?"

"Murdock is listening. Why do you think he let you in here? He wants to hear us talk."

"Who's Murdock?"

Amanda grabbed Jet's shirt through the bars of the cell and shook him for all he was worth.

"He's the policeman! He knows something. He thinks we have the statue and he's trying to make us talk."

Jet swore. "That's why he won't do anything about Gina. He's probably got her tied up somewhere."

"Unless the real killer has her…" said Amanda, then wished she'd kept her mouth shut. The look on Jet's face was something she never wanted to see again. "Jet, I have to tell you something. Right before Murdock arrested me I was on the phone with Gina. She dropped the phone and then she just disappeared."

"Murdock's not working with the killer?"

"Maybe he is!" said Amanda. "All we know is he doesn't have the statue."

"How many people are *in* on this thing?"

Jet put his head in his hands for a moment, as if trying to nurture a thought that was in the very early stages of hatching. Amanda looked at him and realized that somehow she'd wound up hitching her wagon to his star. When had that happened? Her only hope of getting out of this cell was the boy who she credited with as much intelligence as your average soup spoon.

"Don't worry, I'll get you out of here," said Jet.

"And do what?" Amanda asked. "We don't have the first idea who has Gina."

Jet rubbed his hands together. "Wait till you hear what I'm about to say: Winifred Leverett." Jet mimed his head exploding and said, "Mind. Blown."

"Winifred Leverett is *dead*! She's been dead for ages, and before that she spent her life in a padded cell at Dreadnought."

"Dead…?" Jet pondered for a moment. "She still could have murdered her husband."

"Brother."

"Whatever. So, Lawrence commissions Winifred to build a statue where he can hide the money while things cool off. She kills her brother, puts him in the statue, and then maybe she goes crazy from all the guilt. She gets locked up at Dreadnought and never gets to spend the dough." Jet facepalmed, muttering to himself, "But that still leaves whoever stole the statue now."

Amanda looked on while Jet seemed to free-associate. She didn't want to break his train of thought in case he might actually be on to something.

"What if they knew it was going to be taken down?" he said. "The council has been trying to replace it for years. Someone figures Leverett stashed the cash in the statue, same as we did, but before they can get it taken down we go busting the thing open. They nab the statue, figure out the money isn't there, and now they have Gina."

Jet looked up. "What do you think?"

Amanda stood dumbstruck for a moment. "Jet, never remind me I said this, but that's not completely asinine."

Jet did a little bow. "Thank you, thank you, you've been a great audience. I'll be here all week."

"But I thought Winifred had been in Dreadnought since she was a girl?" said Amanda.

Jet shrugged. "Who cares? The important thing is, who else knows about the statue? That's who we're looking for."

"Problem is, half the town had a stake in that thing," Amanda sighed.

A floorboard creaked in the hall, reminding Amanda that the sergeant was still lurking nearby, probably with a glass pressed against the wall.

"And that's why the 49ers are a bunch of sell-outs who should never be allowed back within city limits," she proclaimed.

"What are you talking about? Did you just try and make sports talk?"

She nodded pointedly at the doorway and Jet fell silent.

"Stay put," he whispered in her ear. "I'll get you out of here."

"Hey," she said with a smile that looked a little too much like tears. "Where am I going?"

"I'll get a posse together. Bye now."

And with that Jet took his leave. Amanda slumped back down into the corner and rubbed her temples. Jet might be playing cowboys and Indians, but he was her best hope. And, now that she considered it, he wasn't all that bad a hope. If anyone had to bust her out of this hole, she was almost glad it was Jet.

Amanda leaned her head back against the gritty concrete wall. She'd just had a nasty thought about out who had Gina. If she was right, this wasn't going to be pretty.

Chapter 25

"Doc's here to see you," grunted the deputy as he pushed open the door to the cell.

Spillane had been sitting on the bed with his eyes clenched, trying to ignore the excruciating pain in his shoulder. Now he opened his eyes cautiously and caught sight of the doctor gazing into the jail cell like a mildly curious tourist. He was wearing a moth-eaten morning coat in a hideous shade of blue and green plaid. Aside from that he looked respectable enough with his graying goatee, pince-nez, and authoritative black bag loaded to the brim with ointments, unguents, and tonics. He looked at Spillane, as if noticing him for the first time.

"Doc, I need fixin'," said Spillane. "I got me a dislocated shoulder."

"Now then, m'boy, you just lie back easy now and leave the doctorin' to me."

The doctor's voice was just as dusty as his coat. He peered through his lenses at the unfortunate patient, and Spillane could only wonder whether the doctor could see anything at all, or if the lenses in those eyeglasses were just for show.

"You're the expert, doc," said Spillane uncertainly.

"Yip, sure am. Graduated just last week," he said, tapping his head, "so it's all still fresh in my... uh... *memory*."

"You just graduated? But you're a hundred years old."

"Age is no barrier to knowledge, sonny. You'll find that out when you get to my age, in 60 or 70 years."

The doctor started rooting around inside his black bag. He withdrew a knee hammer and started tapping Spillane's foot tentatively.

"It's up here!" shouted Spillane. "I dislocated my shoulder."

"If y'don't mind, I'm conductin' a full and detailed medical examination of this here corpse — uh, that is, patient. When I'm done, *I'll* tell you what's wrong with you."

Over the next hour the doctor inspected the wax in Spillane's ears, shoved sharp metal points into his gums, took precise measurements of his head, and finished by producing a sketch-pad, removing Spillane's pants, and sketching his privates in breathtaking detail. Spillane endured this ordeal without bumping his arm too much, except for when the doctor seemed to go out of his way to jostle it and made Spillane shriek in pain.

Every time Spillane let out another howl, the doctor would just look at him strangely and say, "I wish you'd stop doing that. Makes me think there's somethin' wrong in your head. What you need is a head doctor, git them ants outta your pants."

Finally the doctor put all his implements back into the bag and cast an eye over Spillane approvingly.

"Well?" asked Spillane.

"You need to brush your teeth."

"Do *what* to my teeth?"

"Brush 'em. It's the latest thing. Everyone's doin' it. Does wonders for your love life which, if I'm any judge of self-abuse, you could surely use."

Spillane glanced down to where the doctor was looking and suddenly caught his drift.

"Hey!" Spillane snapped. "That ain't my fault. It moves on its own and —"

"Oh sure, sure, it held a gun to your head."

"What about my shoulder?" Spillane roared.

The doctor pinched Spillane's good shoulder and said, "Seems all right to me."

"THE OTHER ONE."

"Look, kid, ain't nobody got time to loiter around jail cells all day sketchin' willies and pinchin' shoulders. I got doctorin' to do."

The doctor looked on as Spillane staggered to his feet. He stared at the concrete wall with steely determination. Then Spillane gritted his teeth, let out a bone-chilling war-cry, and rammed his shoulder into the wall of the cell. With an excruciating crunch the joint popped back into place and Spillane sucked air into his deeply flushed face.

The doctor stroked his goatee at Spillane and said, "See now this is exactly the kinda thing I been talkin' about. What you need's a head doctor. Got some loose screws need tightenin'."

With that he marched out of the cell, but Spillane managed to catch him before he left for good.

"Wait! Just before you go, what happened to the other man? Is he gonna live?"

The doctor furrowed his brow and murmured, "Other man?" as if hearing the words for the first time.

"Yes! Alabama Sam, the man who was with me when I got taken in. He was burned — all over."

"No-one's come to me with *burns*, m'boy. Two pregnancies, one armpit-clamping, an' a goiter the size of a dead horse, but no burns. Or was it two goiters an' one pregnancy? I always get them mixed up."

From behind bars Spillane watched the doctor stroll out into town. Could Alabama Sam really have survived the burns? Of course he had. Spillane wasn't lucky enough that any mere fire could stop Sam. So where was he, then? What was he plotting? What was his next move? He was a specter, a shade, a whisper that could vanish into the air before you even —

"Howdy," said Alabama Sam.

Spillane stumbled backwards in surprise at the man who was suddenly standing on the other side of the bars. If he hadn't spoken Spillane would never have recognized him. He was covered in bandages from head to toe. His hat rested on top of a head so tightly wrapped that not even a wisp of hair was poking out. Although, Spillane caught himself, he didn't know how much hair the man had left after the fire. The only expression on Sam's empty face came from the two dark holes where his eyes must be, though Spillane couldn't see the eyes themselves — just the black gaps in Sam's face, staring at him like bottomless pits, drilling through him as if he were nothing but a soggy meringue.

"You," breathed Spillane. "I shoulda known I weren't lucky enough."

"You seem awful relaxed," said Sam.

"I don't care any more. Leave me here forever."

Sam's blank face stared back at Spillane for a moment before he turned to go. One step. Two. Three.

"No, wait," said Spillane.

"If you love something, set it free..." murmured Sam.

"Just tell me one thing," said Spillane. "Who was that who hung himself in my room the other day? Who did I burn?"

Sam scoffed. "The rattlesnake that bites last gets all the credit, don't you reckon? I spent weeks starvin' him, beatin' him, torturin' him in ways you can't even imagine, until he looked enough like me. He lost a hundred twenty-nine pounds, all up. By the end, he was beggin' me to kill him. But I ain't a monster. In the end I let him have that pleasure himself, and I let you take the credit. Who says I ain't got a generous spirit? That kinda talk can really wound a man right in the feelin's."

"Who was he?"

"The screams," Sam crowed. "The begging. The blood. I ain't had so much fun since grade school."

"Who was he?" Spillane demanded.

Sam turned to Spillane as if he had only just remembered he was there. "Now what in the hell does that matter?"

Sam sounded genuinely nonplussed. The rage and frustration choking up Spillane's throat suddenly came tearing out.

"WHAT WAS HIS NAME?" Spillane screamed.

"George Hartree," Sam said. His bandages crinkled about where his mouth should be, like ancient skin being stretched too tightly across his skull. Spillane wondered if Sam was smiling. "Didn't you ever wonder what happened to the mayor?"

Spillane recoiled in horror, but Sam only let out a hoarse, bestial wheeze through lungs still ravaged by fire and smoke. Now he really was laughing.

"When I rode into town, he was the only man who didn't believe I was you — the only man who saw through me. Don't ask me how. Most people are, well, dumb. Tell 'em any old horse shit an' they're only too happy to take you at your word. You idiots think everything you need to know about a man is on his face. Then a man comes along whose face means nothin' an' takes you all for a ride. Sometimes it's just too easy.

"But Hartree, I dunno. Maybe he was like me, only he came down on the other side of the law. It's funny, now I think of it. I always thought I was the only one."

"And you still killed him?"

Sam nodded pensively. "I had to. He was dangerous."

Spillane didn't like where this conversation was going. "Why am I still alive?" he whispered.

Sam wheezed again, this time so hard Spillane saw flecks of blood spread on the bandages around Sam's mouth.

"Because you ain't a danger to no-one but yourself!" choked Sam. "You think you're dangerous? You think you're smart? Lemme spell it out for you, Jack. You're stupid. You're weak. You're —"

"Just go," begged Spillane, cutting him off. "What do you need me for now? I ain't no good to you. Take the treasure, I don't want it. Just leave."

"You crossed me, Spillane. Ain't nobody crosses me an' gets away with it. You're my favorite toy and it's nearly time to put you away for good. But what d'you say? One last game before the end? For old time's sake?"

Spillane shook his head. "No," he choked. "Please, no."

"That gold ain't goin' nowhere. It'll keep till I come collect it. But till then you're just too much fun."

Sam began to stride towards the door. He waved goodbye over his shoulder.

"You'll be seein' me again, Spillane. You can count on that."

Chapter 26

"Ladies and gentlemen of the jury," announced Jet's mom.

Jet tried to hide his face with his hand. There was no jury — it wasn't a criminal hearing — but for some reason his mother had seen one too many episodes of *Law and Order* and now she thought she was Casey Novak.

His father was sitting at the counsel table looking understandably nervous and trying not to make eye contact with Emily Beagle, the FedEx delivery woman. Every now and then he casually let his eyes wander across the courtroom towards her, trying to divine what she was thinking, but every time she snapped her head around and glared at him with so much force he was afraid her eyeballs might shoot out of their sockets. Mr. Allan quickly faced back to the front of the court.

Although Mr. Allan had opted for state-appointed representation, his wife insisted that she should handle the proceedings on the basis of one year of law school which she had subsequently ditched in favor of clown college. That single year of law had left her with a decade of student loans, but she maintained that she didn't regret it for a second. Jet suspected his father was regretting it now, though. If any of that legal training had stuck to his mother, then it can only have been to the underside of her shoe.

"Mrs. Ashwood," boomed the judge, "please dispense with your attempts at rhetoric and get on with the case."

"Your Honor, I would like to present to the court the facts that we know for a fact the defendant is actually guilty of. *One*, this is my husband," she said, pointing accusingly at Mr. Allan. "He is certainly guilty of that. *Two*, despite his timid and kitten-like demeanor, he has the sexual drive of a teenage Lord Byron and the animal magnetism of Humphrey Bogart. He is most certainly guilty of that. *Three*, that on the second of June he tried to talk me out of executing a brilliantly conceived acrobatic and operatic extravaganza at my daughter's birthday party. Yes, ladies and gentlemen, he is guilty of that too. Guilty!" she shrieked, jabbing a finger at her husband. "Guilty, guilty, guilty!"

"Little scarab," he whispered, tugging at her sleeve. "I really don't think you're sending the right message."

"But is it not also true," she declaimed, ignoring her husband, "that on the second of June my son received a package via Federal Express, and that *that woman there*," she said, indicating the startled Miss Beagle, "is guilty of delivering it!"

A vaguely scandalized whisper started traveling around the courtroom.

"But does this mean that my client — my husband — is guilty of sexually assaulting this fine employee of Federal Express? After all, it was a crazy party. There was booze, drugs, and a massive freakin' cake. Hell, anything could have happened, right? WRONG," she shrieked, slamming her hand down on the table so hard that it reverberated around the courtroom. "*Not* anything could have happened! Because you forget that I was there and that my husband is a good man. He may be guilty of practically everything else, but he is not guilty of assaulting that woman.

"I rest my case."

The judge watched Mrs. Ashwood sit back down and clasp her hands smugly on the table. In all his years he had never seen such a performance. As a rule he did not allow cell phones in his courtroom, but when he saw one man in the gallery filming the proceedings he chose to pretend he hadn't seen it. He kind of wanted a copy of that himself, and he had a sneaking suspicion the thing could go viral on YouTube.

"Thank you Mrs. Ashwood for a defense that, I dare say, none of us could equal. The prosecution may call their first witness."

Beagle's lawyer rose and said, "Your Honor, we call Mr. Maximilian Allan."

The security guard escorted Mr. Allan up to the witness box, where he fidgeted for a moment while the prosecuting lawyer warmed up his knuckle-dusters.

"Mr. Allan, is it true that on the second of June you and your wife were holding a birthday party for your daughter Gina?"

"It's a trick!" shouted Mrs. Ashwood.

"Order," boomed the judge with a tap of his gavel. "If you do not keep your place, Mrs. Ashwood, I shall have you ejected from this court. Mr. Allan, please answer the question."

Mr. Allan nodded.

"Out loud, if you please," insisted the judge.

"Yes, we threw a party for our daughter," he said, noticing now that the stenographer had started up again. He grew distant for a moment watching her fingers orchestrate the keys. He could have sworn she was wearing a really bad wig.

"Answer the question, Mr. Allan!" said the judge.

"Sorry, what?"

"I asked you," said the prosecution, pointing at a receipt he had presented to the court, "if this is the receipt for a seven-foot birthday cake with a candy Wolverine on top which you ordered for the orgiastic festivities at this so-called 'party?'"

"Well give me half a chance," grumbled Mr. Allan.

The prosecution handed him the receipt and Mr. Allan inspected it through a pair of pre-War granny specs that he produced from his pocket.

"Yes, this is the receipt," he said.

"And was it not with that same candy Wolverine that you molested my client?" he demanded.

Mr. Allan leaned forward and spoke into the microphone, "No."

The prosecution raised a smug eyebrow at the courtroom. "Mr. Allan, there is no point in lying. You have already admitted to the receipt of the candy Wolverine that my client has reported being assaulted with. Now does that or does that not make you guilty of the charge being brought against you today of sexual assault with a candy Wolverine?"

"Not guilty," said Mr. Allan. "It was a candy Batman, not a Wolverine."

The prosecution whipped around and hissed at his client, "You told me it was Wolverine!"

"It was!" Beagle insisted. "He has the black mask with the ears and the English butler. And he's enemies with Heath Ledger — Wolverine."

The courtroom audibly groaned.

"That's Batman, you witless woman, *Batman*! Don't you know the difference between Batman and Wolverine?"

"Well which one's Wolverine then?" she asked.

"How should I know?" exploded the lawyer. "Do I look like a 12-year-old? I don't give a shit about Wolverine."

"Oh, but *I'm* supposed to know everything."

"IT'S BATMAN, EVERYONE ON THE PLANET KNOWS BAT-MAN."

"Order!" said the judge. "I'm dismissing this case. Between the prosecution and the defense, I have never seen such a ham-fisted bunch of morons in this courtroom in my life. It's a miracle you passed the bar," he said to the prosecution, "and it's a mercy you didn't," he said to Mrs. Ashwood. "Mr. Allan, you'd be well advised to stay away from delivery women, superheroes, and candy in the future, and if I ever see you in this courtroom again I'm going to throw the whole damn book at you. Do we understand each other?"

Mr. Allan nodded mutely.

"Case dismissed," said the judge. "Now get the hell out of my court."

Starbucks didn't really seem like the right place to foment a revolution, but then Jet's friend Josue was only ever a champagne socialist to begin with so he didn't think he'd mind. It turned out he'd guessed correctly. When Jet arrived he found Josue and Steve already there. Josue was dressed as Che Guevara — unruly curls jammed into a communist cap, a red t-shirt with a yellow star, and the wisps of revolutionary beard smattered across his face. He was standing on a chair waving a white-chocolate mocha in the air and holding forth on the benefits of income caps. Steve was quiet, sitting effortlessly outside Josue's sphere of crazy.

Jet felt slightly better knowing that even with a murderer on the loose, some things would never change.

"Comrade!" said Josue when he spotted Jet come in. "Take a seat and tell us where the party is."

"What party?" asked Jet.

"The Revolution party! You told us to dress for revolution."

"Yes, an *actual* revolution, not a theme party."

Josue looked disappointed.

"You mean I put all this on for nothing? I didn't know it was an actual revolution. My shirt could get ruined. My mom got this for me in Vietnam."

"You know it was probably made by children in sweatshops, right?"

"Wrong," said Josue. "It was made by children in the *best* sweatshops. Look at the quality of that stitching. Feel it. That's world class."

"Stop telling people to feel your clothes," said Steve. "It's like the sixth time you've said that."

"You just don't appreciate fine workmanship. That much is clear from looking at your slipshod ensemble. You look like a Mexican bag-lady."

"Gentlemen," said Jet, trying to steer the ship back on course. "We're here on serious business. We're just waiting on one more person to arrive."

After only a few more minutes the café door tinkled and in walked Bentley. He pretended not to notice them at first, instead spending a few seconds eying the café with supercilious pupils.

"Oh hello!" he said when he spotted Jet. "This is jolly. I don't suppose it's too much to ask why we're all here?"

"You're probably wondering why you're all here," said Jet.

"Yes, that's... what I said."

"We're on a rescue mission: we have to bust Amanda out of jail."

"Is the espresso here any good?" asked Bentley. "It feels like an espresso kind of night."

"Did you hear me?" Jet demanded.

"Oh I heard you, I just haven't had nearly enough caffeine for this."

"Amanda's in jail?" asked Josue. "You're joking! Did she speak out against the administration? Is this about the NSA? I bet she and Snowden are like this," he said, crossing his fingers tightly.

Jet sighed. He'd known this moment would come, but he had no idea how he was going to go about explaining everything to Josue, Steve, and Bentley. He was going to sound like he was insane, but he had to try. He explained that Amanda had been locked up by sinister forces, though he did his very best to avoid mentioning the treasure or the murder. This business was complicated enough without spreading it around that there was a killer on the loose.

When he'd finished the others were still gazing at him critically.

"You don't believe me," he said.

"Of course I don't believe you," said Steve. "But your slow descent into madness is good entertainment value. I'll help."

"To the Bastille!" yelled Josue.

"Those revolutionaries were just as corrupt as —"

Josue jabbed his finger at Steve and said, "That sounds like aristocrat talk to me, Marie Antoinette, if that *is* your real name."

While Josue and Steve started arguing again, Bentley took Jet's arm and whispered, "Is Amanda really in trouble?"

Jet nodded.

"I figured something was up — she's been acting really strangely, breaking into your house and everything."

"Was that you?" said Jet. "Oh my God. No wonder Mom's been so happy lately."

"I take the fifth. Also, it was Amanda's idea."

Steve interrupted: "So how are we supposed to stage this great escape?"

Jet grinned from ear to ear. "Steven, I'm glad you asked me that question."

If it weren't for the cicadas sizzling in the night, Skunks Dance would have been quiet. The evening had taken the edge off the day's heat, leaving the small town wrapped in a pleasant, comforting glow. Only the occasional breeze stole through the eucalyptus trees, rustling the leaves like gentle chimes before evaporating back into the air. It was, Jet thought, the most boring thing he'd ever seen.

It was a good thing that was about to change.

He made sure he was well hidden behind the concrete steps and pressed the luminescent button his watch. The sudden backlight looked like an otherworldly blue glow bobbing disembodied in mid air before shutting off sharply, leaving Jet's eyes swimming in the dark.

Any minute now.

Jet peeked over the steps and saw the police station sitting in a cone of light. A car was parked out front and if he really strained he could hear some gentle murmurs coming from inside. He ducked back down and checked his watch again, but the seconds ticked by so slowly. This was unbearable.

"Stop doing that," said Bentley. "You shouldn't be wearing those anyway. You'll get testicular cancer."

"Really?"

"Yes," sighed Bentley, "that's why they sell them to small children and teenagers. What happened to your phone anyway? That watch is more '90s than Hammer pants."

"It got broken by a swarm of demented black widows," Jet mumbled.

"Fine, don't tell me."

"What's the group noun for a swarm of spiders?"

"Oh, you meant spiders. I thought you were talking about African-American women with dead husbands."

"*Why* would you —"

"It's a clutter," said Bentley.

"A clutter of spiders? Huh."

Jet conceded that was actually pretty good. He found himself almost liking Bentley. He was still kind of a twit, but he wasn't completely useless.

Jet was just about to speak again when a gunshot ripped through the night. It must have reverberated off every building in town. Every car alarm in the vicinity went off at once, but they could only add to the chorus of bells and piercing bleeps coming from the dark interior of the bank. In minutes the plaza was going to be swarming with people. Jet had to hand it to them — Josue and Steve had actually pulled this off.

The cops came running out of the station and into their car. The siren kicked off with a roar before the car launched itself down the road and into town.

Jet and Bentley looked at each other in amazement. It was working.

Jet crept around the back of the station, being careful to keep out of sight of any CCTV cameras that might be watching. He was wearing as much black as he could find, but this mostly meant a turtle-neck that gave him an unfortunate resemblance to Steve Jobs.

Above him he could make out the reinforced steel bars set deep inside the concrete wall — a window into the cells. It was a bit high, but having circus performers for parents had certain advantages. With a bit of care and ingenuity, and by carefully and ingeniously scraping up both his knees, Jet managed to hoist himself up to the ledge and put his face to the bars.

"Finally!" said Amanda as she spotted him.

"Shut up!" Jet hissed. "Just wait a sec."

They paused for a moment until they heard voices at the front of the station. It was Bentley and Murdock.

"...really appreciate the help. It's due at the start of term and I always start late."

"Listen kid, beat it. It's the middle of the night, I can't have —"

"Did you know this place used to be the sheriff's office? You can even look up the old survey maps and see they used to hang people here. Probably on that big tree out front. You can tell by the branches, that's a good hangin' tree."

"I don't care."

"You work in a historic place. You must feel so lucky every day."

Amanda turned back to Jet. "Is that Ben?"

"Yes, now hurry up!"

Jet produced a crowbar and managed to wedge the thing between the bars on the window. By using the weight of his whole body he was just about able to bend one of the bars out of shape. He suddenly wished he were fatter — he could barely move the bar enough to squeeze Amanda through.

"I can't get through that," she protested.

"You'll have to. It's not coming any —"

Jet didn't get any further before the whole bar wrenched away from the window and sent Jet tumbling onto the ground. He landed hard on his tailbone and swore just a bit too loudly.

"What was that?" said Murdock.

"It was me *trying* to tell you about how they invented the hangtown fry in the Gold Rush," Bentley insisted. "Now listen, do you like oysters?"

"*No.*"

Amanda was already scrambling halfway through the window. She had to squeeze, but she was just about able to jam herself into the space between the bars, and with one big pull from Jet she was free.

Murdock's voice floated from inside the station. "Hold on, kid, I need to check on something."

Jet and Amanda bolted into the night. As soon as Murdock turned to check on the cells, Bentley legged it too, following Jet and Amanda by only a few seconds.

As they sprinted through the empty streets, Jet puffed to Amanda, "Not a bad rescue, eh?"

"Eight and a half out of ten," she panted.

Chapter 27

The judge peered over a pair of half-moon spectacles at Spillane, who by this time was emitting a distinct odor. The judge wrinkled his nose and pretended to shuffle some papers.

"I call this court of Skelton county to order. Ladies and gentlemen I am here today to hear the case against one 'Spivvy Spillane' of Tennessee in the matter of the murder of Alabama Sam, alias Clancy Wellwater, alias Jebediah Balthrop, alias… Heck, this list doesn't half go on, does it?"

"Spivey, your honor."

"I beg your pardon?" snapped the judge.

"I'm Spivey, your honor."

"I'll be the judge of that. Now since it is obvious you cannot afford legal representation I have approved a representative for you. Mr. Lang, please take your seat."

The doors at the back of the courtroom flew open and a heavy footstep fell onto the wooden floorboards. Before he even turned around to see, Spillane could feel a savage prickling on the back of his neck. He shut his eyes and sank into his chair. *Please, no.*

Lang drew even with Spillane and looked down at his client through thick bandages.

"Good morning, Mr. Spillane. Don't you worry now. I'm a lawyer."

Spillane forced his eyes upwards to where they met those familiar black holes. He couldn't tell if "Lang" was smiling now, but the specks of blood still stained the bandages around his mouth from the last time he'd tried.

"Mr. Spillane," murmured the judge, leaning over his desk. "Is something the matter?"

"Yes, your honor! That man is Alabama Sam," he screamed.

"Alabama Sam is dead, Mr. Spillane. You said so yourself when you were found with the body."

"No, that wasn't him. It was all a trick. This is the real Sam."

Lang raised his hand. "Your honor, with your indulgence I would like to make a short demonstration."

"Go on," said the judge warily.

"I would like to present the latest in humane interrogation techniques. This serum," he announced, producing a large, rusty hypodermic needle with a three-fingered plunger, "is specially formulated to oblige the subject to tell the truth. When I administer it to my client here, it will guarantee that he believes everything he says."

"No," Spillane moaned, pushing his chair back.

He made to get up, but the deputy was on him in an instant, forcing him back into his seat and clamping down on his arms. Lang drew closer with the needle, the large gauge in the tip spitting some unmentionable substance.

"What's in that thing?" Spillane gasped.

Lang didn't answer, but Spillane could have sworn he saw Lang shrug his shoulders mischievously. "No!" he cried. "You can't do this. You can't do this."

Lang seized Spillane's arm and his disgusting fingers pried at the veins. Spillane squirmed, but the deputy held him too tight. The cold tip of the needle brushed against Spillane's skin like an insect about to bite. Then Lang drove it in, one hand twisting the barrel of the syringe while the other pressed down on the plunger.

Spillane watched as the liquid disappeared into his arm.

Suddenly it was over. Lang stepped back and the deputy let him go, but it was too late. Spillane slumped in resignation. His arm ached dully. Somewhere inside the muscle he could feel a big lump like a spider's poison.

"Now we will get to the truth of the matter, your honor," said Lang. "Mr. Spillane, you say this 'Alabama Sam' died and now he's me?"

"It is you!" Spillane said. He turned to the judge and said, "How do you think he got burned? He was Aurelio Nunes when I got arrested. That's when he fell into the fire. You already know about Balthrop and Wellwater. Who knows how many other people he is."

"Do you remember the girl who brought you dinner in your cell last night? You thought she was pretty," said Lang, making sure to murmur just loud enough that the court could hear.

"Oh my God, was that you too?" said Spillane. "He's everyone, your honor. He's insane."

"And doesn't his honor the judge look a bit familiar?"

"It's him!" screamed Spillane. "Arrest the judge!"

"There you have it," said Lang, whipping around to face the judge. "Alabama Sam is everywhere and everyone. I think this makes it quite clear that my client is hopelessly feeble-minded and sees the shadow of this imaginary threat everywhere he looks."

"What can have brought on this feeble-mindedness?" asked the judge.

"Perhaps his failure on the gold fields, or perhaps simply the damage inflicted by self-abuse."

"It's true," nodded Spillane's doctor at the back of the court. "I seen it."

"This town has already seen the appalling display of indecency and perversion which the accused calls *Heliogabalus' Pursuit of the Sugar Plum Faeries*," Lang continued.

"Which you made me do!" Spillane shouted.

"There he goes again," said Lang. "The man sees demons everywhere. I'll wager there is not one ill wind in this man's life that he does not attribute to Alabama Sam. He was after all only a man, was he not, Mr. Spillane?"

"Sam," he growled, "you are no man. You are the Devil himself. And if I ever do kill you, it won't be murder. It'll be an act of God."

"Delusions of grandeur!" said Lang. "Your honor, it would be cruel and unmerciful to parade this poor man's illness about in public any further. I move to have Mr. Spillane committed on the grounds of severe and incontinent idiocy."

"I concur," said the judge. "Mr. Spillane, you are not guilty by reason of insanity and must live out the rest of your days at Dreadnought Hospital."

Lang smugly put his hands on his hips. As he did so his hand pushed back the hem of his jacket, revealing the butt of a revolver sticking out of its holster. Spillane's eyes caught the glint of the metal, and in a flash the gun was in his hand.

A shot echoed through the courtroom. Everyone dived for the ground, except for the sheriff who was already diving for Spillane. He tackled Spillane to the ground and wrestled the gun from his grip.

The judge peered back up from behind his desk and, when he was sure everything was safe again, resumed his seat.

"Mr. Spillane, you do not make my job any easier. Recent events — *very* recent events — have made it clear that your insanity knows no bounds. You are not just a danger to yourself, but also to the good folk of Skelton county. If they don't wind up watching grown men prance around in tutus then they'll wind up with your bullets in their brains. I'm afraid you leave me with no choice but to sentence you to be hanged — the sooner the better."

But Spillane was not paying any attention. He was still staring at Sam. "I hit you," said Spillane, growing pale. "*What are you?*"

Sam stared back at Spillane through empty eye-holes. No expression was detectable on his face, and for a moment Spillane recoiled in horror as if he had just seen into the eyes of the Devil.

Spillane's hand still trembled from the memory of the shot. It hadn't felt right — something was amiss.

"Blanks," he breathed. "You let me have that gun on purpose."

"You sure do walk inta these things, don't you, Spillane? Ain't no matter. Soon enough you ain't gonna walk inta anything ever again."

The judge turned to the sheriff. "What does your schedule look like tomorrow, sheriff?"

"I have to check my notebook, your honor, but I reckon we got time for a hangin'."

"Then so be it," said the judge. "Mr. Spillane shall be hanged tomorrow at your earliest convenience."

In the audience Jacqueline Hyde rolled her eyes. It had been a long time since she'd witnessed such a catastrophic display of incompetence. She'd almost let herself believe Spillane could take care of himself for five minutes, but it turned out he was just another helpless man. So what else was new?

She rose from her seat and left in disgust.

Spillane pressed his face to the bars in the window of his cell. Freedom felt so near and so far. Just a few short inches away the inhabitants of Skunks Dance were enjoying the afternoon, walking and talking like the world was not about to end. A few short inches. What was an inch? It was everything to him now.

The sheriff watched him press his face to the bars and scoffed, "Son, ain't no way out that way, 'less you're made o' spaghetti."

But Spillane did not turn to face him. He didn't want to give him the satisfaction. For all Spillane knew he'd have his face pressed to these bars until the hour of his death, but he had to try. He had a woman on the outside, and as long as there was even the slightest chance that she might come for him, he would not give up hope.

Hour by hour the town went about their business until the sun began to set and the only lights in town were thrown by flickering candle flames. Spillane's eyelids felt heavy and his body ached. This was the last night of his life. Surely he was entitled to some rest? He shook his head, snapping himself out of it and maintaining his vigil. There was still time. She could still come.

"Jackie!" he hissed, catching sight of a bustle in the dark. He couldn't believe it. Was it her? Was it happening at last?

The figure strolling back from the Belle and Bullethole stepped into the shaft of light shining through the bars of the cell. With relief Spillane saw that it really was her. She had come for him!

"Jackie!" he hissed again.

She stopped guiltily in her tracks and gazed sadly up at the window. "Yes?" she said.

"The sheriff is asleep," Spillane whispered. "You can bust me outta here now."

"I'm not going to bust you out of anywhere, Spillane. You're not my responsibility. Frankly I've already helped you more than I should have and you still managed to louse it up. Keeping you alive is a full-time job, and I already got a store."

"Please — just one more time. They're gonna kill me."

"Then you'll be in good company," said Jackie. "Most of my favorite people are dead. Say hi to them for me."

She took a step and disappeared from the light. Spillane remained with his face pressed to the bars for another minute before her footsteps vanished into the night. Then he finally took himself away from the window and slumped down against the wall.

Chapter 28

"Starbucks?" said Amanda. "*This* is where you planned my break-out?"

"Fomented," insisted Josue. "We fomented. Oh how we fomented. The fomenting was fierce and potent. I have never seen the likes of such a fomentation."

"Shut up," said Jet.

"Bourgeois pig…"

The five were having celebratory drinks at the same Starbucks table they were at an hour ago, only this time with the addition of one Amanda Spillane, fugitive at large. As Josue explained to her in great detail and with more references to communism than Amanda thought were necessary, what had happened was this.

Jet had been able to appropriate a pistol from among his parents' bag of tricks. If he remembered correctly they had once used it in their act, where Max had to shoot Cerise off the horns of a charging bull. The act was a huge hit, but they got shut down for breaking about seven different regulations, among them endangering the public, discharging a firearm in an enclosed space, cruelty to animals, and indecent exposure. Cerise boasted that Max's aim was so good he could shoot her pubic hairs off at a distance of 20 feet without adversely affecting her womanhood. Max, however, declined to demonstrate and reluctantly had to retire the act.

The pistol itself must have been much older than that, though. It looked like an antique six-shooter. Jet hadn't look all that closely, but on the handle were the initials SS — it had probably belonged to Mr. and Mrs. Hitler or something.

This pistol he gave, somewhat hesitantly, into the care of Josue and Steve. He tried to hand it directly to Steve who was obviously the safer pair of hands, but somehow Josue's hands were there instead. He petted and stroked the thing like it was a shivering kitten.

When the four split up, Josue and Steve set up camp opposite the bank. It was on the main street, flooded with light even at this hour, but the lights inside were dark and it wasn't too hard to find a side-street that gave them a good view of the façade. When the time came, Steve made sure to take the gun off Josue and fire a single shot through the window of the bank. Every alarm in town must have gone off, bringing the police scurrying out of the station, but the two teens were already legging it as fast as they could.

When the five all met back up they were out of breath and buzzing with adrenaline, so Jet got everyone a round of hot drinks. Amanda didn't think sugar and caffeine were the best things to calm them down right now, but she also knew they were approaching the second, more dangerous stage of the operation. They were going to need this buzz to carry them through the rest of the night.

Amanda grabbed Jet by the arm and guided him towards the ladies' toilets.

"A word?" she said.

"Hey, this is the girls' toilet. I can't go in there."

"It's just a sign on the door, Jet, it's not going to give you lady-parts."

She hauled Jet inside and watched as he marveled at the glorious cornucopia that opened up before him — the pristine sinks, the floral soaps, the mellow, poop-inducing music that floated down from speakers in the ceiling. There was even a sofa.

"Oh my God," he breathed. "It's everything I ever dreamed and more."

He collapsed onto the sofa and started running his hands over the plush upholstery. He started moaning and attempting to give the sofa a full-body hug. Amanda just cocked an eyebrow at him until he noticed and said, "Oh, right. What's up?"

"I think I know where to find Gina," she said, "and we're going to get her tonight. We can't leave her in the hands of that thieving, turkey-necked idiot one more minute."

Jet looked like he was about to ask a question when he halted, eyes going wide. "*Franklin?*"

"Who else could have arranged the police to lock me up? Why else do you think he was petitioning the council to replace the statue? Once they got a new statue, he'd be free to scoop up the old one."

"Then if he thinks the treasure is inside the statue, he can't have murdered Leverett."

"We hope. He would have been like ten years old at the time, but maybe he's working with the murderer. Or he saw it happen. I don't know," she said, rubbing her head.

"We have to ditch the others," Jet said, suddenly serious.

Amanda nodded. It would hurt to get rid of their backup, but they couldn't risk this thing getting any bigger. Bentley was grateful to go home and put the evening behind him. So was Josue, who kept breathing in the fumes from his espresso and complaining about how the night's heroism had left him enervated.

Steve, however, was the only one who seemed to notice that more was afoot than he was being told. He didn't say anything, but on his way out Amanda could have sworn she saw him shoot Jet a look that might have been suspicious but might also have been resentful. He seemed to be uncommonly perceptive for someone who was friends with Jet.

When the others had gone, the Jet and Amanda of them were left staring at each other over the table.

"Here we are again," said Amanda.

"Steed and Peel," said Jet.

"Thelma and Louise."

"Let's go then," said Jet, getting up from the table and heading for the door.

It took until she and Jet were walking down the empty street before Amanda scoffed, "Steed and Peel?"

"Yeah. I rock the house down in a cat-suit. And you'd be dynamite in a derby."

It was easily one of the bigger houses on the street. It had an ornate Grecian portico out front and tall, well-trimmed hedges lining the driveway. Amanda wondered whose money had paid for all this — the tax-payers'? Or had Franklin got into politics after he was already rich? Either way, the house had the air of a bloated, inflamed appendix ready to burst.

Amanda eyed it from the car and grimaced as if she had a bad taste in her mouth. It was usually her policy to smile and be friendly. She didn't know why. It just seemed like life was supposed to work that way — if you were nice to people, they were nice to you back. And now Franklin had done this. How long had he been a bag of scum? How long had she not noticed? All her smiles and pleases and thank-yous hadn't been enough to tell her when she was talking to a skid mark like him. Then she wondered, what else could she have done? Scowled? Said something rude? She didn't know how. Inside herself she felt something missing, as if she'd been this way for too long. She was beginning to wonder if smiles and pig-tails were all she had left.

She swore she was going to tear Franklin a new ass in his face.

"I think I've seen that look on people's faces when they're about to whip out a semiautomatic and go to town on a bunch of people they've never met."

Amanda looked back at Jet and smiled weakly. "Yeah. You're not far off."

Jet offered her a fist-bump. She awkwardly returned something that was half fist-bump and half handshake, which sort of worked out when Jet turned it into a squid. Amanda sighed. At least when Jet was being douchey he was kind of good at it.

They left the car on the other side of the street, waited till its interior light went out, and made their way towards the darkened house. The night had been cooling fast and now the air nipped at her exposed skin. She shivered with the memory of the warm day and tried to focus on the house. There wasn't much sign of life.

A movement startled them and they ducked behind a car parked in the street.

A figure was making its way towards them from the house. Amanda

226

kept her head down and tried not to breathe. Footsteps fell sinisterly on the pebble garden, and the moonlight illuminated flashes of skin. And — Amanda looked closer — long hair. Her heart almost burst with joy. In a second she was on her feet and running towards the house.

"Gina!" said Jet.

"Finally!" said Gina. "Just in the nick of time, then. Nice of you to wait until I escaped." She turned to Amanda. "This was my brother's idea, wasn't it?"

"Like 80 to 90%, yeah."

"You're like a bull in a Chinese shop," she said to Jet. "Thanks a million, Ruggles."

"Chinese shop?" said Jet.

"*Ruggles?*" said Amanda.

"Oh hasn't he told you his middle name?" asked Gina. "It's Ruggles."

Amanda stared at him with a look of sheer jubilation.

"Look," he said, "it's after Thomas Pynchon, all right? My parents' favorite book is *Vineland.*"

She cocked an eyebrow at him. "Even *I've* never finished a Pynchon novel."

"I didn't say they finished it."

"I thought it might be after the Civil War general."

"There was a general called Ruggles?" said Jet. "How did I not know about this? They'd never have called me Ruggles if they knew… God damn it!"

Everyone was quiet for a moment before Amanda and Jet looked at each other and burst out laughing. She was tired, dirty, and hungry, but after everything she'd been through in the last day there wasn't anything she could do except laugh. She supposed it was just the blessed relief that everything was, after all, going to be okay.

A sharp snap nearby interrupted them.

She looked around but it was so dark she could only really make out the silhouettes of Jet and Gina.

"Is someone there?" hissed Amanda.

Franklin's porch light blazed into life, blinding them temporarily. When her eyes started to adjust, she made out two figures ensconced in a ring of fire.

"Miss Spillane. How very gratifying."

As her vision became sharper Amanda managed to bring the two men into focus. It was Franklin. She might have known — but he was not the one who'd spoken. That would have been impossible with the gag in his mouth and the gun to his head. The one who'd spoken was Mr. Snodgrass.

"I think it's time we compared notes, don't you?" he said.

Chapter 29

The bowl of water they'd given him was cold. Spillane swirled his razor in it and attempted to shave, but when he dragged the blade across his skin he could feel it catch on every hair with a metallic *ping*. Alabama Sam had come to gloat, but Spillane simply ignored him. For a moment he held the razor up again but instead of bringing it to his chin he gazed forlornly at the blade. Let Sam do his worst. He didn't care any more.

Spillane looked up into the mirror and realized he had nicked himself. There was a nasty little gouge in his neck. He'd never even felt the razor slide into his skin, but already the blood was oozing out. Spillane rubbed his neck with one hand, and then his eyes wandered, sparking with faint hope, to the rafters in the ceiling. He put down the razor and slowly began to undo his belt. The leather felt strong.

"P'raps now you know what you're dealin' with, Spillane," drawled Alabama Sam. Still swathed in bandages, he was marking his territory outside Spillane's jail cell, pacing slowly back and forth, letting each second burn in Spillane's mind. "In a few hours you'll be hangin' from that there tree like a strangely-shaped bird-feeder."

He whipped around to face Spillane. If he had been expecting to see Spillane's defeat, he didn't show it. Instead Sam's gaze wandered upwards. Perhaps he'd done his work too well. What he saw was Spillane's body swinging from a rafter.

Sam cocked his head at Spillane and regarded the man's gentle motion to and fro, the stoic look that had settled on Spillane's features in the last moments of his life. It was funny. They always thought suicide was an escape. And it's true, Sam intended that Spillane should die. But there was no way he was going to give Spillane the dignity of doing it himself.

In his own time Sam drew his pistol and shot the belt that suspended Spillane from the rafter. He crashed onto the floor of his cell, choking and spluttering.

The sheriff came tumbling in, eyes wide at the sight of Lang standing over Spillane with a gun.

"What in God's name happened?" he spluttered.

"My client attempted to hang himself," said Lang.

"Why didn't you let him?" drawled the deputy. "You coulda saved us the cost of a hangin'."

"Deputy, I'm surprised at you. Spillane should be hanged when the county of Skelton says so, not whenever he damn well pleases. And besides, I should never like to deprive the hangman of his job satisfaction. Call for the doctor. Make sure Spillane's well enough to execute."

The sheriff turned to the deputy and said, "He's right, y'know. It's no fun if they don't struggle."

Spillane propped himself up against the bed while the deputy went to fetch the doctor. Sam tipped his hat at Spillane and told the sheriff, "Keep an eye on him. I'll be back when it's showtime."

"Don't you worry yerself, Mr. Lang," said the sheriff as Sam strolled out the door. "He won't get away from us."

A few minutes later the doctor bumbled into the cell, clamping on his pince-nez helter-skelter and fishing for a piece of rock candy in his jacket pocket.

"Root canal, is it?" he asked.

Spillane gingerly shook his head.

"Now boy, we had this conversation before. You just let me do my job an' I'll let you do yours."

Spillane eyed the doctor humorlessly and croaked, "I have a sore throat."

The doctor suddenly seemed to notice the ugly bruising on Spillane's neck. He paused and looked Spillane in the eyes for the first time. With that one look Spillane thought he might have found the only actual sane person in Skunks Dance.

"Son, this ain't no time for jokes. What happened to you?"

"It's a real long story," he wheezed.

"No, don't talk," said the doctor. "Just rest an' let me get you patched up."

Spillane rested his eyes while the doctor wound bandages around his angry bruises.

"Look at that," said the sheriff, stomping hard on the scaffolding. "That's quality workmanship. Ain't seen carpentry like that in donkey's years."

The deputy nodded wearily. Ever since they'd got this gallows it was the apple of the sheriff's eye. Now they finally had the chance to use the thing and if he thought that would keep the sheriff quiet he was wrong.

"Do you know what kind of wood that is?" asked the sheriff.

The deputy shook his head.

"Pine," the sheriff announced. "100% pure, California pine. Makes you proud to be an American, don't it?"

A thought seemed to occur to the deputy. "You do know how to operate one o' these contraptions, don't you sheriff?"

"Course I do! Think I was born yesterday, yojimbo? I executed more'n fifty men in my time. Every one snapped clean through at the neck — no mess, no fuss. I'll let you in on a little secret — it's all in how you position the noose. Some hangmen'll tie it wrong an' leave the poor sucker stranglin' to death for twenty minutes or more. Sure, that's got a certain kind o' appeal to it, but there ain't no sense o' climax. When that neck cracks and the head goes limp, then the crowd knows the job's well an' done."

The gallows was little more than a wooden platform with steps leading up one side, a place for the priest to stand and distribute holy water with a liberal arm, and a trapdoor in the middle for the unfortunate soul to drop the few feet required to separate the vertebrae in his neck. The sheriff was particularly proud of this set-up because instead of using a crossbeam they were using a sturdy branch on the tree outside the sheriff's office. This, he felt, was more than just economical — it lent a personalized air to the proceedings. This wasn't just any gallows. It was his gallows.

The townsfolk were beginning to gather. They had never seen a proper execution before, and the crowd was a curious one. The men came in from the gold fields and the saloons. The women came from their stores and homes, making sure to bring their children to show them the fate that awaits outlaws in the West. The more enterprising businessmen of Skunks Dance were selling beer and popcorn to the onlookers.

All in all it was a good day for a hanging.

Spivey Spillane grasped the bars of his cell. From this angle he could just about see out the front door to where the sheriff and his deputy had set up shop under the big sycamore.

The sheriff came strolling back into the office and regarded Spillane coldly.

"Well?" said the sheriff. "I warned you, didn't I?"

Spillane nodded.

"I hope you made peace with yer God, son."

Spillane nodded, this time a little smaller.

"Come on, then. No sense in draggin' it out all day. The town's a-waitin'."

Spillane tenderly touched the bandages on his neck and mumbled, "Sure."

The sheriff led Spillane out into the burning sunlight by one arm. The crowd erupted into a mix of cheers and boos when they saw the condemned man. For his part Spillane kept his head down and tried not to catch anyone's eye as they pelted him with rotten fruit and vegetables. To his small satisfaction a few of these went astray and managed to wallop the sheriff, who glared back at the crowd resentfully.

They climbed the short steps to the platform where a Catholic priest was already waiting.

"I'm a Baptist," croaked Spillane.

"Yeah? Well you'll be dead soon," snapped the priest.

While the priest recited a passage in rapid Latin and flung holy water to and fro, the sheriff and his deputy moved Spillane into position over the trapdoor. The boards creaked ominously under Spillane's boots. He wondered how strong the latches were on that door. He didn't fancy falling through prematurely, even now. His chest gripped tight around his heart. Every beat felt strangulated. Every beat, he realized, might be his last.

The sheriff brought the noose down around Spillane's head and tightened it hard against his neck. It was getting hard to breathe now. Spillane felt the eyes of the town upon him.

Then, to the sheriff's consternation, Spillane smiled.

"Any last words?" the sheriff demanded.

Spillane adjusted his head as well he could with his hands tied behind his back.

"Yes," he said at last. "As some o' you folks may know, I'm a long way from home. I traveled all the way here from Tennessee. I stopped in a lotta towns and met a lotta different folks, but the folks in Skunks Dance are without a doubt the biggest bunch o' flea-bitten shit-for-brains lunatics I ever had the misfortune to meet. If everyone in California is like this, then I hope you all eat each other before the crazy spreads to the next state."

The crowd was booing him before he even finished. As soon as Spillane had got out the last word, the sheriff pulled the lever.

The floor dropped away beneath Spillane's feet. The sudden fall was dizzying. The rope tightened unbearably around his neck, sending a blinding pain washing over him, cutting off his air, biting into the bruises still raw beneath the bandages.

And then, Spillane hit the ground. Before anyone knew what had happened he was running.

The sheriff grabbed the rope and hauled the noose up to his face. He didn't know how, but by some devilry the noose had been cut clean through. He swore. It wasn't possible. He'd tied that noose himself like he'd tied a dozen others.

"Get him!" screamed the sheriff, and the town was thundering at once, pouring past the hanging tree and chasing the escaped man.

Jacqueline Hyde, safely hidden on a balcony across the street, watched Spillane hoofing it away from the roaring crowd. She took her eye away from the sight of the rifle where she had, just moments ago, had the rope in easy aim.

Well that was unexpected, she thought.

She had never even fired a shot.

Chapter 30

Jet felt the throbbing on one side of his face and tried to angle himself so it didn't hurt quite so much. He must have winced as he did it, because the next thing he knew the throbbing was a searing pain. He was beginning to think this whole undertaking had been a bad idea.

Jet had always thought that if someone pulled a gun on him, he'd naturally figure out a way to kung-fu it out of their hand, or do some kind of incredibly slow-motion bullet-time to dodge it. Whenever he watched action movies he always tried to remember how the hero managed to jump out of a plane without a parachute or avoid being shot by a firing squad, just in case he ever had to do it. There was always a way. Or maybe he'd just balls it out — go right up to the gunman, put his finger in the barrel, look him in the eye and say, "Go on then. Pull the trigger, punk."

That was, of course, how he came to be lying tied up, gagged, and concussed in the back of a van being driven by the gunman. When it came down to it, after everything that had happened to them, when someone shoved a gun in his face there was nothing he could do about it. The comics and movies were useless. Who'd have thought.

"Argh ee oh ooh eh illeh ee," said Jet.

And that was another thing he always thought he'd be really good at — talking through a gag. It was just a bit of fabric. How hard could it be?

"Uh uh," quipped Amanda, and Jet didn't need to understand the words to know she'd just told him to shut up.

Only five minutes ago they'd been free, reunited, and happy, but when Snodgrass cornered them with the gun it all seemed to evaporate into the night. One by one he had them tie each other up until Gina was the only one left free. Snodgrass tied her up himself.

"Tackling the girl yourself?" Jet had said. "Real big of you."

"I don't take risks," Snodgrass said. "But if you think this feeble old man doesn't have it in him any more, just remember this."

"A kiss is just a kiss?" asked Gina.

"A sigh is just a sigh?" said Jet.

Snodgrass kicked him viciously in the face and hissed, "The girl gets the next one."

That had seemed to end the conversation.

Minutes later Snodgrass had them gagged and bundled into the back of his van. Now they were bumping along through the suburban streets, heading for God knew where and God knew what. If he angled his head just right and ignored the pain, Jet could make out the little window between the front and the back where Snodgrass sat silhouetted in the driver's seat. The old man sucked noisily on his dentures. Click-tap, click-tap, click-tap.

Jet slumped back onto the floor of the van in despair.

The smell of Snodgrass' basement was incredible. They were locked underground behind feet of concrete with absolutely no ventilation. Jet wondered if this even was a basement and not some kind of old bomb shelter from the Cold War. Whatever it was it tended to trap smells, and when that smell came from a 40-year-old decomposing body it made for a less than comfortable way to spend an evening. The only illumination came from a naked bulb swinging perilously from a cord, but the ancient light was enough to see the head and torso of Spivey Spillane in the other corner. The statue still contained the remains of Lawrence Leverett.

"You knew about this," hissed Amanda.

There was no need for gags down here. No-one was going to hear them.

Franklin shook his head emphatically and sent his jowls quivering. "I only wanted the statue," he whined. "I thought Leverett had hidden the treasure inside it."

"So did we," said Amanda with resignation.

"You still kidnapped my sister," spat Jet. "I guess you don't get to be a politician in this country without a lot of bastard running through your veins."

Franklin didn't even try to make an excuse. For her part Gina remained quiet. Jet didn't think he'd ever seen her go so long without talking, but it seemed like she'd finally found a reason not to. He almost wished they got tied up by murderous statue-thieves more often. He shivered as a wave of guilt crashed over him. He didn't want to admit it, but right now he'd have given anything to have Gina kick him in the shins and say something annoying.

"What do we reckon, then?" asked Amanda. "We know Leverett found the gold. Then, what, he commissions his mentally ill sister to make a statue of Spivey Spillane? Why make a statue at all?"

"There's still our first theory," said Jet. "He thought he was about to be found out, so he was going to hide the gold in the statue."

"But Snodgrass got to him first," Amanda breathed. "He killed Leverett, and hid the body inside the statue."

Franklin groaned. "*That's* what he was doing."

"What who was doing?"

"I saw him do it. I was only a boy, but I saw it happen. It was dark. I never knew who it was — I always assumed it was Leverett. But I saw him in his pick-up with the statue in the back. He took it out and put it back in the plaza, only now it had a head on it."

Jet nodded. "It was the only way he could fit the whole body inside."

"I just thought he'd hidden the gold," Franklin blubbered. "I didn't know it was Snodgrass. I didn't know it was a body."

"So as far as you knew there was a hidden fortune inside that statue. But the only way you could get at it was to have the statue replaced."

"That's the only reason I ever ran for mayor," said Franklin. "I tried every which way. Petitions. Bribery. Blackmail. Nothing worked.

"Please help me," he begged. "I'm not young any more. I never wanted any of this."

Amanda eyed him with distaste. "To think I was going to vote for you."

"Yes," said Jet. "I too withdraw my political support."

A silence fell over the four of them as they contemplated what was going to happen. There was no escape, as far as they could tell. The only door was at the top of the stairs and that led directly into Snodgrass' house. And that was if they could get their ropes undone. It didn't seem likely.

Amanda cleared her throat. "You know…"

"What?" asked Jet.

"Nevermind."

"No, go on. Help take our minds off things."

"I just never thought I'd die like this."

"Well that's helped take our minds off it, thanks Amanda."

"No, I mean there's something I always wanted to say and, and if I'm going to die, I'd rather be me."

"You're not you? Who are you then?"

"If I'm going to die, then I want at least one person to know I'm gay."

"Reeeeeeally? Amanda! I had no idea you were a scissor sister."

"This is exactly why I knew I shouldn't tell you," she huffed.

"No no, sorry. That didn't come out how I imagined it."

"Neither did I," sighed Amanda. "You know, though, I kind of wanted to ask Nina out for ages."

"Nina? You have a crush on *Nina*? I could have told you you were barking up the wrong tree there."

"How do you know?" asked Amanda.

"Because *I* went out with Nina," said Jet.

"You what? And she said yes? How far did you get? First base? Second?"

"I caught the Snitch, if that's what you mean."

Amanda was quiet for a moment before she asked, "How was it?"

"Humorless," he replied. "And grim. Like the Siege of Leningrad."

Gina startled both of them by interjecting, "The death of Mallory."

"What?" asked Jet.

"I heard you say it was like the death of Mallory — alone, in an icy cave on top of a mountain."

Gina started giggling. Then Jet and Amanda laughed too. It didn't feel like real laughter, but it felt good anyway. Mayor Franklin didn't seem to appreciate the humor of the situation and just looked at them, confused and appalled.

The basement door swung open hard and slammed into the wall. They could see Snodgrass' profile outlined against the light at the top of the stairs. "What's that noise?" he snapped.

"We were laughing at a joke," said Jet.

"Well stop it. I never heard such an awful racket, and I won't have you telling off-color jokes about bosoms and buttocks and all kinds of prurience in my house."

"You can't stop us laughing."

"What's that? Why do you keep talking?" said Snodgrass. "Who made you leader, eh? You're only 12 years old."

"I'm 17," said Jet. "I'm a full grown man."

Before Jet knew what was happening, Snodgrass had a straight razor in his hand. He unfolded it slowly. The blade was so polished and finely honed that it looked like a surgical instrument.

Snodgrass sauntered down the stairs, each foot creaking on the old wooden staircase. He approached Jet with horrible deliberateness. When he was within striking distance he leaned in close and grabbed Jet's hair, pulling his head back viciously. Jet tried to jerk away but he was still tied up. He couldn't do more than wriggle like a worm. Snodgrass brought the blade in close against Jet's neck, and suddenly Jet stopped struggling. One wrong move and that razor would slice straight into his skin.

With cruel roughness Snodgrass dragged the blade up Jet's throat. The edge collected the sweat off Jet's skin, now flushed with terror. When Snodgrass reached Jet's chin he flicked the blade upwards and examined it closely.

"Not a hair," Snodgrass scoffed. "Some man. I think I'll just kill you now."

He pressed the razor back against Jet's throat, this time letting the blade push into the skin.

"Boy," said Snodgrass, "it's been a long time since I did this."

Jet felt the blade begin to slice.

Chapter 31

It seemed like a bad idea to light a fire. It was true, the night was warm enough, but even if Spillane bothered catching a rabbit he wouldn't be able to cook it without one. He'd rather go hungry than let the towns-folk catch him. So he lay in the shelter of a log and pretended that the growling in his stomach was really a warm, juicy steak.

Occasionally his hand wandered up to his neck where he rubbed the bruises. They had turned dark brown but had not stopped aching yet. The pain made him smile. That escape was worthy of Alabama Sam himself. His fondest memory in all his 20 years on this Earth was when he hit the ground and turned for the hills. In that moment he'd caught a single glimpse of Alabama Sam. He hadn't seen Sam's face, of course, but he could imagine the expression behind the evil little eye-slits in his bandages. Was it outrage, he wondered? Or horror? Or maybe a delicious combination of both.

The snap of twigs and leaves disturbed his reverie just as he'd begun to drift off. He sat bolt upright and listened carefully. The sound happened again. It was regular, and getting closer.

A fist closed around Spillane's heart. He'd thought he'd have more time to prepare to face Sam. He knew it was going to happen. Sam was the kind of man who had to have control — there was no way he'd let Spillane simply make a getaway. But it was okay now. Spillane felt like he had already won, had already pulled his great victory over Sam. All that was left now was to finish him off, and there was no power in Heaven or Earth that would stop him killing that man.

Spillane scrambled up a tree to hide and hopefully get the drop on Sam. His feet scraped against the bark and the footsteps stopped — he'd been heard. When they started up again they seemed to have more purpose. Good, let him come. Spillane was ready.

A slender, shadowy figure stepped into view. He'd been so intent on killing Alabama Sam that at first Spillane couldn't make sense of what he was seeing.

"Jackie?" he hissed.

"Spivey? Where are you?"

"Up here!"

She squinted up into the branches and said, "We must stop meeting in trees. They wreak havoc with my bustle."

Spillane climbed down and found to his enormous relief that Jackie had brought some provisions. It was mostly jerky and dried fruit, but he didn't care. He ate with undisguised relish.

"In return for this bountiful repast," said Jackie, "you have to tell me how you effected your escape from the hangman. In all my years I've never yet seen a man escape a hanging once the noose was around his neck. At least, not on his own. If I may be perfectly honest, I was all set to shoot you down myself."

"Thought I wasn't your responsibility," grunted Spillane.

"You're not. But you are fun to keep around."

Spillane smiled to himself and continued to eat, leaving Jackie's question unanswered. She accepted the challenge.

"It was something to do with the bandages, wasn't it?"

"Faked tryin' to hang myself in jail. They got me down and patched up my neck, like I knew they would. Sam was never gonna let me out the easy way. That's when I snapped the blade off my razor and fixed it under the bandages."

Jackie clicked her tongue. "Cunning devil."

"The rope pretty much cut itself."

She looked at him strangely. Spillane recognized it — it was the same look she'd given him when he beat her at poker.

The next thing he knew she was on top of him, holding his arms down and kissing him hard. Spillane was frozen. Every part of his body tingled with a strength he'd never known. He didn't have the heart to tell her he'd never kissed a woman before.

"Marry me," he said. "Come away with me and we'll get married."

Jackie paused for a second before she burst out in a fit of hysterical laughter.

"Hey," he said, trying to wriggle out from under her. "Quit laughin'. What's so funny?"

"You don't know me as well as you think you do, Mr. Spillane. I'm not the marrying type."

"Get off me," he said. "I don't even know why you came here. I got work to do."

"You spoil everything when you talk," said Jackie. "Just keep your mouth shut and look pretty."

Then she started pressing her weight against his hips and Spillane thought he might just die here and now, and he'd be okay with that.

Maybe, he thought, California wasn't all bad.

Chapter 32

The razor slipped beneath Jet's skin and Amanda could see the blood beginning to flow. Snodgrass was panting with excitement.

"It's in the statue!" she blurted.

Snodgrass stopped, the razor poised to cut deeper and finish Jet off. Amanda could hear Jet breathing raggedly, verging on a whimper.

"What?" Snodgrass said. "You think the gold is inside the statue?" Then he burst out laughing so violently that Amanda thought the razor might just slip and cut Jet's throat anyway. "The gold isn't inside the statue!" he crowed. "Is that why you knocked its block off? Looking for hidden treasure?"

"It's not *inside* the statue, it's *in* the statue." Amanda was talking so fast now she could barely keep her thoughts straight. It would be a miracle if she could pull this off, but her heart was racing and there was no going back now.

"What do you think it's made of?" she asked. "Bronze? You might be right, but it's bronze and something else. You never found out where Leverett hid that gold. How many years did you waste looking when it was right under your nose?"

"Son of a bitch!" he shrieked.

In a second he was up off the floor and on the other side of the room. The shattered fragments of the statue lay on the ground oozing slowly into the damp cement.

As Amanda looked on, Snodgrass slowly began to assemble something in the middle of the basement. He was old and the parts were unfamiliar to him, but he'd done this once before and he was determined to do it again. He hurried back and forth, consulting manuals and textbooks, ancient and moldy, about forging, foundry, and alloys. Amanda had to guess that all of this equipment had once belonged to poor Winifred Leverett.

Jet inched his way over to Amanda like a worm. His hands were still tied so he just moved slowly and hoped Snodgrass was too distracted to notice.

"How long were you going to hold onto that?" he whispered.

"It just came to me," she said, half wondering at her own ingenuity. The thrill of adrenaline was running through her veins. It felt like flexing a muscle she'd always had but never used — something that had lain dormant for a very long time. But could she be right, even if by accident? She and Jet had thought the gold was hidden in the statue. Maybe it still was.

"Well your timing could use some work, but aside from that… thanks."

"That's all well and good, but now what do we do?" she asked. "Once he gets that gold he's still going to kill us."

"I was hoping you'd ask me that," said Jet, waving his hands in front of her — he'd cut himself free, and in one hand he was holding Snodgrass' razor. He must have dropped it in his excitement.

Amanda waved her hands too.

"How did you do that?" asked Jet.

Amanda shrugged mischievously and said, "Foot-hands, remember? Do you still have your parents' gun?"

Jet shook his head and indicated Snodgrass. The old man had confiscated it when he bundled them into the back of his van.

Amanda and Jet lay back down and pretended to be tied up. They kept their eyes on Snodgrass the entire time, but he was far too distracted by setting up the furnace and the crucible to pay any attention to them.

Minutes later she was blinded by the light of an acetylene torch. Snodgrass methodically cut the statue into smaller pieces while the furnace heated up. Now the entire furnace was boiling, radiating an intense light that flooded the basement and threw wicked shadows against the walls.

246

Piece by piece Amanda watched as Snodgrass fed the statue into the crucible. The metal was molten now, burning with its own light. The remains of Lawrence Leverett that still clung to the inside of the statue hissed and screamed when they hit the heat, then boiled off into a stench that was even worse than the smell of the decomposing body. The whole basement reeked of rotting barbecue.

Snodgrass rooted through the old supplies and produced a beaker of mercury. He held it on the end of a pair of tongs and slowly began to pour it into the crucible, watching keenly for the mercury to bind with the gold and separate from the rest of the alloy. Amanda and Jet watched on, holding their breaths.

Nothing happened.

He dumped the rest of the mercury in at once, and it crackled as it met the molten mixture. A cloud of mercury gas rose into the air, forcing Snodgrass to cover his mouth and nose with his sleeve.

He howled and threw the beaker into the crucible, then kicked it over, sending fiery streaks of lava snaking across the ground. The four captives bunched up against the walls, the heat searing their legs even from here.

Snodgrass whipped around on them, eyes ringed with fatigue. Amanda had no doubt in her mind that if he wasn't unbalanced before, he was totally deranged now.

Slowly he withdrew the gun.

"So what did that buy you?" he hissed. "A few hours? You're not half the liar your ancestor was."

"Spivey Spillane was not a liar."

"Some historian! You're not descended from Spivey Spillane. You're descended from his impostor, the con-man who arrived in Skunks Dance a few weeks before Spillane did. He knocked up some two-bit Jezebel who never heard from him again. *That's* who fathered this town's great line of Spillanes. A huckster."

Amanda's skin was flushed and her eyes were dark.

"Hey, Snodgrass!" yelled Jet. "Look, no hands."

Jet was up on his feet and doing jazz hands for Snodgrass' benefit. Snodgrass followed him cautiously, being careful to keep the gun pointed at him. His finger tightened on the trigger. Then, without a word, Snodgrass smiled.

Amanda kicked Snodgrass just as he fired. Jet ducked as the bullet ricocheted off the concrete, and Snodgrass fell to the ground. He landed in the pool of molten metal, splashing the his face and body. He screamed. The metal burnt his skin and cooled fast in the open air. The screaming never stopped, now mixed with sobbing, as Jet and Amanda hurried to untie the others.

The four of them legged it up the stairs to the tune of Snodgrass' whimpers. Gina was last out the door, and held back as she watched Snodgrass curl up on the damp concrete and cry. Without waiting for the others she dashed back down the stairs.

"Gina!" called Jet.

Gina turned Snodgrass face-up.

"Get away from him!" said Jet. Then, after a moment, "Is he dead?"

Gina shook her head. "But he's gonna need an ambulance."

Jet nodded.

"I'll call 911," said Amanda. "You keep an eye on those two," she said, indicating Franklin and Snodgrass.

Chapter 33

The light this early in the morning wasn't golden or bright, but a kind of gray that seemed to come out of the earth with the dew and the beetles and the centipedes. The earliest birds were beginning to rustle and call to each other across the trees. If you put your ear close to the ground you could almost discern, deep down, the sounds of worms making mysterious tunnels through the soil. The ground was damp and sticky.

Jackie lay with her arms around Spillane. She had wrapped around him in the night to share their warmth and the two had not parted, but now she was wide awake and completely still. She let the dew soak into her petticoats. She shut her eyes in frustration, hoping somehow that by blocking out her vision she might be able to hear better. The noises of the morning — the clicks, the rustles, the wet crawling sounds all around her — and something else.

She ever so gently put her hand over Spillane's mouth. She felt the oil on his skin and the prickle of his stubble against her hand. She didn't have to move far to whisper in his ear, so softly she was almost just mouthing the words, "We're being followed."

Spillane started awake, but Jackie's hand over his mouth kept him quiet while he processed what she had said.

When she removed her hand, he whispered, "Sam."

"You stay here. Pretend to make breakfast. I'll circle around, take him from behind."

"No. We keep goin'. I got a plan."

"But —" she began to protest.

"Trust me," he said.

And she did.

She made coffee and twist bread using the few provisions she had left, while Spillane wandered and returned a short while later with two squirrels. They skinned them together and cooked them over the fire. Jackie worried that the townsfolk might see the smoke, but then she observed that theirs was not the only pillar of smoke in the sky. With any luck the manhunt had died down overnight and they would be left to their own devices, with the exception of Sam. The thought chilled Spillane again with a prickling on the back of his neck. Somehow it always boiled down to the same problem: Sam.

They covered the fire with rocks and began their hike through the woods. They climbed higher and higher into the mountains where the trees seemed to capture the heat from the sun and concentrate it on the hikers. The light wasn't gray any more, but a suffocating yellow that pricked their skin with sweat and baked them slowly in their clothes. Still they walked on, stopping only to rest and eat.

"Aren't you gonna ask me where we're goin'?" asked Spillane.

"Where are we going?" whispered Jackie.

"Louder," he hissed.

"Where are we going?" she said, trying to make it just loud enough for their pursuer to hear them.

"Calaveras Ridge."

As the sun began to fade the ground beneath them became flatter and sturdier. The leaves and soil gave way to old cobblestones peppered with the ruins of walls and battlements.

Up ahead the walls came together in an arch. The night was closing in around them and the interior of the ruins was pitch black.

"It's too dark," said Jackie. "We should wait until tomorrow."

Spillane shook his head. "It has to be now."

He took off his shirt and tore it into strips. Jackie eyed him approvingly and said, "I don't know why I didn't suggest this sooner."

Spillane just grinned at her as he he coated the strips of cloth in whatever fat he'd managed to save from breakfast. He wrapped them around one end of a stick, and after a few minutes produced a primitive grease torch. He lit it from a match, and as the flames began to spread the light flooded Jackie's smiling face, and that of the man behind her.

Jackie followed Spillane's gaze and whipped around to see Alabama Sam. His bandages were gone now, revealing a ruined face encrusted with scabs and traces of blood. Inexplicably he was smiling.

"I believe congratulations are in order," murmured Sam, "on finally losin' your virginity. Look, I baked you a cake," he said, waving his pistol at Spillane.

"What now?"

"It's what I like to call Plan A," said Sam. "You can try as hard as you like to get away from me, Spillane, but you oughta remember who you're dealin' with. From now until the day you die, I will be your shadow. Death's the only way you'll ever be free o' me." He motioned to the arch in front of them. "Walk."

Spillane and Jackie walked ahead of Sam through the stone entry. The torch threw flickering shadows onto the walls. Every vine, every startled possum and crumbling stone cast phantoms all around them.

"Stop!" said Sam.

His ears listened keenly and his eyes searched out as much of the courtyard as he could. Something was amiss.

"Now we're gonna find out just how clever those Dagos were," said Sam. "Spillane, it's your time to shine." He motioned Spillane ahead with the barrel of the gun.

Spillane breathed deeply. Things were getting out of hand. This wasn't how it was supposed to happen — Sam had found them too soon — but he knew there was only one way to play it now. The slightest hesitation would ruin everything. He swaggered across the courtyard. He shivered and his skin was goosebumped from head to toe, but he didn't let it show. He swaggered on. He felt like a drowning man coming to the surface for air. His lungs were bursting, mere feet from the surface.

A twang broke the night.

The arrows were coming at him before he could register what was happening. He hit the ground as they slammed into the wall to his left, but it was only when he looked down that he saw one sticking out from his own leg. He'd never even felt it strike.

Alabama Sam's hysterical laughter echoed all around him. Jackie was at his side attempting to staunch the bleeding, but a cold dread was already filling Spillane's limbs. He was going to die in these hills — he knew that now.

Sam crowed, "Oh my God, that was worth you escapin' from bein' hanged. They gotta make that into a pop-up book so I can enjoy it again later."

Spillane grunted as Jackie tied up the wound with a piece of her skirt.

"The arrow…" Spillane gasped, but Jackie shook her head.

"If we take it out now you might bleed to death."

"No slackin'," said Sam. "Keep goin'."

Spillane struggled to his feet. He could just about put weight on his injured leg, but the pain was incredible. He could feel the arrow digging into his flesh with every step. Jackie looked him in the eye, and Spillane knew that if they didn't do something now it would be too late.

Jackie spun around and, even in her skirts and heels, managed to kick the pistol out of Sam's grip. It flew off into the darkness. The next thing Sam knew he had Spillane's fist in his face. If Spillane was honest with himself he'd admit he'd hesitated a moment before hitting Sam. The thought of pulping that brittle, burnt face was almost too horrific. But it hadn't taken a fraction of a second to overcome that nausea. Sam was no ordinary man.

Even though the punch took him down, Sam was already scrambling. In an instant he had latched onto Spillane's leg and bit deep. Spillane howled and tried to shake him off, but Sam was like a feral animal. The punch had only enraged him.

Jackie dived onto Sam and tried to wrestle him off Spillane. The man was impossible to budge. He had an untameable strength that neither she nor Spillane could match. He continued to fight the both of them off until the cobblestones, weakened by Jackie's added weight, seemed to shift.

The ground opened up beneath them and the three plummeted into darkness. They all landed hard. The torch slammed onto the ground beside them, sending up great splashes of fire. It must have been at least ten feet down, but even now Spillane refused to relinquish his grip on Alabama Sam.

"I've got a little somethin' I been meanin' to give you," grunted

Spillane. He yanked the arrow out of his thigh and plunged it viciously into Sam's.

Sam screeched, twisting in agony, unable to see a thing except the shard of night sky above him and the guttering flames beside his head.

Spillane leaped up off Sam and grabbed the torch. Sam struggled to his feet as Spillane thrust the torch towards him. He backed away from it, the memory of another fire still blazing in his mind. Spillane felt Jackie by his side. The two of them backed Sam further and further into the cavernous room until he was up against the wall. The torch caught the glints of Sam's teeth, smiling even now. Why was he smiling?

"Give me the torch," growled Sam.

"Ain't never appreciated your sense of humor, Sam," said Spillane.

"You don't have a choice. After last time, I took a few precautions."

Sam opened his coat to reveal several packets of gunpowder encircling his body. One touch of the flame, even one good gunshot, would annihilate Sam and anyone in the vicinity.

Spillane felt himself handing the torch to Sam. With every inch he extended his hand, the closer he felt himself getting to defeat. This was the last weapon he had. Sam snatched it from his hand unceremoniously.

"Now," said Sam. "March."

A rusty grinding noise echoed through the chamber. All three of them peered into the darkness as best they could.

A great iron gate slammed to the ground, trapping Sam against the wall. Spillane and Jackie backed slowly away. Now doubt flooded Sam's features for the first time. He had just enough time to make eye contact with Spillane in a look that Spillane would wonder about for years to come. There was fear, yes, but he could have sworn there was something else too.

A metal blade swooped through the air and embedded itself in the wall, taking Alabama Sam with it. The torch dropped to the ground with Sam's body, now separated from his head. The next thing Spillane knew the floor was tilting away. The body and the torch both disappeared downwards to where Spillane could hear the sound of rushing water. Then with a grinding of heavy metal gears it was dark again.

Spillane stared at where Sam had been. He had thought Sam was dead twice already — but it felt different this time.

"It's over," said Spillane. "He's dead!" He turned to Jackie and said, "He's really, finally dead! The gold is ours."

Although Spillane couldn't see it, Jackie shook her head. "Spivey, let's go home."

"But —" he started, then felt Jackie take his hand. Her skin was tender against his. A new understanding washed over him.

Together they began to make their way back.

Chapter 34

The aftermath was almost more exhausting than the experience itself. First Jet had to give his account of the night's events to the ambulance crew. Then, of course, the police were called in and he had to tell the story again. He knew Amanda and Gina would back him up, but at the back of his mind he wondered how much Franklin was going to tell the cops. If Jet had anything to do with it, that ass was going to wind up begging for spare change on the corner of the street.

Fortunately, as he discovered later, Murdock had flipped on Franklin and backed them up. The police decided not to press charges against Jet for busting Amanda out of jail, but Franklin was going to feel the full weight of the law. Someone needed to be held responsible, and hanging Franklin out to dry would show the town's commitment to flushing corruption out of their government.

Snodgrass did not make it through the day. The doctors treated him as best they could, but Snodgrass was an old man and his injuries were too severe. That was the one that really worried Jet. Amanda had killed Snodgrass, although everyone acknowledged it had been in self-defense. She was lucky the law saw things her way. There could be little doubt that Snodgrass had been about to kill them — his gun had clearly been fired, and Jet had bled a fair bit from the cut on his neck, though it looked worse than it really was. Still, Amanda had attended one counseling session already. Jet tip-toed around her, tried to invite her out, and kept asking how she was. He got a little pissed off when the most he got out of her was, "Why do you keep asking me that? I'm not a mental patient, you know. I'm fine."

However he still caught her glancing behind herself every now and then, and when she raised a coffee to her lips he could detect a little tremor in her hand.

It was Jet's idea to go see Spackle. Neither had seen him in some time, and he thought Amanda could do with a friendly visit.

They buzzed silently at the front door and it didn't take long for Spackle to answer. His fierce eyebrows were already cocked in disapproval.

"What?" he demanded. "This place is never quiet any more. I blame you two," he said with an evil look.

"Didn't you hear what happened?" asked Jet.

"Of course I heard! Take me for some kind of shut-in? There isn't anything in this town that you know that I didn't know first."

"There was the body," Jet said with a wry grin.

Spackle grunted something that couldn't quite be taken for concession. "Well? You going to block up my doorway all day?"

They supposed that was as much of an invitation as they were going to get.

Jet sat down in a cracked leather chair overlooked by a statue of the dog from the RCA logo. It was weird having someone peering over your shoulder the whole time, even if it was just a plastic dog. Spackle brought out some cracked enamel mugs and over three cups of tea Jet and Amanda related what had happened. Although a few details about the murder of Lawrence Leverett had been released to the public, the majority of the story was still under investigation. The police and the papers made no mention of the statue of Spivey Spillane. There were some things you didn't want to drop onto an unsuspecting town right away.

When Jet and Amanda got to Snodgrass melting the statue, Spackle shrieked, "He melted it down? Vandals, the lot of you. That statue was part of this town's history."

"*We* didn't do it," Amanda protested.

"You gave him the damn fool idea. Now we'll never get it back."

"Anyway," said Jet pointedly. "We managed to escape."

"Never trusted that parasite an inch."

"Who, Snodgrass?" asked Jet.

"Man was a tit, but I'm talking about Franklin. Trying to destroy Skunks Dance's heritage. Replacing the town statue," he scoffed.

Amanda tried to console him by saying, "Is there any more of Winifred Leverett's work still around? We can remember her by that."

Spackle snorted so hard his tea nearly came out his nose.

"Winifred Leverett never sculpted that statue. Bunch of uneducated hooligans. Never know a thing about art. Don't you listen? Woman was in the loony bin, she never sculpted a thing in her life."

"But —"

"Leverett must have got someone else to make it, passed it off as his sister's."

"Who?" said Amanda.

"Can tell by the style. Looks like a Huntsman to me."

Now it was Amanda's turn to choke. "*Alexander* Huntsman — the sculptor?"

"No, the pest exterminator!" roared Spackle.

"But that must have cost Leverett a fortune. And it would only have got more valuable since then. Where did he get the money?"

"How should I know?" demanded Spackle.

Jet and Amanda turned to each other in horror.

"The treasure wasn't in the statue, it *was* the statue. We just watched a million dollars' worth of statue get melted down into scrap," she groaned.

"A million dollars," scoffed Spackle. "I wouldn't give three cents for it."

"But you said —"

"I said it was part of this town's history. What the hell do I care about a hack like Huntsman?"

Amanda set her cup down on the table and mumbled, "I feel ill. I think I want to go home."

When the two said goodbye, Spackle turned around and said, "What? Are you two still here? Go, already. I'm busy."

They walked a little way together. Amanda was looking aimlessly at her shoes.

"We did pretty good," he said. "We solved a murder."

"Do you think it's true?" she asked. "I mean what Snodgrass said, that I'm not really a Spillane?"

"Seriously? Who cares?" said Jet, then regretted it. "He didn't know what he was talking about. Dude was deranged."

"He was the town archivist. He'd know."

"Did you ever look up my family?" Jet said curiously.

"Yeah. Nothing too interesting. Far as I could tell your mom's descended from someone with a stupid name like Thomas Jefferson Ashwood. His wife owned a gun store in town." Amanda sighed. "Tell you what, let's give it a rest, huh? I don't feel like talking. Oh, but before I go…" Amanda reached into her bag and pulled out Jet's comic book. "Here, this is yours."

Jet watched Amanda stroll dejectedly off home while he took a different route. Poor Amanda. They'd come all this way for nothing. Then a second thought interrupted him. Poor Amanda? Poor him! He'd been going to do so much with that money. He was annoyed with himself for thinking of Amanda first. He'd have to fix that.

Jet lay on the sofa at home and stared up at the ceiling. After everything that had gone down, he discovered that he didn't know what to do with himself next. Even Nina had stopped pestering him. It took him a while to figure out why, until Josue messaged him in a tizzy and blurted out that he and Bentley had got to talking after they'd left Starbucks. Between the two of them, they'd managed to convince Nina that the young gym teacher, Mr. Graves, had a crush on her. She'd been scribbling romantic poems ever since, and word had it she'd even tried to friend him on Facebook — a request he'd rejected three times already. Bentley even reported spotting Mr. Graves run into Nina in the plaza, and the look of horror on his face was priceless. Ben had never seen anyone run away from Nina so fast. Josue laughed evilly, and Jet had to admit this was one of his better schemes.

"Hey Jet?" said Gina.

"No," he mumbled.

"No what?"

"No I don't want to play Spaceteam."

Gina flopped down onto a chair and said, "Well fine. It's not my fault you're all moody and teenagery."

"I can't anyway. I don't have a phone."

"You only just bought one!"

"Yeah well it's gone, isn't it? I have to get a new one. Again."

Jet sighed and idly thumbed through *Fantastic Firecat*. He began to wonder whether $400 might not buy a new car for Amanda.

Chapter 35

The sheriff was desperately curious to know about this Ashwood fellow who'd managed to hook the attentions of Jacqueline Hyde. She'd kept her gun store full of bizarre and unusual weaponry, and the townsfolk still refused to play her at cards, but now she lived on the edge of town with the man she married. At least she wasn't parading around the saloon so much and drinking everyone under the table, but then the barman complained that business just wasn't the same without her. If the saloon couldn't find another town hellion with her qualifications then they were going to have to form a merger with the whorehouse next door.

The sheriff leaned back in his chair and sighed. Life in Skunks Dance was never easy. He never did find out what happened to the mayor. Or that Spivey Spillane character, come to think of it. All they knew was his body washed up in the river one day, headless, if you could believe it, and without a single clue what in hell had happened to him other than the fact he'd been shot in the leg and badly burned. It looked like one of the lynch mob had worked him over good. The sheriff tried not to let it bother him too much. Someone, somewhere, had given him his comeuppance.

Jackie rode onto the ranch and stabled her horse. While she was in town running her store, "Thomas" did a pretty good job of running the farm and keeping the baby out of trouble.

When she pushed open the door she was delighted to find him pouring out two generous portions of whiskey.

"Mr. Ashwood," she said.

"Mrs. Ashwood," he replied with a grin and handed her a glass.

She downed the whiskey in one. "You always know just how to get me in the mood. Put it on for me?"

"Put what on?" he asked disingenuously. She eyed him skeptically until he said, "Oh. Well, if you insist."

He reached behind the table and produced a pink tutu. She pounced on him and kissed him hard before the two collapsed onto the ground, helpless in fits of laughter.

St John is an ornamental hermit who likes to live near exciting things so he can not go to them. He has an undying love for the unusual, the Bonzo Dog Doo-Dah Band, and toast. He spends his time plotting his own spectacular demise. *Skunks Dance* is his second novel. His first, *Radium Baby*, is also a thing that happened.